The Merry Adventures

of ROBIN
HOOD

of Great Renown, in Nottinghamshire

By HOWARD PYLE

Illustrated by
PAUL BUSCH

WHITMAN PUBLISHING COMPANY
RACINE, WISCONSIN

CONTENTS

CHAPTER 1 · · ·

How Robin Hood Became an Outlaw

IN MERRY England in the time of old, when good King Henry the Second ruled the land, there lived within the green glades of Sherwood Forest, near Nottingham Town, a famous outlaw whose name was Robin Hood. No archer ever lived that could speed a gray goose shaft with such skill and cunning as his, nor were there ever such yeomen as the seven-score merry men that roamed with him through the green-wood shades. Right merrily they dwelt within the depths of Sherwood Forest, suffering neither care nor want, but passing the time in merry games of archery or bouts of cudgel play, living upon the King's venison, washed down with drafts of ale of October brewing.

Not only Robin himself but all the band were outlaws and dwelt apart from other men, yet they were beloved by the country people round about, for no one ever came to jolly Robin for help in time of need and went away again with an empty fist.

And now I will tell you how it first came about that Robin

Hood fell afoul of the law.

When Robin was a youth of eighteen, stout of sinew and bold of heart, the Sheriff of Nottingham proclaimed a shooting match and offered a prize of a butt of ale to whoever should shoot the best shaft in Nottinghamshire. "Now," quoth Robin, "will I go too, for fain would I draw a string for the bright eyes of my lass and a butt of good October brewing." So up he got and took his good stout yew bow and a score or more of broad clothyard arrows, and started off from Locksley Town through Sherwood Forest to Nottingham.

It was at the dawn of day in the merry May-time, when hedge-rows are green and flowers bedeck the meadows; daisies pied and yellow cuckoo buds and fair primroses were all along the briery hedges; when apple buds blossom and sweet birds sing, the lark at dawn of day, the throstle cock and cuckoo; when lads and lassies look upon each other with sweet thoughts; when busy housewives spread their linen to bleach upon the bright green grass. Sweet was the greenwood as he walked along its paths, and bright the green and rustling leaves, amid which the little birds sang with might and main; and blithely Robin whistled as he trudged along, thinking of Maid Marian and her bright eyes, for at such times a youth's thoughts are wont to turn pleasantly upon the lass that he loves the best.

As thus he walked along with a brisk step and a merry whistle, he came suddenly upon some foresters seated beneath a great oak tree. Fifteen there were in all, making themselves merry with feasting and drinking as they sat around a huge pasty, to which each man helped himself, thrusting his hands into the pie, and washing down that which they ate with great horns of ale which they drew all foaming from a barrel that stood nigh. Each man was clad in Lincoln green, and a fine show they made, seated upon the sward beneath that fair, spreading tree. Then one of them, with his mouth full, called out to Robin, "Hulloa, where goest thou, little lad, with thy one-penny bow and thy farthing shaft?"

Then Robin grew angry, for no stripling likes to be taunted with his green years.

"Now," quoth he, "my bow and eke [also] mine arrows are as good as thine; and moreover, I go to the shooting-match at Nottingham Town, which same has been proclaimed by our good Sheriff of Nottinghamshire; there I will shoot with other stout yeomen, for a grand prize has been offered of a fine butt of ale."

Then one who held a horn of ale in his hand, said, "Ho! Listen to the lad! Why, boy, thou pratest of standing up with good stout men at Nottingham butts [targets], thou who art scarce able to draw one string of a two stone bow."

"I'll hold the best of you twenty marks," quoth bold Robin, "that I hit the clout [cloth target] at threescore rods, by the good help of Our Lady fair."

At this all laughed aloud, and one said, "Well boasted, thou fair infant, well boasted! And well thou knowest that no target is nigh to make good thy wager."

And another cried, "He will be taking ale with his milk next."

At this Robin grew right angry. "Hark ye," said he; "yonder, at the glade's end, I see a herd of deer, even more than threescore rods distant. I'll hold you twenty marks that, by leave of Our Lady, I cause the best hart among them to die."

"Now done!" cried he who had spoken first. "And here are twenty marks. I wager that thou causest no beast to die, with or without the aid of Our Lady."

Then Robin took his good yew bow in his hand, and placing

the tip at his instep, he strung it right deftly; then he nocked
[fitted to the string] a broad clothyard arrow, and, raising the
bow, drew the gray goose-feather to his ear; the next moment
the bow-string rang and the arrow sped down the glade as a
sparrow-hawk skims in a northern wind. High leaped the
noblest hart of all the herd, only to fall dead, reddening the
green path with his heart's blood.

"Ha!" cried Robin, "how likest thou that shot, good fellow?
I wot [know] the wager were mine, an it were three hundred
pounds."

Then all the foresters were filled with rage, and he who had
spoken the first and had lost the wager was more angry than
all.

"Nay," cried he, "the wager is none of thine, and get thee
gone, straightway, or, by all the saints of heaven, I'll baste
thy sides until thou wilt ne'er be able to walk again."

"Knowest thou not," said another, "that thou hast killed the
King's deer, and, by the laws of our gracious lord and sovereign, King Harry, thine ears should be shaven close to thy
head?"

"Catch him!" cried a third.

"Nay!" said a fourth, "let him e'en go because of his tender
years."

Never a word said Robin Hood, but he looked at the foresters
with a grim face; then, turning on his heel, strode away from
them down the forest glade. But his heart was bitterly angry,
for his blood was hot and youthful and prone to boil.

Now, well would it have been for him who had first spoken
had he left Robin Hood alone; but his anger was hot, both because the youth had gotten the better of him and because of the
deep drafts of ale that he had been quaffing. So, of a sudden,
without any warning, he sprang to his feet and seized upon

his bow and fitted it to a shaft. "Ay," cried he, "and I'll hurry thee anon," and he sent the arrow whistling through the air after Robin.

It was well for Robin Hood that that same forester's head was spinning with ale, or else he would never have taken another step; as it was, the arrow whistled within three inches of his head.

Then Robin turned around and quickly drew his own bow, and sent an arrow back in return. "Ye said I was no archer," cried he aloud, "but say so now again!"

The shaft flew straight; the archer fell forward with a cry, and lay on his face upon the ground, his arrows rattling about him from out of his quiver, the gray goose shaft wet with his heart's blood. Then, before the others could gather their wits about them, Robin Hood was gone into the depths of the greenwood. Some started after him, but not with much heart, for each feared to suffer the death of his fellow; so presently they all came and lifted the dead man up and bore him away to Nottingham Town.

Meanwhile Robin Hood ran through the greenwood. Gone was all the joy and brightness from everything, for his heart was sick within him, and it was borne in upon his soul that he had slain a man.

"Alas!" cried he. "Thou hast found me an archer that will make thy wife to wring [grieve deeply]! I would that thou had'st ne'er said one word to me, or that I had never passed thy way, or e'en that my right forefinger had been stricken off ere that this had happened! In haste I smote, but grieve I sore at leisure!" And then, even in his trouble, he remembered the old saw that "What is done is done; and the egg cracked cannot be cured."

And so he came to dwell in the greenwood that was to be his

home for many a year to come, never again to see the happy days with the lads and lasses of sweet Locksley Town; for he was outlawed, not only because he had killed a man, but also because he had poached upon the King's deer, and two hundred pounds were set upon his head, as a reward for whoever would bring him to the court of the King.

Now the Sheriff of Nottingham swore that he himself would bring this knave, Robin Hood, to justice, and for two reasons: first, because he wanted the two hundred pounds, and next, because the forester that Robin Hood had killed was of kin to him.

But Robin Hood lay hidden in Sherwood Forest for one year, and in that time there gathered around him many others like himself, cast out from other folk for this cause and for that. Some had shot deer in hungry winter time, when they could get no other food, and had been seen in the act by the foresters, but had escaped, thus saving their ears; some had been turned out of their inheritance, that their farms might be added to the King's lands in Sherwood Forest; some had been despoiled by a great baron or a rich abbot or a powerful esquire—all, for one cause or another, had come to Sherwood to escape wrong and oppression.

So, in all that year, fivescore or more good stout yeomen gathered about Robin Hood, and chose him to be their leader and chief. Then they vowed that even as they themselves had been despoiled they would despoil their oppressors, whether baron, abbot, knight, or squire, and that from each they would take that which had been wrung from the poor by unjust taxes, or land rents, or in wrongful fines; but to the poor folk they would give a helping hand in need and trouble, and would return to them that which had been unjustly taken from them. Beside this, they swore never to harm a child nor to wrong a woman, be she maid, wife, or widow; so that, after a while, when the people began to find that no harm was meant to them, but that money or food came in time of want to many a poor family, they came to praise Robin and his merry men, and to tell many tales of him and of his doings in Sherwood Forest, for they felt Robin Hood to be one of themselves.

Up rose Robin Hood one merry morn when all the birds were singing blithely among the leaves, and up rose all his merry men, each fellow washing his head and hands in the cold brown brook that leaped laughing from stone to stone. Then said Robin: "For fourteen days have we seen no sport, so now I will go abroad to seek adventures forthwith. But tarry ye, my merry men all, here in the greenwood; only see that ye mind well my call. Three blasts upon the bugle horn I will blow in my hour of need; then come quickly, for I shall want your aid."

So saying, he strode away through the leafy forest glade until he had come to the verge of Sherwood. There he wandered for a long time, through highway and byway, through dingly dell and forest skirts. Now he met a fair buxom lass in a shady lane, and each gave the other a merry word and passed their way; now he saw a fair lady upon an ambling pad [easy-going horse], to whom he doffed his cap, and who bowed sedately in return to the fair youth; now he saw a fat monk on a pannier-laden ass; now a gallant knight, with spear and shield and armor that flashed brightly in the sunlight; now a page clad in crimson; and now a stout burgher from good Nottingham Town, pacing along with serious footsteps; all these sights he saw, but adventure found he none. At last he took a road by the forest skirts; a bypath that dipped toward a broad, pebbly stream spanned by a narrow bridge made of a log of wood. As he drew nigh this bridge he saw a tall stranger coming from the other side. Thereupon Robin quickened his pace, as did the stranger likewise; each thinking to cross first. "Now stand thou back," quoth Robin, "and let the better man cross first."

"Nay," answered the stranger, "then stand back thine own self, for the better man, I wot [know] am I."

"That will we presently see," quoth Robin; "and meanwhile stand thou where thou art, or else, by the bright brow of Saint Ælfrida, I will show thee right good Nottingham play with a clothyard shaft betwixt thy ribs."

"Now," quoth the stranger, "I will tan thy hide till it be as many colors as a beggar's cloak, if thou darest so much as touch a string of that same bow that thou holdest in thy hands."

"Thou pratest like an ass," said Robin, "for I could send this shaft clean through thy proud heart before a curtal [short-frocked] friar say grace over a roast goose at Michaelmas-tide."

"And thou pratest like a coward," answered the stranger, "for thou standest there with a good yew bow to shoot at my heart, while I have nought in my hand but a plain blackthorn staff wherewith to meet thee."

"Now," quoth Robin, "by the faith of my heart, never have I had a coward's name in all my life before. I will lay by my trusty bow and eke [also] my arrows, and if thou darest abide my coming, I will go and cut a cudgel to test my manhood withal."

"Ay, marry, that will I abide thy coming, and joyously, too," quoth the stranger; whereupon he leaned sturdily upon his staff to await Robin.

Then Robin Hood stepped quickly to the coverside and cut a

good staff of ground oak, straight, without flaw, and six feet
in length, and came back trimming away the tender stems
from it, while the stranger waited for him, leaning upon his
staff, and whistling as he gazed round about. Robin observed
him furtively as he trimmed his staff, measuring him from top
to toe from out the corner of his eye, and thought that he had
never seen a lustier or a stouter man. Tall was Robin, but
taller was the stranger by a head and a neck, for he was seven
feet in height. Broad was Robin across the shoulders, but
broader was the stranger by twice the breadth of a palm,
while he measured at least an ell [forty-five inches] around
the waist.

"Nevertheless," said Robin to himself, "I will baste thy
hide right merrily, my good fellow." He said aloud, "Lo, here
is my good staff, lusty and tough. Now wait my coming, an
thou darest, and meet me, an thou fearest not; then we will
fight until one or the other of us tumble into the stream by
dint of blows."

"Marry [indeed], that meeteth my whole heart!" cried the
stranger, twirling his staff about his head, betwixt his fingers
and thumb, until it whistled again.

Never did the Knights of Arthur's Round Table meet in a
stouter fight than did these two. In a moment Robin stepped
quickly upon the bridge where the stranger stood; first he made
a feint and then delivered a blow at the stranger's head that,
had it met its mark, would have tumbled him speedily into the
water; but the stranger turned the blow right deftly and in
return gave one as stout, which Robin also turned as the
stranger had done. So they stood, each in his place, neither
moving a finger's breadth back, for one good hour, and many
blows were given and received by each in that time, till here
and there were sore bones and bumps, yet neither thought

of crying, "Enough," or seemed likely to fall from off the bridge. Now and then they stopped to rest, and each thought that he never had seen in all his life before such a hand at quarter-staff. At last Robin gave the stranger a blow upon the ribs that made his jacket smoke like a damp straw thatch in the sun. So shrewd was the stroke that the stranger came within a hair's breadth of falling off the bridge; but he regained himself right quickly, and, by a dexterous blow, gave Robin a crack on the crown that caused the blood to flow. Then Robin grew mad with anger, and smote with all his might at the other; but the stranger warded the blow, and once again thwacked Robin. And this time he thwacked so fairly that Robin fell heels over head into the water, as the queen pin falls in a game of bowls.

"And where art thou now, good lad?" shouted the stranger, roaring with laughter.

"Oh, in the flood and floating adown with the tide," cried Robin, nor could he forbear laughing himself at his sorry plight. Then, gaining his feet, he waded to the bank, the little fish speeding hither and thither, all frightened, at his great splashing.

"Give me thy hand," cried he, when he had reached the bank. "I must needs own thou art a brave and sturdy soul, and, withal, a good stout stroke with the cudgels. By this and by that, my head hummeth like to a hive of bees on a hot June morning."

Then he clapped his horn to his lips and winded a blast that went echoing sweetly down the forest paths. "Ay, marry," quoth he again, "thou art a tall lad, and eke [also] a brave one, for ne'er, I trow [believe], is there a man betwixt here and Canterbury Town could do the like to me that thou hast done."

"And thou," quoth the stranger, laughing, "takest thy cudgeling like a brave heart and a stout yeoman."

But now the distant twigs and branches rustled with the coming of men, and suddenly a score or two of good stout yeomen, all clad in Lincoln green, burst from out the covert, with merry Will Stutely at their head.

"Good master," cried Will, "how is this? Truly thou art all wet from head to foot, and that to the very skin."

"Why, marry," answered jolly Robin, "yon stout fellow hath tumbled me neck and crop into the water and hath given me a drubbing beside."

"Then shall he not go without a ducking and eke a drubbing himself!" cried Will Stutely. "Have at him, lads!"

Then Will and a score of yeomen leaped upon the stranger, but though they sprang quickly, they found him ready and felt him strike right and left with his stout staff, so that, though he went down with press of numbers, some of them rubbed cracked crowns before he was overcome.

"Nay, forbear!" cried Robin, laughing until his sore sides ached again. "He is a right good man and true, and no harm shall befall him. Now hark ye, good youth, wilt thou stay with me and be one of my band? Three suits of Lincoln green shalt thou have each year, besides forty marks in fee, and share with us whatsoever good shall befall us. Thou shalt eat sweet venison and quaff the stoutest ale, and mine own good right-hand man shalt thou be, for never did I see such a cudgel-player in all my life before. Speak! Wilt thou be one of my good merry men?"

"That know I not," quoth the stranger, surlily for he was angry at being so tumbled about. "If ye handle yew bow and apple shaft no better than ye do oaken cudgel, I wot ye are not fit to be called yeomen in my country; but if there be any man here that can shoot a better shaft than I, then will I bethink me of joining with you."

"Now by my faith," said Robin, "thou art a right saucy varlet, sirrah; yet I will stoop to thee as I never stooped to man before. Good Stutely, cut thou a fair white piece of bark four fingers in breadth, and set it fourscore yards distant on yonder oak. Now, stranger, hit that fairly with a gray goose shaft and call thyself an archer."

"Ay, marry, that will I," answered he. "Give me a good stout bow and a fair broad arrow, and if I hit it not strip me and beat me blue with bowstrings."

Then he chose the stoutest bow amongst them all, next to Robin's own, and a straight gray goose shaft, well-feathered and smooth, and stepping to the mark—while all the band, sitting or lying upon the greensward, watched to see him shoot—he drew the arrow to his cheek and loosed the shaft right deftly, sending it so straight down the path that it clove the mark in the very center. "Aha!" cried he, "mend [better] thou that if thou canst," while even the yeomen clapped their hands at so fair a shot.

"That is a keen shot, indeed," quoth Robin. "Mend it I cannot, but mar it I may, perhaps."

Then taking up his own good stout bow and nocking an arrow with care he shot with his very greatest skill. Straight flew the arrow, and so true that it lit fairly upon the stranger's shaft and split it into splinters. Then all the yeomen leaped to their feet and shouted for joy that their master had shot so well.

"Now by the lusty yew bow of good Saint Withold," cried the stranger, "that is a shot indeed, and never saw I the like in all my life before! Now truly will I be thy man henceforth and for aye. Adam Bell was a fair shot, but never shot he so!"

"Then have I gained a right good man this day," quoth jolly Robin. "What name goest thou by, good fellow."

"Men call me John Little whence I came," answered the stranger.

Then Will Stutely, who loved a good jest, spoke up. "Nay, fair little stranger," said he, "I like not thy name and fain would I have it otherwise. Little art thou indeed, and small of bone and sinew, therefore shalt thou be christened Little John, and I will be thy godfather."

Then Robin Hood and all his band laughed aloud until the stranger began to grow angry.

"An [if] thou make a jest of me," quoth he to Will Stutely, "thou will have sore bones and little pay, and that in short season."

"Nay, good friend," said Robin Hood, "bottle thine anger, for the name fitteth thee well. Little John shall thou be called henceforth, and Little John shall it be. So come, my merry men, and we will go and prepare a christening feast for this fair infant."

So turning their backs upon the stream, they plunged into the forest once more, through which they traced their steps till they reached the spot where they dwelt in the depths of the woodland. There had they built huts of bark and branches of trees and made couches of sweet rushes spread over with skins of fallow deer. Here stood a great oak tree with branches spreading broadly around, beneath which was a seat of green moss where Robin Hood was wont to sit at feast and at merry-making with his stout men about him. Here they found the rest of the band, some of whom had come in with a brace of fat does. Then they all built great fires and after a time roasted the does and broached a barrel of humming [frothing] ale. Then when the feast was ready they all sat down, but

Robin Hood placed Little John at his right hand, for he was henceforth to be the second in the band.

Then when the feast was done Will Stutely spoke up. "It is now time, I ween [think], to christen our bonny babe, is it not so, merry boys?"

"Aye! Aye!" cried all, laughing till the woods echoed with their mirth.

"Then seven sponsors shall we have," quoth Will Stutely; and hunting among all the band he chose the seven stoutest men of them all.

"Now by Saint Dunstan," cried Little John, springing to his feet, "more than one of you shall rue it an you lay finger upon me."

But without a word they all ran upon him at once, seizing him by his legs and arms and holding him tightly in spite of his struggles, and they bore him forth while all stood around to see the sport. Then one came forward who had been chosen to play the priest because he had a bald crown, and in his hand he carried a brimming pot of ale. "Now who bringeth this babe?" asked he right soberly.

"That do I," answered Will Stutely.

"And what name callest thou him?"

"Little John call I him."

"Now Little John," quoth the mock priest, "thou has not lived heretofore, but only got thee along through the world, but henceforth thou wilt live indeed. When thou livedst not, thou wast called John Little, but now that thou dost live indeed, Little John shalt thou be called; so christen I thee." And at these last words he emptied the pot of ale upon Little John's head.

Then all shouted with laughter as they saw the good brown ale stream over Little John's beard and trickle from his nose and chin, while his eyes blinked with the smart of it. At first he was of a mind to be angry, but found he could not because the others were so merry; so he, too, laughed with the rest. Then Robin took this sweet, pretty babe, clothed him all anew from top to toe in Lincoln green, and gave him a good stout bow, and so made him a member of the merry band.

And thus it was that Robin Hood became outlawed; thus a band of merry companions gathered about him, and thus he gained his right-hand man, Little John.

CHAPTER 2

Robin Hood and the Tinker

NOW IT was told before how two hundred pounds were set upon Robin Hood's head, and how the Sheriff of Nottingham swore that he himself would seize Robin, both because he would fain [gladly] have the two hundred pounds and because the slain man was a kinsman of his own. Now the Sheriff did not yet know what a force Robin had about him in Sherwood, but thought that he might serve a warrant for his arrest, as he could upon any other man that had broken the laws; therefore he offered fourscore golden angels [coins] to any one who would serve this warrant.

But men of Nottingham Town knew more of Robin Hood and his doings than the Sheriff did, and many laughed to think of serving a warrant upon the bold outlaw, knowing well that all they would get for such service would be cracked crowns; so that no one came forward to take the matter in hand. Thus a fortnight passed, in which time none came forward to do the Sheriff's business. Then said he: "A right good reward have I offered to whoever would serve my warrant upon Robin Hood, and I marvel that no one has yet come to me to undertake the task."

Then one of his men who was near him said: "Good master, thou wottest not [knowest not] the force that Robin Hood has about him and how little he cares for warrant of king or sheriff. Truly, no one likes to go on this service, for fear of cracked crowns and broken bones."

"Then I hold all Nottingham men to be cowards," said the Sheriff. "And let me see the man in all Nottinghamshire that dare disobey the warrant of our sovereign lord, King Harry, for, by the shrine of Saint Edmund, I will hang him forty cubits high! But if no man in Nottingham dare win fourscore angels, I will send elsewhere, for there should be men of mettle somewhere in this land."

Then he called up a messenger in whom he placed great trust, and bade him saddle his horse and make ready to go to Lincoln Town to see whether he could find anyone there that would do his bidding and win the reward. That same morning the messenger started forth upon his errand.

Bright shone the sun upon the dusty highway that led from Nottingham to Lincoln, stretching away all white over hill and dale. Dusty was the highway and dusty the throat of the messenger, so that his heart was glad when he saw before him the sign of the Blue Boar Inn, when somewhat more than half his journey was done. The inn looked fair to his eyes, and the shade of the oak trees that stood around it seemed cool and pleasant, so he alighted from his horse to rest himself for a time, calling for a pot of ale to refresh his thirsty throat.

There he saw a party of right jovial fellows seated beneath the spreading oak that shaded the greensward in front of the door. There was a tinker, two barefoot friars, and a party of six of the King's foresters all clad in Lincoln green, and all of

them were quaffing humming ale and singing merry ballads
of the good old times. Loud laughed the foresters, as jests
were bandied about between the singing, and louder laughed
the friars, for they were lusty men with beards that curled
like the wool of black rams; but loudest of all laughed the
Tinker, and he sang more sweetly than any of the rest. His
bag and his hammer hung upon a twig of the oak tree, and
near by leaned his good stout cudgel, as thick as his wrist and
knotted at the end.

"Come," cried one of the foresters to the tired messenger,
"come join us for this shot. Ho. Landlord! bring a fresh pot
of ale for each man."

The messenger was glad enough to sit down along with the
others who were there, for his limbs were weary and the ale
was good.

"Now what news bearest thou so fast?" quoth one. "And
whither ridest thou today?"

The messenger was a chatty soul and loved a bit of gossip
dearly; besides the pot of ale warmed his heart; so that,
settling himself in an easy corner of the inn bench, while the
host leaned upon the doorway and the hostess stood with her
hands beneath her apron, he unfolded his budget of news
with great comfort. He told all from the very first: how Robin
Hood had slain the forester, and how he had hidden in the
greenwood to escape the law; how that he lived therein, all
against the law, God wot, slaying his Majesty's deer and levy-
ing toll on fat abbot, knight, and esquire, so that none dare
travel even on broad Watling Street or the Fosse Way for fear
of him; how that the Sheriff, Heaven save his worship, who
paid him, the messenger, sixpence every Saturday night, of
good broad money stamped with the King's head, besides ale at
Michaelmas and a fat goose at Christmas-tide, had a mind to

serve the king's warrant upon this same rogue, though little would he mind either warrant of king or sheriff, for he was far from being a law-abiding man. Then he told how none could be found in all Nottingham Town to serve this warrant, for fear of cracked pates and broken bones, and how that he, the messenger, was now upon his way to Lincoln Town to find of what mettle the Lincoln men might be, and whether there were any there that dared to serve this same warrant; wherefore was he now sitting among the prettiest lads he had ever known, and the ale was the best ale he had tasted in all his life.

To this discourse they listened with open mouths and eyes, for it was a fair piece of gossip to them. Then when the messenger had done the jolly Tinker broke silence.

"Now come I, forsooth, from good Banbury Town," said he, "and no one nigh Nottingham—nor Sherwood either, an that be the mark—can hold cudgel with my grip. Why lads, did I not meet that mad wag, Simon of Ely, even at the famous Fair at Hertford Town, and beat him in the ring at that place before Sir Robert of Leslie and his lady! This same Robin Hood, of whom, I wot, I never heard before, is a right merry blade, but gin [if] he be strong, am I not stronger? And gin he be sly, am not I slyer? Now by the bright eyes of Nan o' the Mill and by mine own name, and that's Wat o' the Crabstaff, and by mine own mother's son, and that's myself, will I, even I, Wat o' the Crabstaff, meet this same sturdy rogue, and gin he mind not the seal of our glorious sovereign, King Harry, and the warrant of the good Sheriff of Nottinghamshire, I will so bruise, beat, and bemaul his pate, that he shall never move finger or toe again! Here ye that, bully boys? Come, let us have another bout."

"Now art thou the man for my farthing," cried the messenger. "And back thou goest with me to Nottingham Town."

"Nay," quoth the Tinker, shaking his head slowly from side to side. "Go I with no man gin it be not with mine own free will."

"Nay, nay," said the messenger, "no man is there in Nottinghamshire could make thee go against thy will, thou brave fellow."

"Ay, that be I brave," said Tinker.

"Ay, marry," said the messenger, "thou art a brave lad; but our good Sheriff hath offered fourscore angels of bright gold to whosoever shall serve the warrant upon Robin Hood, though little good will it do."

"Then I will go with thee, lad. Do but wait till I get my bag, hammer, and my cudgel. Ay, let me but meet this same Robin Hood, and let me see whether he will not mind the King's warrant."

So, after having paid their score, the messenger, with the Tinker striding beside his nag, started back to Nottingham again.

One bright morning soon after this time, Robin Hood started off to Nottingham Town to find what was a-doing there, walking merrily along the roadside where the grass was sweet with daisies, his eyes wandering and his thoughts also. His bugle-horn hung at his hip and his bow and arrows at his back, while in his hand he bore a good stout oaken staff, which he twirled with his fingers as he strolled along.

As thus he walked down a shady lane he saw a tinker coming, trolling a merry song as he drew nigh. On his back hung his bag and his hammer, and in his hand he carried a right stout crabstaff full six feet long.

"Halloa, good friend!" cried Robin, shouting above the song.

The Tinker went on singing.

"Halloa! Art thou deaf, man? Good friend, say I!"

"And who art thou dost so boldly check a fair song?" quoth the Tinker, stopping his singing. "Halloa, thine own self, whether thou be good friend or no. But let me tell thee, thou stout fellow, gin thou be a good friend it were well for us both; but gin thou be no good friend it were ill for thee."

"Then let us be good friends," quoth jolly Robin, "for ill would it be to be ill, and ill like I thine oaken staff full well to make it but well, so good friends let us be."

"Ay, marry, then let us be," said the Tinker. "But, good youth, thy tongue runneth so nimbly that my poor and heavy wits can but ill follow it, so talk more plainly, I pray thee, for I am a plain man, forsooth."

"And whence comest thou, my lusty blade?" quoth Robin.

"I come from Banbury," answered the Tinker.

"Alas," quoth Robin, "I hear sad news this merry morn."

"Ha! It is indeed so?" cried the Tinker eagerly. "Prythee tell it speedily, for I am a tinker by trade, as thou seest, and as I am in my trade I am greedy for news, even as a priest is greedy for farthings."

"Well then," quoth Robin, "list thou and I will tell, but bear thyself up bravely, for the news is sad, I wot. Thus it is: I hear that two tinkers are in the stocks for drinking ale and beer!"

"Now a murrain [plague] seize thee and thy news, thou scurvy dog," quoth the Tinker, "for thou speakest but ill of good men. But sad news it is indeed, gin there be two stout fellows in the stocks."

"Nay," said Robin, "thou hast missed the mark and dost but weep for the wrong sow. The sadness of the news lieth in that there be but two in the stocks, for the others do roam the country at large."

"Now by the pewter platter of Saint Dunstan," cried the Tinker, "I have a good part of a mind to baste thy hide for thine ill jest. But gin men be put in the stocks for drinking ale and beer, I trow thou wouldst not lose thy part."

Loud laughed Robin and cried: "Now well taken, Tinker, well taken! Why, thy wits are like beer, and do froth up most when they grow sour! But right art thou, man, for I love ale and beer right well. Therefore come straightway with me hard by to the sign of the Blue Boar, and if thou drinkest as thou appearest—and I wot thou wilt not belie thy looks—I will drench thy throat with as good homebrewed as ever was tapped in all broad Nottinghamshire."

"Now by my faith," said the Tinker, "thou art a right good fellow in spite of thy scurvy jests. I love thee, my sweet chuck, and gin I go not with thee to that same Blue Boar thou mayest call me a heathen."

"Tell me thy news, good friend, I prythee," quoth Robin as they trudged along together, "for tinkers, I ween [think], are all as full of news as an egg of meat."

"Now I love thee as my brother, my bully blade," said the Tinker, "else I would not tell thee my news; for sly am I, man, and I have in hand a grave undertaking that doth call for all my wits, for I come to seek a bold outlaw that men, hereabouts, call Robin Hood. Within my pouch I have a warrant, all fairly written out on parchment, forsooth, with a great red seal for to make it lawful. Could I but meet this same Robin Hood I would serve it upon his dainty body, and if he minded it not, I would beat him till every one of his ribs would cry Amen. But thou livest hereabouts; mayhap thou knowest Robin Hood thyself, good fellow."

"Ay, marry, that I do somewhat," quoth Robin, "and I have seen him this very morn. But, Tinker, men say that he is but a sad, sly thief. Thou hadst better watch thy warrant, man, or else he may steal it out of thy very pouch."

"Let him but try!" cried Tinker. "Sly may he be, but sly am I, too. I would I had him here now, man to man!" And he made his heavy cudgel to spin again. "But what manner of man is he, lad?"

"Much like myself," said Robin, laughing, "and in height and build and age nigh the same; and he hath blue eyes, too, like mine."

"Nay," quoth the Tinker, "thou art but a green youth. I thought him to be a great bearded man, Nottingham men feared him so."

"Truly, he is not so old nor so stout as thou art," said Robin. "But men do call him a right deft hand at quarter-staff."

"That may be," said the Tinker, right sturdily; "but I am more deft than he, for did I not overcome Simon of Ely in a fair bout in the ring at Hertford Town? But if thou knowest him, my jolly blade, wilt thou go with me and bring me to him? Fourscore bright angels hath the Sheriff promised me if I serve the warrant upon the knave's body, and ten of them will I give to thee if thou showest me him."

"Ay, that will I," quoth Robin; "but show me thy warrant, man, until I see whether it be good or no."

"That will I not do, even to mine own brother," answered the Tinker. "No man shall see my warrant till I serve it upon yon fellow's own body."

"So be it," quoth Robin. "An thou show it not to me I know not to whom thou wilt show it. But here we are at the sign of the Blue Boar, so let us in and taste his brown October."

No sweeter inn could be found in all Nottinghamshire than that of the Blue Boar. None had such lovely trees standing around, or was so covered with trailing clematis and sweet woodbine; none had such good beer and such humming ale; nor, in winter time, when the north wind howled and snow drifted around the hedges, was there to be found, elsewhere, such a roaring fire as blazed upon the hearth of the Blue Boar. At such times might be found a goodly company of yeomen or country folk seated around the blazing hearth, bandying merry jests, while roasted crabs [small sour apples] bobbed in bowls of ale upon the hearthstone.

Well known was the inn to Robin Hood and his band, for there had he and such merry companions as Little John or Will Stutely or young David of Doncaster often gathered when all the forest was filled with snow. As for mine host, he knew how to keep a still tongue in his head, and to swallow his words before they passed his teeth, for he knew very well which side of his bread was spread with butter, for Robin and his band were the best of customers and paid their scores without having them chalked up behind the door. So now, when Robin Hood and Tinker came thereto and called for two great pots of ale, none would have known from look or speech that the host had ever set eyes upon the outlaw before.

"Bide thou here," quoth Robin to the Tinker, "while I go and see that mine host draweth ale from the right butt, for he hath good October, I know, and that brewed by Withold of Tamworth." So saying, he went within and whispered to the host to add a measure of Flemish strong waters to the good English ale, which the latter did and brought it to them.

"By our Lady," said the Tinker, after a long draught of the ale, "yon same Withold of Tamworth—a right good Saxon name, too, I would have thee know—breweth the most humming ale that e'er passed the lips of Wat o' the Crabstaff."

"Drink, man, drink," cried Robin, only wetting his own

lips meanwhile. "Ho, landlord! Bring my friend another pot of the same. And now for a song, my jolly blade!"

"Ay, that will I give thee a song, my lovely fellow," quoth the Tinker, "for I never tasted such ale in all my days before. By'r Lady, it doth make my head hum even now! Hey, Dame Hostess, come listen, an thou wouldst hear a song; and thou too, bonny lass, for never sing I so well as when bright eyes do look upon me the while."

Then he sang an ancient ballad of the time of good King Arthur, called "The Marriage of Sir Gawaine," which you may sometime read, yourself, in stout English of early times; and as he sang, all listened to that noble tale of noble knight and his sacrifice to his king. But long before the Tinker came to the last verse his tongue began to trip and his head to spin, because of the strong waters mixed with the ale. First his tongue tripped, then it grew thick of sound; then his head wagged from side to side, until at last he fell asleep.

Then Robin Hood laughed aloud and quickly took the warrant from out the Tinker's pouch with his deft fingers. "Sly art thou, Tinker," quoth he, "but not yet, I trow, art thou as sly as that same sly thief, Robin Hood."

Then he called the host to him and said, "Here, good man, are ten broad shillings for the entertainment thou has given us this day. See that thou takest good care of thy fair guest there, and when he wakes thou mayst again charge him ten shillings also, and if he hath it not, thou mayst take his bag and hammer, and even his coat, in payment. Thus do I punish those that come into the greenwood to deal dole to me. As for thine own self, never knew I landlord yet that would not charge twice an he could."

At this the host smiled slyly, as though saying to himself the rustic saw [saying], "Teach a magpie to suck eggs."

The Tinker slept until the afternoon drew to a close and the shadows grew long beside the woodland edge, then he awoke. First he looked up, then he looked down, then he looked east, then he looked west, for he was gathering his wits together, like barley-straws blown apart by the wind. First he thought of his merry companion, but he was gone. Then he thought of his stout crabstaff, and that he had within his hand. Then of his warrant, and of the fourscore angels he was to gain for serving it upon Robin Hood. He thrust his hand into his pouch, but not a scrap nor a farthing was there. Then he sprang to his feet in a rage.

"Ho, landlord!" cried he. "Whither hath that knave gone that was with me but now?"

"What knave meaneth your worship?" quoth the landlord, calling the Tinker worship to soothe him, as a man would pour oil upon angry water. "I saw no knave with your worship, for I swear no man would dare call that man knave so nigh to Sherwood Forest. A right stout yeoman I saw with your worship, but I thought that your worship knew him, for few there be about here that pass him by and know him not."

"Now, how should I, that ne'er have squealed in your sty, know all the swine therein? Who was he, then, an thou knowest him so well?"

"Why, yon same is a right stout fellow whom men hereabouts do call Robin Hood; which same"—

"Now, by'r Lady!" cried the Tinker hastily, and in a deep voice like an angry bull. "Thou didst see me come into thine inn, I, a staunch, honest craftsman, and never told me who my company was, well knowing thine own self who he was. Now, I have a right round piece of a mind to crack thy knave's pate for thee!" Then he took up his cudgel and looked at the landlord as though he would smite him where he stood.

"Nay," cried the host, throwing up his elbow, for he feared the blow, "how knew I that thou knewest him not?"

"Well and truly thankful mayst thou be," quoth the Tinker, "that I be a patient man and so do spare thy bald crown, else wouldst thou ne'er cheat customers again. But as for this same knave, Robin Hood, I go straightway to seek him, and if I do not score his knave's pate, cut my staff into fagots and call me a woman." So saying, he gathered himself together to depart.

"Nay," quoth the landlord, standing in front of him and holding out his arms like a gooseherd driving his flock, for money made him bold, "thou goest not till thou has paid me."

"But did not he pay thee?"

"Not so much as one farthing, and ten good shillings' worth of ale have ye drunk this day. Nay, I say, thou goest not away without paying me, else shall our good sheriff know of it."

"But nought have I to pay thee with, good fellow," quoth the Tinker.

" 'Good fellow' not me," said the landlord. "Good fellow am I not when it cometh to lose ten shillings! Pay me that thou owest me in broad money, or else leave thy coat and bag and hammer; yet, I wot they are not worth ten shillings, and I shall lose thereby. Nay, an thou stirrest, I have a great dog within and I will loose him upon thee. Maken, open thou the door and let forth Brian if this fellow stirs one step."

"Nay," quoth the Tinker—for, by roaming the country, he had learned what dogs were—"take thou what thou wilt have, and let me depart in peace, and may a murrain go with thee. But oh, landlord! An I catch yon scurvy varlet, I swear he shall pay full with usury for that he hath had!"

So saying, he strode away toward the forest, talking to himself, while the landlord and his worthy dame and Maken stood looking after him and laughed when he had fairly gone.

"Robin and I have stripped yon ass of his pack main neatly," quoth the landlord.

Now it happened about this time that Robin Hood was going through the forest to Fosse Way, to see what was to be seen there, for the moon was full and the night gave promise of being bright. In his hand he carried his stout oaken staff, and at his side hung his bugle horn. As thus he walked up a forest path, whistling, down another path came the Tinker, muttering to himself and shaking his head like an angry bull; and so, at a sudden bend, they met sharply face to face. Each stood still for a time, and then Robin spoke. "Halloa, my sweet bird," said he, laughing merrily, "how likest thou thine ale? Wilt not sing to me another song?"

The Tinker said nothing at first, but stood looking at Robin with a grim face. "Now," quoth he at last, "I am right glad I have met thee, and if I do not rattle thy bones within thy hide this day, I give thee leave to put thy foot upon my neck."

"With all my heart," cried merry Robin. "Rattle my bones, an thou canst." So saying, he gripped his staff and threw himself upon his guard. Then the Tinker spat upon his hands, and grasping his staff, came straight at the other. He struck two or three blows, but soon found that he had met his match, for Robin warded [guarded] and parried all of them, and, before the Tinker thought, Robin gave him a sharp rap upon the ribs in return.

At this Robin laughed aloud, and the Tinker grew angrier than ever and smote again with all his might and main. Again Robin warded two of the strokes, but at the third, his staff broke beneath the mighty blows of the Tinker. "Now, ill betide thee, traitor staff," cried Robin, as it fell from his hands. "A foul stick art thou to serve me thus in mine hour of need."

"Now yield thee," quoth the Tinker, "for thou art my captive; and if thou do not, I will beat thy pate to a pudding."

To this Robin Hood made no answer, but clapping his horn to his lips, he blew three blasts, loud and clear.

"Ay," quoth the Tinker, "blow thou mayest, but go thou must with me to Nottingham Town, for the Sheriff would fain see thee there. Now wilt thou yield thee, or shall I have to break thy pretty head?"

"An I must drink sour ale, I must," quoth Robin, "but never have I yielded me to man before, and that without wound or mark upon my body. Nor, when I bethink me, will I yield now. Ho, my merry men! Come quickly!"

Then from the forest leaped Little John and six stout yeomen clad in Lincoln green.

"How now, good master," cried Little John, "what need hast thou that thou dost wind thy horn so loudly?"

"There stands a tinker," quoth Robin, "that would fain take me to Nottingham, there to hang upon the gallows tree."

"Then shall he himself hang forthwith," cried Little John, and he and the others made at the Tinker, to seize him.

"Nay, touch him not," said Robin, "for a right stout man is he. A metal man he is by trade, and a mettled [brave] man by nature; moreover, he doth sing a lovely ballad. Say, good fellow, wilt thou join my merry men all? Three suits of Lincoln green shalt thou have a year, beside twenty marks in fee; thou shalt share all with us and lead a right merry life in the greenwood; for cares have we not and misfortune cometh not upon us within the sweet shades of Sherwood, where we shoot the dun deer and feed upon venison and sweet oaten cakes, and curds and honey. Wilt thou come with me?"

"Ay, marry, will I join with you all," quoth the Tinker, "for I love a merry life, and I love thee, good master, though thou didst thwack my ribs and cheat me into the bargain. Fain am I to own thou art both a stouter and a slyer man than I; so I will obey thee and be thine own true servant."

So all turned their steps to the forest depths, where the Tinker was to live henceforth. For many a day he sang ballads to the band, until the famous Allan a Dale joined them, before whose sweet voice all others seemed as harsh as a raven's; but of him we will learn hereafter.

CHAPTER 3

The Shooting-Match at Nottingham

THEN the Sheriff was very wroth because of this failure to take jolly Robin, for it came to his ears, as ill news always does, that the people laughed at him and made a jest of his thinking to serve a warrant upon such a one as the bold outlaw; and a man hates nothing so much as being made a jest of. So he said: "Our gracious Lord and Sovereign King himself shall know of this, and how his laws are perverted and despised by this band of rebel outlaws. As for yon traitor Tinker, him will I hang, if I catch him, upon the very highest gallows tree in all Nottinghamshire."

Then he bade all his servants and retainers to make ready to go to London Town, to see and speak with the King.

At this there was bustling at the Sheriff's castle, and men ran hither and thither upon this business and upon that, while the forge fires of Nottingham glowed red far into the night like twinkling stars, for all the smiths of the town were busy making or mending armor for the Sheriff's troop of escort. For two days this labor lasted; then, on the third, all was

ready for the journey. So forth they started in the bright
sunlight, from Nottingham Town to Fosse Way and thence to
Watling Street; and so they journeyed for two days, until they
saw at last the spires and towers of great London Town and
many folks stopped, as they journeyed along, and gazed at the
show they made riding along the highways with their flashing
armor, and gay plumes and trappings.

In London King Henry and his fair Queen Elinor held their
court, gay with ladies in silks and satins and velvets and
cloth of gold, and also brave knights and gallant courtiers.
Thither came the Sheriff and was shown into the King's
presence.

"A boon, a boon," quoth he, as he knelt upon the ground.

"Now what wouldst thou have?" said the King. "Let us hear
what may be thy desires."

"O good my Lord and Sovereign," spake the Sheriff, "in
Sherwood Forest, in our own good shire of Nottingham, liveth
a bold outlaw whose name is Robin Hood."

"In good sooth [truth]," said the King, "his doings have
reached even our own royal ears. He is a saucy, rebellious
varlet, yet, I am fain [glad] to own, a right merry soul withal."

"But hearken, O my most gracious Sovereign," said the
Sheriff. "I sent a warrant to him with thine own royal seal
attached, by a right lusty knave, but he beat the messenger
and stole the warrant. And he killeth thy deer and robbeth
thine own liege subjects even upon the great highways."

"Why, how now," quoth the King, wrathfully. "What
wouldst thou have me do? Comest thou not to me with a
great array of men-at-arms and retainers and yet art not able
to take a single band of lusty knaves without armor on breast,
in thine own county! What wouldst thou have me do? Art
thou not my Sheriff? Are not my laws in force in Nottingham-

shire? Canst thou not take thine own course against those that break the laws or do an injury to thee or thine? Go, get thee gone, and think well; devise some plan of thine own but trouble me no further. But look well to it, Master Sheriff, for I will have my laws obeyed by all men within my kingdom, and if thou art not able to enforce them thou art no sheriff for me. So look well to thyself, I say, or ill may befall thee as well as all the thieving knaves in Nottinghamshire. When the flood cometh it sweepeth away grain as well as chaff."

Then the Sheriff turned away with a sore and troubled heart and sadly he rued his fine show of retainers, for he saw that the King was angry because he had so many men about him and yet could not enforce the laws. So, as they all rode back to Nottingham, the Sheriff was thoughtful and full of care. Not a word did he speak to anyone, and no one of his men spoke to him, but all the time he was busy devising some plan to take Robin Hood.

"Aha!" he cried suddenly, smiting his hand upon his thigh. "I have it now! Ride on, my merry men all, and let us go back to Nottingham Town as speedily as we may. And mark well my words: before a fortnight is passed, that evil knave, Robin Hood, will be safely clapped into Nottingham gaol."

But what was the Sheriff's plan?

As a miser takes each one of a bag of silver angels, feeling each coin to find whether it be clipped or not, so the Sheriff, as all rode slowly and sadly back toward Nottingham, took up thought after thought in turn, feeling around the edges of each, but finding in everyone some flaw. At last he thought of the daring soul of jolly Robin and how, as the Sheriff knew, he often came even within the walls of Nottingham.

"Now," thought the Sheriff, "could I but persuade Robin nigh to Nottingham Town so that I could find him, I warrant

I would lay hands upon him so stoutly that he would never get away again." Then of a sudden it came to him like a flash that were he to proclaim a great shooting-match and offer some grand prize, Robin Hood might be over-persuaded by his spirit to come to the butts; and it was this thought which caused him to cry "Aha!" and smite his palm upon his thigh.

So, as soon as he had returned safely to Nottingham, he sent messengers north and south, and east and west, to proclaim through town, hamlet, and countryside, this grand shooting-match, and everyone was bidden that could draw a long bow, and the prize was to be an arrow of pure beaten gold.

When Robin Hood first heard the news of this he was in Lincoln Town, and hastening back to Sherwood Forest he soon called all his merry men about him and spoke to them thus: "Now hearken, my merry men all, to the news that I have brought from Lincoln Town today. Our friend the Sheriff of Nottingham hath proclaimed a shooting-match, and hath sent messengers to tell of it through all the countryside, and the prize is to be a bright golden arrow. Now I fain would have one of us win it, both because of the fairness of the prize and because our sweet friend the Sheriff hath offered it. So we will take our bows and shafts and go there to shoot, for I know right well that merriment will be a-going. What say ye, lads?"

Then young David of Doncaster spoke up and said: "Now listen, I pray thee, good master, unto what I say. I have come straight from our friend Eadom o' the Blue Boar, and there I heard the full news of this same match. But, master, I know from him, and he got it from the Sheriff's man Ralph o' the Scar, that this same knavish Sheriff hath but laid a trap for thee in this shooting-match and wishes nothing so much as to see thee there. So go not, good master, for I know right well he doth seek to beguile thee, but stay within the greenwood lest we all meet dole and woe."

"Now," quoth Robin, "thou art a wise lad and keepest thine ears open and mouth shut, as becometh a wise and crafty woodsman. But shall we let it be said that the Sheriff of Nottingham did cow bold Robin and seven-score as fair archers as are in all merry England? Nay, good David, what thou tellest me maketh me to desire the prize even more than I else should do. But what sayeth our good gossip Swanthold? Is it not 'A hasty man burneth his mouth, and the fool that keepeth his eyes shut falleth into the pit?' Thus he says, truly; therefore we must meet guile with guile. Now some of you clothe yourselves as curtal friars, and some as rustic peasants, and some as tinkers, or as beggars, but see that each man taketh a good bow or broadsword, in case need should arise. As for myself, I will shoot for this same golden arrow, and should I win it, we will hang it to the branches of our good greenwood tree for the joy of all the band. How like you the plan, my merry men all?"

Then, "Good, good!" cried all the band right heartily.

A fair sight was Nottingham Town on the day of the shooting-match. All along upon the green meadow beneath the town wall stretched a row of benches, one above the other, which were for knight and lady, squire and dame, and rich burghers and their wives; for none but those of rank and quality were to sit there. At the end of the range, near the target, was a raised seat bedecked with ribbons and scarfs and garlands of flowers, for the Sheriff of Nottingham and his dame. The range was twoscore paces broad. At one end stood the target, at the other a tent of striped canvas, from the pole of which fluttered many-colored flags and streamers. In this booth were casks of ale, free to be broached by any of the archers.

Across the range from where the seats for the better folk
were raised was a railing to keep the poorer people from
crowding in front of the target. Already, while it was early,
the benches were beginning to fill with people of quality, who
kept constantly arriving in little carts, or upon palfreys [sad-
dle horses] that curveted gayly to the merry tinkle of silver
bells at bridle-reins; with these came also the poorer folk, who
sat or lay upon the green grass near the railing that kept them
from off the range.

In the great tent the archers were gathering by twos and
threes; some talking loudly of the fair shots each man had
made in his day; some looking well to their bows, drawing a
string betwixt the fingers to see that there was no fray upon
it, or inspecting arrows, shutting one eye and peering down a
shaft to see that it was not warped, but straight and true, for
neither bow nor shaft should fail at such a time and for such
a prize.

And never were such a company of yeomen as were gathered at Nottingham Town that day, for the very best archers
of merry England had come to this shooting-match. There was
Gill o' the Red Cap, the Sheriff's own head archer, and Diccon Cruikshank of Lincoln Town, and Adam o' the Dell, a man
of Tamworth, of threescore years and more, yet hale and
lusty still, who in his time had shot in the famous match at
Woodstock, and had there beaten that renowned archer, Clym
o' the Clough. And many more famous men of the long bow
were there, whose names have been handed down to us in
goodly ballads of the olden time.

But now all the benches were filled with guests, lord and
lady, burgher and dame, when at last the Sheriff himself came
with his lady, he riding with stately mien upon his milk-white
horse and she upon her brown filly. Upon his head he wore a

purple velvet cap, and purple was his robe, all trimmed about with rich ermine; his jerkin and hose were of sea-green silk, and his shoes of black velvet, the pointed toes fastened to his garters with golden chains. A golden chain hung about his neck, and at his collar was a great carbuncle set in red gold. His lady was dressed in blue velvet, all trimmed with swan's down. So they made a gallant sight as they rode along side by side, and all the people shouted from where they crowded across the space from the gentlefolk; so the Sheriff and his lady came to their place, where men-at-arms, with hauberk and spear, stood about, waiting for them.

Then when the Sheriff and his dame had sat down, he bade his herald wind upon his silver horn; who thereupon sounded three blasts that came echoing cheerily back from the gray walls of Nottingham. Then the archers stepped forth to their places, while all the folk shouted with a mighty voice, each man calling upon his favorite yeoman. "Red Cap!" cried some; "Cruikshank!" cried others; "Hey for William o' Leslie!" shouted others yet again, while ladies waved silken scarfs to urge each yeoman to do his best.

Then the herald stood forth and loudly proclaimed the rules of the game as follows: "Shoot each man from yon mark, which is sevenscore yards and ten from the target. One arrow shooteth each man first, and from all the archers shall the ten that shooteth the fairest shafts be chosen to shoot again. Two arrows shooteth each man of these ten, then shall the three that shoot the fairest shafts be chosen to shoot again. Three arrows shooteth each man of those three, and to him that shooteth the fairest shafts shall the prize be given."

Then the Sheriff leaned forward, looking keenly among the press of archers to find whether Robin Hood was amongst them; but no one was there clad in Lincoln green, such as was worn by Robin and his band. "Nevertheless," said the Sheriff to himself, "he may still be there, and I miss him among the crowd of other men. But let me see when but ten men shoot, for I wot he will be among the ten, or I know him not."

And now the archers shot, each man in turn, and the good folk never saw such archery as was done that day. Six arrows were within the clout, four within the black, and only two smote the outer ring; so that when the last arrow sped and struck the target, all the people shouted aloud, for it was noble shooting.

And now but ten men were left of all those that had shot before, and of these ten, six were famous throughout the land, and most of the folk gathered there knew them. These six men were Gilbert o' the Red Cap, Adam o' the Dell, Diccon Cruikshank, William o' Leslie, Hubert o' Cloud, and Swithin o' Hertford. Two others were yeomen of merry Yorkshire, another was a tall stranger in blue, who said he came from London Town, and the last was a tattered stranger in scarlet, who wore a patch over one eye.

"Now," quoth the Sheriff to a man-at-arms who stood near him, "seest thou Robin Hood amongst the ten?"

"Nay, that do I not, your worship," answered the man. "Six of them I know right well. Of those Yorkshire yeomen, one is too tall and the other too short for that bold knave. Robin's beard is as yellow as gold, while yon tattered beggar in scarlet hath a beard of brown, besides being blind in one eye. As for the stranger in blue, Robin's shoulders, I ween, are three inches broader than his."

"Then," quoth the Sheriff, smiting his thigh angrily, "yon knave is a coward as well as a rogue, and dares not show his face among good men and true."

Then, after they had rested a short time, those ten stout

men stepped forth to shoot again. Each man shot two arrows, and as they shot, not a word was spoken, but all the crowd watched with scarce a breath of sound; but when the last had shot his arrow another great shout arose, while many cast their caps aloft for joy of such marvellous shooting.

"Now by our gracious Lady fair," quoth old Sir Amyas o' the Dell, who, bowed with fourscore years and more, sat near the Sheriff, "ne'er saw I such archery in all my life before, yet have I seen the best hands at the long bow for threescore years and more."

And now but three men were left of all those that had shot before. One was Gill o' the Red Cap, one the tattered stranger in scarlet, and one Adam o' the Dell of Tamworth Town. Then all the people called aloud, some crying, "Ho for Gilbert o' the Red Cap!" and some, "Hey for stout Adam o' Tamworth!" but not a single man in the crowd called upon the stranger in scarlet.

"Now, shoot thou well, Gilbert," cried the Sheriff, "and if thine be the best shaft, fivescore broad silver pennies will I give to thee beside the prize."

"Truly I will do my best," quoth Gilbert, right sturdily. "A man cannot do aught but his best, but that will I strive to do this day." So saying, he drew forth a fair smooth arrow with a broad feather and fitted it deftly to the string, then drawing his bow with care he sped the shaft. Straight flew the arrow and lit fairly in the clout, a finger breadth from the centre. "A Gilbert, a Gilbert!" shouted all the crowd; and, "Now, by my faith," cried the Sheriff, smiting his hands together, "that is a shrewd shot."

Then the tattered stranger stepped forth, and all the people laughed as they saw a yellow patch that showed beneath his arm when he raised his elbow to shoot, and also to see him aim

with but one eye. He drew the good yew bow quickly and
quickly loosed a shaft; so short was the time that no man
could draw a breath betwixt the drawing and the shooting;
yet his arrow lodged nearer the centre than the other by
twice the length of a barleycorn.

"Now by all the saints in Paradise!" cried the Sheriff.
"That is a lovely shaft in very truth!"

Then Adam o' the Dell shot, carefully and cautiously, and
his arrow lodged close beside the stranger's. Then after a short
space they all three shot again, and once more each arrow
lodged within the clout, but this time Adam o' the Dell's was
farthest from the centre, and again the tattered stranger's
shot was the best. Then, after another time of rest, they all
shot for the third time. This time Gilbert took great heed of
his aim, keenly measuring the distance and shooting with
shrewdest care. Straight flew the arrow, and all shouted till the
very flags that waved in the breeze shook with the sound, and
the rooks and daws flew clamoring about the roofs of the old
gray tower, for the shaft had lodged close beside the spot that
marked the very centre.

"Well done, Gilbert!" cried the Sheriff, right joyously.
"Fain am I to believe the prize is thine, and right fairly won.
Now, thou ragged knave, let me see thee shoot a better shaft
than that."

Naught spake the stranger but took his place, while all was
hushed, and no one spoke or even seemed to breathe, so great
was the silence for wonder what he would do. Meanwhile, also,
quite still stood the stranger holding his bow in his hand,
while one could count five; then he drew his trusty yew, holding it drawn but a moment, then loosed the string. Straight
flew the arrow, and so true that it smote a gray goose feather
from off Gilbert's shaft, which fell fluttering through the sun-

lit air as the stranger's arrow lodged close beside his of the red cap, and in the very centre. No one spoke a word for a while and no one shouted, but each man looked into his neighbor's face amazedly.

"Nay," quoth old Adam o' the Dell presently, drawing a long breath and shaking his head as he spoke, "twoscore years and more have I shot shaft, and maybe not all times bad; but I shoot no more this day, for no man can match with yon stranger, whosoe'er he may be." Then he thrust his shaft into his quiver, rattling, and unstrung his bow without another word.

Then the Sheriff came down from his dais and drew near, in all his silks and velvets, to where the tattered stranger stood leaning upon his stout bow, whilst the good folk crowded around to see the man who shot so wondrously well. "Here, good fellow," quoth the Sheriff, "take thou the prize, and well and fairly hast thou won it. What may be thy name, and whence comest thou?"

"Men do call me Jock o' Teviotdale, and thence am I come," said the stranger.

"Then, by Our Lady, Jock, thou art the fairest archer that e'er mine eyes beheld, and if thou wilt join my service I wilt clothe thee with a better coat than that thou hast upon thy back; thou shalt eat and drink of the best, and at every Christmas-tide fourscore marks shall be thy wage. I trow thou drawest better bow than that same coward knave, Robin Hood, that dared not show his face here this day. Say, good fellow, wilt thou join my service?"

"Nay, that will I not," quoth the stranger, roughly. "I will be mine own, and no man in all merry England shall be my master."

"Then get thee gone, and a murrain seize thee!" cried the Sheriff, and his voice trembled with anger. "And by my faith and troth I have a good part of a mind to have thee beaten for thine insolence!" Then he turned upon his heel and strode away.

It was a right motley company that gathered about the noble greenwood tree in Sherwood's depths that same day. A score and more of barefoot friars were there, and some that looked like tinkers, and some that seemed to be sturdy beggars and rustic hinds; and seated upon a mossy couch was one all clad in tattered scarlet, with a patch over one eye; and in his hand he held a golden arrow that was the prize of the great shooting-match. Then, amidst a noise of talking and laughter, he took the patch from off his eye and stripped away the scarlet rags from off his body and showed himself all clothed in fair Lincoln green, and quoth he: "Easy come these things away, but walnut stain cometh not so speedily from yellow hair." Then all laughed louder than before, for it was Robin Hood himself that had won the prize from the Sheriff's very hands.

Then all sat down to the woodland feast and talked amongst themselves of the merry jest that had been played upon the Sheriff, and of the adventures that had befallen each member of the band in his disguise. But when the feast was done, Robin Hood took Little John apart and said, "Truly am I vexed in my blood, for I heard the Sheriff say today, 'Thou shootest better than that coward knave, Robin Hood, that dared not show his face here this day.' I would fain let him know who it was who won the golden arrow from out his hand, and also that I am no coward such as he takes me to be."

Then Little John said, "Good master, take thou me and Will Stutely and we will send yon fat Sheriff news of all this by a messenger such as he doth not expect."

That day the Sheriff sat at meat in the great hall of his

house at Nottingham Town. Long tables stood down the hall, at which sat men-at-arms and household servants and good stout villains [bond servants], in all fourscore and more. There they talked of the day's shooting as they ate their meat and quaffed their ale. The Sheriff sat at the head of the table upon a raised seat under a canopy, and beside him sat his dame.

"By my troth," said he, "I did reckon full roundly that that knave, Robin Hood, would be at the game today. I did not think that he was such a coward. But who could that saucy knave be who answered me to my beard so bravely? I wonder that I did not have him beaten; but there was something about him that spoke of other things than rags and tatters."

Then, even as he finished speaking, something fell rattling among the dishes on the table, while those that sat near started up wondering what it might be. After a while one of the men-at-arms gathered courage enough to pick it up and bring it to the Sheriff. Then everyone saw that it was a blunted gray goose shaft, with a fine scroll, about the thickness of a goose quill, tied near to its head. The Sheriff opened the scroll and glanced at it, while the veins upon his forehead swelled and his cheeks grew ruddy with rage as he read, for this was what he saw:

> *"Now Heaven bless thy grace this day,*
> *Say all in sweet Sherwood,*
> *For thou didst give the prize away*
> *To merry Robin Hood."*

"Whence came this?" cried the Sheriff in a mighty voice.

"Even through the window, your worship," quoth the man who had handed the shaft to him.

CHAPTER 4 · · ·

Will Stutely Rescued

NOW when the Sheriff found that neither law nor guile could overcome Robin Hood, he was much perplexed, and said to himself, "Fool that I am! Had I not told our King of Robin Hood, I would not have gotten myself into such a coil; but now I must either take him captive or have wrath visited upon my head from his most gracious Majesty. I have tried law, and I have tried guile, and I have failed in both; so I will try what may be done with might."

Thus communing within himself, he called his constables together and told them what was in his mind. "Now take ye each four men, all armed in proof [in armor and fully armed]," said he, "and get ye gone to the forest, at different points, and lay in wait for this same Robin Hood. But if any constable finds too many men against him, let him sound a horn, and then let each band within hearing come with all speed and join the party that calls them. Thus, I think, shall we take this green-clad knave. Furthermore, to him that first meeteth with Robin Hood shall one hundred pounds of silver money be given, if he be brought to me, dead or alive; and to him that meeteth with any of his band shall twoscore pounds be given, if such be brought to me dead or alive. So, be ye bold and be ye crafty."

So thus they went in threescore companies of five to Sherwood Forest, to take Robin Hood, each constable wishing that he might be the one to find the bold outlaw, or at least one of his band. For seven days and nights they hunted through the forest glades, but never saw so much as a single man in Lincoln green; for tidings of all this had been brought to Robin Hood by trusty Eadom o' the Blue Boar.

When he first heard the news, Robin said, "If the Sheriff dare send force to meet force, woe will it be for him and many a better man besides, for blood will flow, and there will be great trouble for all. But fain would I shun blood and battle, and fain would I not deal sorrow to women folk and wives because good stout yeomen lose their lives. Once I slew a man, and never do I wish to slay a man again, for it is bitter for the soul to think thereon. So now we will abide silently in Sherwood Forest, so that it may be well for all; but should we be forced to defend ourselves, or any of our band, then let each man draw bow and brand [sword] with might and main."

At this speech many of the band shook their heads, and said to themselves, "Now the Sheriff will think that we are cowards, and folk will scoff throughout the countryside, saying that we fear to meet these men." But they said nothing aloud, swallowing their words, and doing as Robin bade them.

Thus they hid in the depths of Sherwood Forest for seven days and seven nights and never showed their faces abroad in all that time; but early in the morning of the eighth day Robin Hood called the band together and said, "Now who will go and find what the Sheriff's men are at by this time? For

I know right well they will not bide forever within Sherwood shades."

At this a great shout arose, and each man waved his bow aloft and cried that he might be the one to go. Then Robin Hood's heart was proud when he looked around on his stout, brave fellows, and he said, "Brave and true are ye all, my merry men, and a right stout band of good fellows are ye; but ye cannot all go, so I will choose one from amongst you, and it shall be good Will Stutely, for he is as sly as e'er an old dog fox in Sherwood Forest."

Then Will Stutely leaped high aloft and laughed loudly, clapping his hands, for pure joy that he should have been chosen from amongst them all. "Now thanks, good master," quoth he, "and if I bring not news of those knaves to thee, call me no more thy sly Will Stutely."

Then he clad himself in a friar's gown, and underneath the robe he hung a good broadsword in such a place that he could easily lay hands upon it. Thus clad, he set forth upon his quest, until he came to the verge of the forest, and so to the highway. He saw two bands of the Sheriff's men, yet he turned neither to the right nor the left, but only drew his cowl the closer over his face, folding his hands as if in meditation. So at last he came to the Sign of the Blue Boar. "For," quoth he to himself, "our good friend Eadom will tell me all the news."

At the Sign of the Blue Boar he found a band of the Sheriff's men drinking right lustily; so, without speaking to anyone, he sat down upon a distant bench, his staff in his hand, and his head bowed forward as though he were meditating. Thus he sat waiting until he might see the landlord apart, and Eadom did not know him, but thought him to be some poor tired friar, so let him sit without saying a word to him or molesting him, though he liked not the cloth. "For," said he to himself, "it is a hard heart that kicks the lame dog from off the sill."

As Stutely sat thus, there came a great house cat and rubbed against his knee, raising his robe a palm's breadth high. Stutely pushed his robe quickly down again, but the constable who commanded the Sheriff's men saw what had passed and saw also fair Lincoln green beneath the friar's robe. He said nothing at the time, but communed within himself in this wise: "Yon is no friar of orders gray, and also, I wot, no honest yeoman goeth about in priest's garb, nor doth a thief go so for naught. Now I think in good sooth that is one of Robin Hood's own men."

So, presently, he said aloud: "O holy father, wilt thou not take a good pot of March beer to slake thy thirsty soul withal?"

But Stutely shook his head silently, for he said to himself, "Maybe there be those here who know my voice."

Then the constable said again, "Whither goest thou, holy friar, upon this hot summer's day?"

"I go a pilgrim to Canterbury Town," answered Will Stutely, speaking gruffly, so that none might know his voice.

Then the constable said, for the third time, "Now tell me, holy father, do pilgrims to Canterbury wear good Lincoln green beneath their robes? Ha! By my faith, I take thee to be some lusty thief, and perhaps one of Robin Hood's own band! Now, by Our Lady's grace, if thou movest hand or foot, I will run thee through the body with my sword!"

Then he flashed forth his bright sword and leaped upon Will Stutely, thinking he would take him unaware; but Stutely had his own sword tightly held in his hand, beneath his robe, so he drew it forth before the constable came upon him. Then the stout constable struck a mighty blow; but he struck no more in all that fight, for Stutely, parrying the blow right deftly, smote the constable back again and again with all his might. Then he would have escaped, but he could not, for the other, all dizzy with the wound and with the flowing blood, seized him by the knees with his arms even as he reeled and fell. Then the others rushed upon him, and Stutely struck again at another of the Sheriff's men, but the steel cap glanced the blow, and though the blade bit deep, it did not kill. Meanwhile, the constable fainting as he was, drew Stutely downward, and the others, seeing the yeoman hampered so, rushed upon him again, and one smote him a blow upon the crown so that the blood ran down his face and blinded him. Then, staggering, he fell, and all sprang upon him, though he struggled so manfully that they could hardly hold him fast. Then they bound him with stout hempen cords so that he could not move either hand or foot, and thus they overcame him. But it was a doleful day's doings for two of that band; for the constable was sorely wounded, and the other, that Stutely smote upon the crown, lay sick for many a day ere he was the stout man that he had been before this famous fight.

Robin Hood stood under the greenwood tree, thinking of Will Stutely and how he might be faring, when suddenly he saw two of his stout yeomen come running down the forest path, and betwixt them ran buxom Maken of the Blue Boar. Then Robin's heart fell, for he knew they were the bearers of ill tidings.

"Will Stutely hath been taken," cried they, when they had come to where he stood.

"And is it thou that hast brought such doleful news?" said Robin to the lass.

"Ay, marry, for I saw it all," cried she, panting as the hare pants when it has escaped the hounds, "and I fear he is wounded sore, for one smote him main shrewdly i' the crown. They have bound him and taken him to Nottingham Town, and ere I left the Blue Boar I heard that he should be hanged to-morrow day."

"He shall not be hanged tomorrow day," cried Robin, "or, if he be, full many a one shall gnaw the sod, and many shall have cause to cry Alack-a-day!"

Then he clapped his horn to his lips and blew three blasts right loudly, and presently his good yeomen came running through the greenwood until sevenscore bold blades were gathered around him.

"Now hark you all!" cried Robin. "Our dear companion, Will Stutely, hath been taken by that vile Sheriff's men; therefore doth it behoove us to take bow and brand in hand to bring him off again, for I wot that we ought to risk life and limb for him, as he hath risked life and limb for us. Is it not so, my merry men all?"

Then all cried, "Ay!" with a great voice.

"Now," quoth Robin again, "if there be any here that care not to risk life and limb, let them abide within Sherwood shade, for I constrain no man to my will; but tomorrow I will bring Will Stutely back or I will die with him."

Then up spake stout Little John. "Thinkest thou, good master," he said, "that there be one among us all that would not risk life and limb for fellow in trouble? If such there be, then do not I know every man in this company of stout yeomen. And, moreover, if there be such, I wot he should be stripped and beaten from out our merry woodlands. Is it not so, good friends?"

Then all cried, "Ay!" again, for there was not one man amongst them all that would not venture everything for a friend in need.

So the next day they all wended their way from Sherwood

Forest, but by different paths, for it behooved them to be very crafty; so the band separated into parties of twos and threes, which were all to meet again in a tangled dell that lay near to Nottingham Town. Then, when they all had gathered together at the place of meeting, Robin spoke to them thus: "Now we will lie here in ambush until we can get news, for it doth behoove us to be cunning and wary if we would bring our friend, Will Stutely, off from the Sheriff's clutches."

So they lay hidden a long time, until the sun stood high in the sky. The day was warm and the dusty road was bare of travelers, except an aged palmer who walked slowly along the highroad that led close beside the gray castle wall of Nottingham Town. When Robin saw that no other wayfarer was within sight, he called young David of Doncaster, who was a shrewd man for his years, and said to him, "Now get thee forth, young David, and speak to yonder palmer that walks beside the town wall, for he hath come but now from Nottingham Town, and may tell thee news of good Stutely, perchance."

So David strode forth, and when he came up to the pilgrim, he saluted him and said: "Good morrow, holy father, and canst thou tell me when Will Stutely will be hanged upon the gallows tree? I fain would not miss the sight, for I have come from afar to see so sturdy a rogue hanged."

"Now, out upon thee, young man," cried the Palmer, "that thou shouldst speak so when a good stout man is to be hanged for nothing but guarding his own life!" And he struck his staff upon the ground in anger. "Alas, say I, that this thing should be! For even this day, toward evening, when the sun falleth low, he shall be hanged, fourscore rods from the great town gate of Nottingham, where three roads meet; for there the Sheriff sweareth he shall die as a warning to all outlaws in Nottinghamshire. But yet, I say again, alas! For, though

Robin Hood and his band may be outlaws, yet he taketh only from the rich and the strong and the dishonest man, while there is not a poor widow nor a peasant with many children, nigh to Sherwood, but has barley-flour enough all the year long through him. It grieves my heart to see one as gallant as this Stutely die, for I have been a good Saxon yeoman in my day, ere I turned palmer, and well I know a stout hand and one that smiteth shrewdly at a cruel Norman or a proud abbot with fat money-bags. Had good Stutely's master but known how this man was compassed about with perils, perchance he might send succor to bring him out of the hand of his enemies."

"Ay, marry, that is true," cried the young man. "If Robin Hood and his men be nigh this place, I wot right well they will strive to bring him forth from his peril. But fare thee well, thou good old man, and believe me, that if Will Stutely die, he shall be right well avenged."

Then he turned and strode rapidly away; but the Palmer looked after him, muttering, "I wot that youth is no country hind that hath come to see a good man die. Well, well, perchance Robin Hood is not so far away but that there will be stout doings this day." So he went upon his way, muttering.

When David of Doncaster told Robin Hood what the Palmer had said to him, Robin called the band around him and spoke to them thus: "Now let us get straightway into Nottingham Town, and mix ourselves with people there; but keep ye one another in sight, pressing as near the prisoner and his guards as ye can, when they come outside the walls. Strike no man without need, for I would fain avoid bloodshed, but if ye do strike, strike hard, and see that there be no need to strike again. Then keep all together until we come again to Sherwood, and let no man leave his fellows."

The sun was low in the western sky when a bugle-note sounded from the castle wall. Then all was bustle in Nottingham Town and crowds filled the streets, for all knew that the famous Will Stutely was to be hanged that day. Presently the castle gates opened wide and a great array of men-at-arms came forth with noise and clatter, the Sheriff, all clad in shining mail of linked chain, riding at their head. In the midst of all the guard, in a cart, with a halter about his neck, rode Will Stutely. His face was pale with his wound and with loss of blood, like the moon in broad daylight, and his fair hair was clotted in points upon his forehead, where the blood had hardened. When he came forth from the castle he looked up and he looked down, but though he saw some faces that showed pity and some that showed friendliness, he saw none that he knew. Then his heart sank within him like a plummet of lead, but nevertheless he spoke up boldly.

"Give a sword into my hand, Sir Sheriff," said he, "and wounded man though I be, I will fight thee and all thy men till life and struggle be gone."

"Nay, thou naughty varlet," quoth the Sheriff, turning his head and looking right grimly upon Will Stutely, "thou shalt have no sword but shall die a mean death, as beseemeth a vile thief like thee."

"Then do but untie my hands and I will fight thee and thy men with no weapon but only my naked fists. I crave no weapon, but let me not be meanly hanged this day."

Then the Sheriff laughed aloud. "Why, how now," quoth he, "is thy proud stomach quailing? Shrive thyself, thou vile knave, for I mean that thou shalt hang this day, and that where three roads meet, so that all men shall see thee hang, for carrion crows and daws to peck at."

"O thou dastard heart!" cried Will Stutely, gnashing his

teeth at the Sheriff. "Thou coward hind! If ever my good master meet thee thou shalt pay dearly for this day's work! He doth scorn thee, and so do all brave hearts. Knowest thou not that thou and thy name are jests upon the lips of every brave yeoman? Such a one as thou art, thou wretched craven, will never be able to subdue bold Robin Hood."

"Ha!" cried the Sheriff, in a rage. "Is it even so? Am I a jest with thy master, as thou callest him? Now I will make a jest of thee and a sorry jest withal, for I will quarter thee limb from limb, after thou art hanged." Then he spurred his horse forward, and said no more to Stutely.

At last they came to the great town gate, through which Stutely saw the fair country beyond, with hills and dales all clothed in verdure, and far away the dusky line of Sherwood's skirts. Then when he saw the slanting sunlight lying on field and fallow, shining redly here and there on cot and farmhouse, and when he heard the sweet birds singing their vespers, and the sheep bleating upon the hillside, and beheld the swallows flying in the bright air, there came a great fullness to his heart so that all things blurred to his sight through salt tears, and he bowed his head lest the folk should think him unmanly when they saw the tears in his eyes.

Thus he kept his head bowed till they had passed through the gate and were outside the walls of the town. But when he looked up again he felt his heart leap within him and then stand still for pure joy, for he saw the face of one of his own dear companions of merry Sherwood; then glancing quickly around he saw well-known faces upon all sides of him, crowding closely upon the men-at-arms who were guarding him. Then of a sudden the blood sprang to his cheeks, for he saw for a moment his own good master in the press, and, seeing him, knew that Robin Hood and all his band were there.

Yet betwixt him and them was a line of men-at-arms.

"Now, stand back!" cried the Sheriff in a mighty voice, for the crowd pressed around on all sides. "What mean ye, varlets, that ye push upon us so? Stand back, I say!"

Then came a bustle and a noise, and one strove to push between the men-at-arms so as to reach the cart, and Stutely saw that it was Little John that made all that stir.

"Now stand thou back!" cried one of the men-at-arms whom Little John pushed with his elbows.

"Now stand thou back thine own self," quoth Little John and straightway smote the man a buffet beside his head that felled him as a butcher fells an ox, and then he leaped to the cart where Stutely sat.

"I pray thee take leave of thy friends ere thou diest, Will," quoth he, "or maybe I will die with thee if thou must die, for I could never have better company." Then with one stroke he cut the bonds that bound the other's arms and legs, and Stutely leaped straightway from the cart.

"Now as I live," cried the Sheriff, "yon varlet I know right well is a sturdy rebel! Take him, I bid you! Let him not go!"

So saying he spurred his horse upon Little John, and rising in his stirrups smote with might and main, but Little John ducked quickly underneath the horse's belly and the blow whistled harmlessly over his head.

"Nay, good Sir Sheriff," cried he, leaping up again when the blow had passed. "I must e'en borrow thy most worshipful sword." Thereupon he twitched the weapon deftly from out the Sheriff's hand. "Here, Stutely," he cried, "the Sheriff hath lent thee his sword! Back to back with me, man, and defend thyself, for help is nigh!"

"Down with them!" bellowed the Sheriff in a voice like an angry bull; and he spurred his horse upon the two who now

stood back to back, forgetting in his rage that he had no weapon with which to defend himself.

"Stand back, Sheriff!" cried Little John; and even as he spoke, a bugle-horn sounded shrilly, and a clothyard shaft whistled within an inch of the Sheriff's head. Then there came a swaying hither and thither and oaths and cries and groans and clashing of steel, and swords flashed in the setting sun, and a score of arrows whistled through the air, and some cried "Help, help!" and some, "A rescue, a rescue!"

"Treason!" cried the Sheriff in a loud voice. "Bear back! Bear back! Else we be all dead men!" Thereupon he reined his horse backward through the thickest of the crowd.

Now Robin Hood and his band might have slain half of the Sheriff's men had they desired to do so, but they let them push out of the press and get them gone, only sending a bunch of arrows after them to hurry them in their flight.

"Oh, stay!" shouted Will Stutely after the Sheriff. "Thou wilt never catch bold Robin Hood if thou dost not stand to meet him face to face." But the Sheriff, bowing along his horse's back, made no answer but only spurred the faster.

Then Will Stutely turned to Little John and looked him in the face till the tears ran from his eyes and he wept aloud, and kissing his friend's cheeks, "O Little John!" quoth he, "mine own true friend, and he that I love better than man or woman in all the world beside! Little did I reckon to see thy face this day, or to meet thee this side of Paradise." And Little John could make no answer, but wept also.

Then Robin Hood gathered his band together in a close rank, with Will Stutely in the midst, and thus they moved slowly away toward Sherwood and were gone, as a storm-cloud moves away from the spot where a tempest has swept the land. But they left ten of the Sheriff's men lying along the ground wounded—some more, some less—yet no one knew who smote them down.

Thus the Sheriff of Nottingham tried thrice to take Robin Hood and failed each time; and the last time he was frightened, for he felt how near he had come to losing his life. He said, "These men fear neither God nor man, nor King nor King's officers. I would sooner lose mine office than my life, so I will trouble them no more." He kept close within his castle for many a day and dared not show his face outside of his own household. All the time he was gloomy and would speak to no one, for he was ashamed of what had happened that day.

CHAPTER 5 · · ·

Robin Hood Evens Scores

NOW after all these things had happened, and it became known to Robin Hood how the Sheriff had tried three times to make him captive, he said to himself: "If I have the chance, I will make our worshipful Sheriff pay right well for that which he hath done to me. Maybe I may bring him some time into Sherwood Forest, and have him to a right merry feast with us."

He laughed aloud, for when Robin Hood caught a baron or a squire, or a fat abbot or bishop, he brought them to the greenwood tree and feasted them before he lightened their purses.

But in the meantime Robin Hood and his band lived quietly in Sherwood Forest, without showing their faces abroad, for Robin knew that it would not be wise for him to be seen in the neighborhood of Nottingham, those in authority being very wroth with him. But though they did not go abroad, they lived a merry life within the woodlands, spending the days in shooting at garlands hung upon a willow wand at the end of

71

the glade, the leafy aisles ringing with merry jests and laughter; for whoever missed the garland was given a sound buffet, which, if delivered by Little John, never failed to topple over the unfortunate yeoman. Then they had bouts of wrestling and of cudgel play, so that every day they gained in skill and strength.

Thus they dwelt for nearly a year, and in that time Robin Hood often turned over in his mind many means of making an even score with the Sheriff. At last he began to fret at his confinement; so one day he took up his stout cudgel and set forth to seek adventure, strolling blithely along until he came to the edge of Sherwood. There, as he rambled along the sunlit road, he met a lusty young Butcher driving a fine mare, and riding in a stout new cart, all hung about with meat. Merrily whistled the Butcher as he jogged along, for he was going to the market, and the day was fresh and sweet, making his heart blithe within him.

"Good morrow to thee, jolly fellow," quoth Robin; "thou seemest happy this merry morn."

"Ay, that am I," quoth the jolly Butcher; "and why should I not be so? Am I not hale in wind and limb? Have I not the bonniest lass in all Nottinghamshire? And lastly, am I not to be married to her on Thursday next in sweet Locksley Town?"

"Ha," said Robin, "comest thou from Locksley Town? Well do I know that fair place for miles about, and well do I know each hedgerow and gentle pebbly stream, and even all the bright little fishes therein, for in that fair town I was born and bred.

"Now, where goest thou with thy meat, my fair friend?"

"I go to the market at Nottingham Town to sell my beef and my mutton," answered the Butcher. "But who art thou that comest from Locksley Town?"

"A yeoman am I, good friend, and men do call me Robin Hood."

"Now, by Our Lady's grace," cried the Butcher, "well do I know thy name, and many a time have I heard thy deeds both sung and spoken of. But Heaven forbid that thou shouldst take ought of me! An honest man am I, and have wronged neither man nor maid; so trouble me not, good master, as I have never troubled thee."

"Nay, Heaven forbid, indeed," quoth Robin, "that I should take from such as thee, jolly fellow! Not so much as one farthing would I take from thee, for I love a fair Saxon face like thine right well; more especially when it cometh from Locksley Town, and most especially when the man that owneth it is to marry a bonny lass on Thursday next. But come, tell me for what price thou wilt sell all thy meat and thy horse and cart."

"At four marks do I value meat, cart, and mare," quoth the Butcher; "but if I do not sell all my meat I will not have four marks in value."

Then Robin Hood plucked the purse from his girdle, and quoth he, "Here in this purse are six marks. Now, I would fain be a butcher for the day and sell my meat in Nottingham Town. Wilt thou close a bargain with me and take six marks for thine outfit?"

"Now may the blessings of all the saints fall on thine honest head!" cried the Butcher right joyfully, as he leaped down from his cart and took the purse that Robin was holding out to him.

"Nay," quoth Robin, laughing loudly, "many do like me and wish me well, but few call me honest. Now get thee gone back to thy lass and give her a sweet kiss from me."

So saying, he donned the Butcher's apron, and, climbing into the cart, he took the reins in his hand and drove through the forest to Nottingham Town.

When he came to Nottingham, he entered that part of the market where butchers stood and took up his inn [stand for selling] in the best place he could find. Next, he opened his stall and spread his meat upon the bench, then taking his cleaver and steel and clattering them together, he trolled aloud, in merry tones:

> *"Now come, ye lasses, and eke, ye dames,*
> *And buy your meat from me;*
> *For three pennyworths of meat I sell*
> *For the charge of one penny."*

Thus he sang blithely, while all who stood near listened amazedly; then, when he had finished, he clattered the steel and cleaver still more loudly, shouting lustily, "Now, who'll buy? who'll buy? Four fixed prices have I. Three pennyworths of meat I sell to a fat friar or priest for sixpence, for I want not their custom; stout aldermen I charge threepence, for it doth not matter to me whether they buy or not; to buxom dames I sell three pennyworths of meat for one penny, for I like their custom well; but to the bonny lass that hath a liking for a good tight butcher I charge nought but one fair kiss, for I like her custom the best of all."

Then all began to stare and wonder, and crowd around, laughing, for never was such selling heard of in all Nottingham Town; but when they came to buy they found it as he had said, for he gave good wife or dame as much meat for one penny as they could buy elsewhere for three, and when a widow or a poor woman came to him, he gave her flesh for nothing; but when a merry lass came and gave him a kiss, he charged not one penny for his meat; and many such came to his stall, for his eyes were as blue as the skies of June, and he laughed merrily, giving to each full measure. Thus he sold his meat so fast that no butcher that stood near him could sell anything.

Then they began to talk among themselves, and some said, "This must be some thief who has stolen cart, horse, and meat." Others said, "Nay, when did ye ever see a thief who parted with his goods so freely and merrily? This must be some prodigal who hath sold his father's land and would fain live merrily while the money lasts." And these latter being the greater number, the others came round, one by one, to their way of thinking.

Then some of the butchers came to him to make his acquaintance. "Come, brother," quoth one who was the head man of them all, "we be all of one trade, so wilt thou go dine with us? For this day the Sheriff hath asked all the Butcher Guild to feast with him at the Guild Hall. There will be stout fare and much to drink, and that thou likest, or I much mistake thee."

"Now, beshrew his heart," quoth jolly Robin, "that would deny a butcher. And, moreover, I will go dine with you all, my sweet lads, and that as fast as I can hie." Whereupon, having sold all his meat, he closed his stall, and went with them to the great Guild Hall.

There the Sheriff had already come in state, and with him many butchers. When Robin and those that were with him came in, all laughing at some merry jest he had been telling them, those that were near the Sheriff whispered to him, "Yon is a right mad blade, for he hath sold more meat for one penny this day than we could sell for three, and to whatsoever merry lass gave him a kiss he gave meat for nought." And others said, "He is some prodigal that hath sold his land for silver and gold and meanest to spend all that he has right merrily."

Then the Sheriff called Robin to him, not knowing him in his butcher's dress, and made him sit close to him on his right hand; for he loved a rich young prodigal—especially when he thought that he might lighten that prodigal's pockets into his own most worshipful purse. So he made much of Robin and laughed and talked with him more than with any of the others.

At last the dinner was ready to be served and the Sheriff bade Robin say grace, so Robin stood up and said: "Now Heaven bless us all and eke good meat and good sack within this house, and may all butchers be and remain as honest men as I am."

At this all laughed, the Sheriff loudest of all, for he said to himself, "Surely this is indeed some prodigal, and perchance I may empty his purse of some of the money that the fool throweth about so freely." Then he spake aloud to Robin saying: "Thou art a jolly young blade, and I love thee mightily," and he smote Robin upon the shoulder.

Then Robin laughed loudly too. "Yea," quoth he, "I know thou dost love a jolly blade, for didst thou not have jolly Robin at thy shooting-match and didst thou not gladly give him a bright golden arrow for his own?"

At this the Sheriff looked grave and all the guild of butchers, too, so that none laughed but Robin, only some winked slyly at each other.

"Come, fill us some sack!" cried Robin. "Let us e'er be merry while we may, for man is but dust, and he hath but a span to live here till the worm getteth him, as our good gossip Swanthold sayeth; so let life be merry while it lasts, say I. Nay, never look down i' the mouth, Sir Sheriff. Who knowest but that thou mayest catch Robin Hood yet if thou drinkest less good sack and Malmsey and bringest down the fat about thy paunch and the dust from out thy brain. Be merry, man."

Then the Sheriff laughed again, but not as though he liked the jest, while the butchers said, one to another, "Before Heaven, never have we seen such a mad rollicking blade. Mayhap, though, he will make the Sheriff mad."

"How now, brothers," cried Robin, "be merry! Nay, never count over your farthings, for by this and by that I will pay this shot myself, e'en though it cost two hundred pounds. So let no man draw up his lip, nor thrust his forefinger into his purse, for I swear that neither butcher nor Sheriff shall pay one penny for this feast."

"Now thou are a right merry soul," quoth the Sheriff, "and I wot thou must have many a head of horned beasts and many an acre of land, that thou doest spend thy money so freely."

"Ay, that have I," quoth Robin, laughing loudly again, "five hundred and more horned beasts have I and my brothers, and none of them have we been able to sell, else I might not have turned butcher. As for my land, I have never asked my steward how many acres I have."

At this the Sheriff's eyes twinkled, and he chuckled to himself. "Nay, good youth," quoth he, "if thou canst not sell thy cattle it may be I will find a man that wilt lift them from thy hands; perhaps that man may be myself, for I love a merry youth and would help such a one along the path of life. Now how much dost thou want for thy horned cattle?"

"Well," quoth Robin, "they are worth at least five hundred pounds."

"Nay," answered the Sheriff, slowly, and as if he were thinking within himself. "Well do I love thee, and fain would I help thee along, but five hundred pounds in money is a good round sum; besides I have it not by me. Yet I will give thee three hundred pounds for them all, and that in good hard silver and gold."

"Now thou old scoundrel!" quoth Robin. "Well thou knowest that so many horned cattle are worth seven hundred pounds and more, and even that is but small for them, and yet thou, with thy gray hairs and one foot in the grave, wouldst trade upon the folly of wild youth."

At this the Sheriff looked grimly at Robin. "Nay," quoth Robin, "look not on me as though thou hadst sour beer in thy mouth, man. I will take thine offer, for I and my brothers do need the money. We lead a merry life, and no one leads a merry life for a farthing, so, Sir Sheriff, I will close the bargain with thee.

"But mind that thou bring a good three hundred pounds with thee, for I trust not one that driveth so shrewd a bargain as this."

"I will bring the money," said the Sheriff. "But what is thy name, good youth?"

"Men call me Robert o' Locksley," quoth bold Robin.

"Then, good Robert o' Locksley," quoth the Sheriff, "I will come this day to see thy horned beasts. But first my clerk shall draw up a paper in which thou shalt be bound to the sale, for thou gettest not my money without I get thy beasts in return for it."

Then Robin Hood laughed again. "So be it," he cried, smiting his palm upon the Sheriff's hand. "Truly my brothers will be thankful to thee for thy money."

Thus the bargain was closed; but many of the butchers talked among themselves of the Sheriff, saying that it was but a scurvy trick to beguile a poor spendthrift youth in this way, and liking it not.

The afternoon had come when the Sheriff mounted his horse and joined Robin Hood, who stood outside the gateway of the paved court waiting for him, for he had sold his horse and cart to a trader for two marks. Then they set forth upon their way, the Sheriff riding upon his horse and Robin running beside him. Thus they left Nottingham Town and traveled forward along the dusty highway, laughing and jesting together as though they had been old friends; but all the time the Sheriff said within himself, "Thy jest to me of Robin Hood shall cost thee dear, good fellow, even four hundred pounds, thou fool." For he thought he would make at least that much by his bargain.

So they journeyed onward till they came within the verge of Sherwood Forest, when presently the Sheriff looked up and down and to the right and to the left of him and then grew quiet and ceased his laughter. "Now," quoth he, "may Heaven and its saints preserve us this day from a rogue men call Robin Hood."

Then Robin laughed aloud. "Nay," said he, "thou mayst set thy mind at rest, for well do I know Robin Hood and well do I know that thou art in no more danger from him this day than thou art from me."

At this the Sheriff looked askance at Robin saying to himself, "I like not that thou seemest so well acquainted with this bold outlaw, and I wish that I were well out of Sherwood Forest."

But still they traveled deeper into the forest shades, and the deeper they went the more quiet grew the Sheriff. At last they came to where the road took a sudden bend, and before them a herd of deer went tripping across the path. Then Robin

Hood came close to the Sheriff and pointing his finger he said, "These are my horned beasts, good Master Sheriff. How dost thou like them? Are they not wondrously fat and fair to see?"

At this the Sheriff drew rein quickly. "Now fellow," quoth he, "I would I were well out of this forest, for I like not thy company. Go thou thine own path, good friend, and let me but go mine."

But Robin only laughed and caught the Sheriff's bridle rein. "Nay," cried he, "stay a while, for I would thou shouldst see my brothers who own these fair horned beasts with me." So saying he clapped his bugle to his mouth and winded three merry notes, and presently up the path came leaping fivescore good stout yeomen with Little John at their head.

"What wouldst thou have, good master?" quoth Little John.

"Why," answered Robin, "dost thou not see that I have brought goodly company to feast with us today? Fye, for shame! Do you not see our good and worshipful master, the Sheriff of Nottingham? Take thou his bridle, Little John, for he has honored us today by coming to feast with us."

Then all doffed their hats humbly, without smiling, or seeming to be in jest whilst Little John took the bridle rein and led the palfrey still deeper into the forest, all marching in order, with Robin walking beside the Sheriff, hat in hand.

All this time the Sheriff said never a word but only looked about him like one suddenly awakened from sleep; but when he found himself going within the very depth of Sherwood his heart sank within him, for he thought, "Surely my three hundred pounds will be taken from me, even if they take not my life itself, for I have plotted against their lives more than once." But all seemed humble and meek and not a word was said of danger, either to life or money.

So at last they came to that part of Sherwood Forest where a noble oak spread its branches wide, and beneath it was a seat all made of moss, on which Robin sat down, placing the Sheriff at his right hand. "Now busk [prepare] ye, my merry men all," quoth he, "and bring forth the best we have, both of meat and wine, for his worship, the Sheriff, hath feasted me in Nottingham Guild Hall today, and I would not have him go back empty."

All this time nothing had been said of the Sheriff's money, so presently he began to pluck up heart. "For," said he to himself, "maybe Robin Hood hath forgotten all about it."

Then, whilst beyond in the forest bright fires crackled and savory smells of sweetly roasting venison and fat capons filled the glade, and brown pasties warmed beside the blaze, did Robin Hood entertain the Sheriff right royally. First, several couples stood forth at quarterstaff, and so shrewd were they at the game, and so quickly did they give stroke and parry, that the Sheriff, who loved to watch all lusty sports of the kind, clapped his hands, forgetting where he was, and crying aloud, "Well struck! Well struck, thou fellow with the black beard!" Little knew he that the man he called upon was the Tinker that tried to serve his warrant upon Robin Hood.

Then the best archers of the band set up a fair garland of flowers at eightscore paces distant, and shot at it with the cunningest archery practice. But the Sheriff grew grave, for he did not like this so well, the famous meeting at the butts in Nottingham Tower being still green in his memory, and the golden arrow that had been won there hanging close behind him. Then, when Robin saw what was in the Sheriff's mind, he stopped the sport, and called forth some of his band, who sang merry ballads, while others made fair music upon the harp.

When this was done, several yeomen came forward and spread cloths upon the green grass, and placed a royal feast, while others still broached barrels of sack and Malmsey and good stout ale, and set them in jars upon the cloth, with drinking-horns about them. Then all sat down and feasted and drank merrily together until the sun was low and the half-moon glimmered with a pale light betwixt the leaves of the trees overhead.

Then the Sheriff arose and said, "I thank you all, good yeomen, for the merry entertainment ye have given me this day. Right courteously have ye used me, showing therein that ye have much respect for our glorious King and his deputy in brave Nottinghamshire. But the shadows grow long, and I must away before darkness comes, lest I lose myself within the forest."

Then Robin Hood and all his men arose also, and Robin said to the Sheriff, "If thou must go, worshipful sir, go thou must; but thou hast forgotten one thing."

"Nay, I forgot nought," said the Sheriff; yet all the same his heart sank within him.

"But I say thou hast forgot something," quoth Robin. "We keep a merry inn here in the greenwood, but whoever becometh our guest must pay his reckoning."

Then the Sheriff laughed, but the laugh was hollow. "Well, jolly boys," quoth he, "we have had a merry time together to-day, and even if ye had not asked me, I would have given you a score of pounds for the sweet entertainment I have had."

"Nay," quoth Robin seriously, "It would ill beseem us to treat your worship so meanly. By my faith, Sir Sheriff, I would be ashamed to show my face if I did not reckon the King's deputy at three hundred pounds. Is it not so, my merry men all?"

Then "Ay!" cried all, in a loud voice.

"Three hundred devils!" roared the Sheriff. "Think ye that your beggarly feast was worth three pounds, let alone three hundred?"

"Nay," quoth Robin, gravely. "Speak not so roundly, your worship. I do love thee for the sweet feast thou hast given me this day in merry Nottingham Town; but there be those here who love thee not so much. If thou wilt look down the cloth thou wilt see Will Stutely, in whose eyes thou hast no great favor; then two other stout fellows are there here that thou knowest not, that were wounded in a brawl nigh Nottingham Town, some time ago—thou wottest (knowest) when. One of them was sore hurt in one arm, yet he hath got the use of it again. Good Sheriff, be advised by me; pay thy score without more ado, or maybe it may fare ill with thee."

As he spoke the Sheriff's ruddy cheeks grew pale, and he said nothing more but looked upon the ground and gnawed his nether lip. Then slowly he drew forth his fat purse and threw it upon the cloth in front of him.

"Now take the purse, Little John," quoth Robin Hood, "and see that the reckoning is right. We would not doubt our Sheriff, but he might not like it if he should find he had not paid his full score."

Then Little John counted the money and found that the bag held three hundred pounds in silver and gold. But to the Sheriff it seemed as if every clink of the bright money was a drop of blood from his veins, and when he saw it all counted out in a heap of silver and gold, filling a wooden platter, he turned away and silently mounted his horse.

"Never have we had so worshipful a guest before!" quoth Robin. "And as the day waxeth late, I will send one of my young men to guide thee out of the forest depths."

"Nay, heaven forbid!" cried the Sheriff, hastily. "I can find mine own way, good man, without aid."

"Then I will put thee on the right track mine own self," quoth Robin, and, taking the Sheriff's horse by the bridle rein, he led him into the main forest path. Before he let him go, he said, "Now, fare thee well, good Sheriff, and when next thou thinkest to despoil some poor prodigal, remember thy feast in Sherwood Forest. 'Ne'er buy a horse, good friend, without first looking into its mouth,' as our good gaffer [old man] Swanthold says. And so, once more, fare thee well." Then he clapped his hand to the horse's back, and off went nag and Sheriff through the forest glades.

Then bitterly the Sheriff rued the day that first he meddled with Robin Hood, for all men laughed at him and many ballads were sung by folks throughout the country, of how the Sheriff went to shear and came home shorn to the very quick. For thus men sometimes overreach themselves through greed and guile.

Spring had gone since the Sheriff's feast in Sherwood, and summer also, and the mellow month of October had come. All the air was cool and fresh; the harvests were gathered home, the young birds were full fledged, the hops were plucked, and apples were ripe. But though time had so smoothed things over that men no longer talked of the horned beasts that the Sheriff wished to buy, he was still sore about the matter and could not bear Robin Hood's name spoken in his presence.

With October had come the time for holding the great Fair which was celebrated every five years at Nottingham Town, to which folk came from far and near throughout the country. At such times archery was always the main sport of the day, for the Nottinghamshire yeomen were the best hand at the longbow in all Merry England; but this year the

Sheriff hesitated a long time before he issued proclamation of
the Fair, fearing lest Robin Hood and his band might come to
it. At first he had a great part of a mind not to proclaim the
Fair, but second thought told him that men would laugh at
him and say among themselves that he was afraid of Robin
Hood, so he put that thought by. At last he fixed in his mind
that he would offer such a prize as they would not care to
shoot for. At such times it had been the custom to offer a half
score of marks or a tun of ale, so this year he proclaimed
that a prize of two fat steers should be given.

When Robin Hood heard what had been proclaimed he was
vexed and said, "Now beshrew this Sheriff that he should
offer such a prize that none but shepherd hinds will care to
shoot for it! I would have loved nothing better than to have
another bout at merry Nottingham Town, but if I should win
this prize naught would it pleasure or profit me."

Then up spoke Little John: "Nay, but hearken, good master," said he, "only today Will Stutely, young David of Doncaster, and I were at the sign of the Blue Boar, and there we
heard all the news of this merry Fair, and also that the
Sheriff hath offered this prize that we of Sherwood might
not care to come to the Fair; so, good master, if thou wilt, I
would fain go and strive to win even this poor thing among
the stout yeomen who will shoot at Nottingham Town."

"Nay, Little John," quoth Robin, "thou art a sound stout
fellow, yet thou lackest the cunning that good Stutely hath,
and I would not have harm befall thee for all Nottinghamshire. Nevertheless if thou wilt go, take some disguise lest
there be those there who may know thee."

"So be it, good master," quoth Little John; "yet all the disguise that I wish is a good suit of scarlet instead of this of
Lincoln green. I will draw the cowl of my jacket about my

head so that it will hide my brown hair and beard, and then, I trust, no one will know me."

"It is much against my will," said Robin Hood. "Ne'ertheless, if thou dost wish it, get thee gone, but bear thyself accordingly, Little John, for thou art mine own right hand man and I could ill bear to have harm befall thee." So Little John clad himself all in scarlet, and started off to the Fair at Nottingham Town.

Many days later, Little John and a stout companion came back at last to the greenwood tree, where they found Robin Hood and threescore of his merry men lying upon the fresh green grass. When Robin and his men saw who it was that came, they leaped to their feet. "Now welcome!" cried Robin Hood. "Now welcome, Little John! Long hath it been since we have heard from thee, though we all knew that thou hadst joined the Sheriff's service. And how hast thou fared all these long days?"

"Right merrily have I lived at the Lord Sheriff's," answered Little John, "after winning the shooting-match, and I have come straight thence. See, good master! I have brought thee his cook, and even his silver plate." Thereupon he told Robin Hood and his merry men that were there all that had befallen him since he had left them to go to the Fair at Nottingham Town, and especially how he and the cook had fought together and the cook had decided to join the band. Then all shouted with laughter, except Robin Hood, but he looked grave.

"Nay, Little John," said he, "thou art a brave blade and a trusty fellow. I am glad thou hast brought thyself back to us, and with such a good companion as the Cook, whom we all welcome to Sherwood. But I like not so well that thou hast stolen the Sheriff's plate like some paltry thief. The Sheriff hath been punished by us and hath lost three hundred pounds, even as he sought to despoil another; but he hath done nought that we should steal his household plate from him."

Though Little John was vexed with this, he strove to pass it off with a jest. "Nay, good master," quoth he, "if thou thinkest the Sheriff gave us not the plate, I will fetch him, that he may tell us with his own lips he giveth it all to us." So saying, he leaped to his feet, and was gone before Robin Hood could call him back.

Little John ran for full five miles till he came to where the Sheriff of Nottingham and a gay company were hunting near the forest. When Little John came to the Sheriff he doffed his cap and bent his knee. "God save thee, good master," quoth he.

"Why, Reynold Greenleaf!" cried the Sheriff, "whence comest thou and where has thou been?"

"I have been in the forest," answered Little John, speaking amazedly, "and there I saw a sight such as ne'er before man's eyes beheld! Yonder I saw a young hart all in green from top to toe, and about him was a herd of threescore deer, and they, too, were all of green from head to foot. Yet I dared not shoot, good master, for fear lest they should slay me."

"Why, how now, Reynold Greenleaf," cried the Sheriff; "art thou dreaming or art thou mad, that thou dost bring me such a tale?"

"Nay, I am not dreaming nor am I mad," said Little John, "and if thou wilt come with me, I will show thee this fair sight, for I have seen it with mine own eyes. But thou must come alone, good master, lest the others frighten them and they get away."

So the party all rode forward, and Little John led them downward into the forest.

"Now, good master," quoth he at last, "we are nigh where

I saw this herd of deer."

Then the Sheriff descended from his horse and bade them wait for him until he should return; and Little John led him forward through a close copse until suddenly they came to a great open glade, at the end of which Robin Hood sat beneath the shade of the great oak tree, with his merry men all about him. "See, good Master Sheriff," quoth Little John, "yonder is the hart of which I spake to thee."

At this the Sheriff turned to Little John and said bitterly, "Long ago I thought I remembered thy face, but now I know thee. Woe betide thee, Little John, for thou hast betrayed me."

Then Little John laughed aloud. "Good Master Sheriff," said he, "thou dost indeed know me, and I am Little John. But let me tell thee, all this would not have happened had not thy beggarly Steward starved me, and had he given me food to eat when I asked it. But if he gave none to me, the green hart will give thee another feast, and when thou goest back, tell thy Steward the time will come when he and I will have a reckoning."

In the meantime Robin Hood had come to them. "Now welcome, Master Sheriff," said he. "Hast thou come today to take another feast with me?"

"Nay, heaven forbid!" said the Sheriff, in tones of deep earnest. "I care for no feast and have no hunger today."

"Nevertheless," quoth Robin, "if thou hast no hunger, maybe thou hast thirst, and well I know thou wilt take a cup of sack with me. But I am grieved that thou wilt not feast with me, for thou couldst have victuals to thy liking, for there stands thy Cook."

Then he led the Sheriff, will-he-nill-he, to the seat he knew so well beneath the greenwood tree.

"Ho, lads!" cried Robin. "Fill our good friend, the Sheriff, a

right brimming cup of sack and fetch it hither, for he is faint and weary."

Then one of the band brought the Sheriff a cup of sack, bowing low as he handed it to him; but the Sheriff could not touch the wine, for he saw it served in one of his own silver flagons, on one of his own silver plates.

"How now," quoth Robin, "dost thou not like our new silver service? We have gotten a bag of it this day." So saying, he held up the sack of silver that Little John and the Cook had brought with them.

Then the Sheriff's heart was bitter within him; but, not daring to say anything, he only gazed upon the ground. Robin looked keenly at him for a time before he spoke again; then said he, "Now, Master Sheriff, the last time thou camest to Sherwood Forest thou didst come seeking to despoil a poor spendthrift, and thou wert despoiled thine own self; but now thou comes seeking to do no harm, nor do I know that thou hast despoiled any man. I take my tithes from fat priests and lordly squires, to help those that they despoil and to raise up those that they bow down; but I know not that thou hast tenants of thine own whom thou hast wronged in any way. Therefore, take thou thine own again, nor will I dispossess thee today of so much as one farthing. Come with me, and I will lead thee from the forest back to thine own party."

Then, slinging the bag upon his shoulder, he turned away, the Sheriff following him, all too perplexed in mind to speak. So they went forward until they came to within a furlong of the spot where the Sheriff's companions were waiting for him. Then Robin Hood gave the sack of silver back to the Sheriff. "Take thou thine own again," he said, "and, hearken to me, good Sheriff, take thou a piece of advice with it. Try thy servants well ere thou dost engage them again so readily."

Then, turning, he left the other standing bewildered, with the sack in his hands.

The company that waited for the Sheriff were all amazed to see him come out of the forest bearing a heavy sack upon his shoulders; but though they questioned him, he answered never a word, acting like one who walks in a dream. Without a word, he placed the bag across his nag's back, and then, mounting, rode away, all following him; but all the time there was a great turmoil of thoughts within his head, tumbling one over the other.

CHAPTER 6 • • •

Little John and the Tanner

IT OFTEN comes about in this world that unlucky happenings fall upon one in such measure that it seems, as the saying is, that every cat that one strokes flies into one's face. Thus it was with Robin Hood and Little John one bright day in the merry May-time; so listen and you shall hear how Dame Luck so buffeted them that their bones were sore for many a day thereafter.

One fine day, not long after Little John had left abiding with the Sheriff and had come back with his worship's cook to the merry greenwood, Robin Hood and a few chosen fellows of his band lay upon the soft sward beneath the greenwood tree where they dwelt. The day was warm and sultry, so that whilst most of the band were scattered through the forest upon this mission and that, these few stout fellows lay lazily beneath the shade of the tree, in the soft afternoon, passing jests among themselves and telling merry stories, with laughter and mirth.

All the air was laden with the bitter fragrance of the May,

and all the bosky shades of the woodlands beyond rang with the sweet song of birds—the throstle-cock, the cuckoo, and the wood-pigeon—and with the song of birds mingled the cool sound of the gurgling brook that leaped out of the forest shades and ran fretting amid its rough, gray stones across the sunlit open glade before the trysting-tree. And a fair sight was that halfscore of tall, stout yeomen, all clad in Lincoln green, lying beneath the broad-spreading branches of the great oak tree, amid the quivering leaves of which the sunlight shivered and fell in dancing patches upon the grass.

The good old times have gone by when such men grow as grew then; when sturdy quarterstaff and long bow toughened a man's thews [muscles] till they were like leather. Around Robin Hood that day lay the very flower of English yeomanrie. Here lay the great Little John, with limbs as tough as the gnarled oak, yet grown somewhat soft from good living at the Sheriff's house in Nottingham Town; there, Will Stutely, his face as brown as a berry from sun and wind, but, for all that, the comeliest yeoman in the mid-country, only excepting Allan a Dale, the minstrel, of whom you shall hear anon. Beside these was Will Scathelock, as lank as a greyhound, yet as fleet of foot as a buck of three years' growth; young David of Doncaster, with great stout limbs only less than those of Little John in size, the tender beard of early youth now just feathering his chin, and others of great renown both far and near. Suddenly Robin Hood smote his knee.

"By Saint Dunstan," quoth he, "I had nigh forgot that quarterday cometh on apace, and yet no cloth of Lincoln green in all our store. It must be looked to, and that in quick season. Come, busk thee, Little John! Stir those lazy bones of thine, for thou must get thee straightway to our good gossip, the draper, Hugh Longshanks of Ancaster. Bid him send us straightway twentyscore yards of fair cloth of Lincoln green; and mayhap the journey may take some of the fat from off thy bones, that thou has gotten from lazy living at our dear Sheriff's."

"Nay," muttered Little John (for he had heard so much upon this score that he was sore upon the point) "nay, truly, mayhap I have more flesh upon my joints than I once had, yet flesh or no flesh, I doubt not that I could still hold my place and footing upon a narrow bridge against e'er a yeoman in Sherwood, or Nottinghamshire, for the matter of that, even though he had no more fat about his bones than thou hast, good master."

At this reply a great shout of laughter went up, and all looked at Robin Hood, for each man knew that Little John spake of a certain fight that happened between their master and himself, through which they first became acquainted.

"Nay," quoth Robin Hood, laughing louder than all, "Heaven forbid that I should doubt thee, for I care for no taste of thy staff myself, Little John. I must needs own that there are those of my band can handle a seven-foot staff more deftly than I; yet no man in all Nottinghamshire can draw graygoose shaft with my fingers. Nevertheless, a journey to Ancaster may not be ill for thee; so go thou, as I bid, and thou hadst best go this very evening, for since thou hast abided at the Sheriff's many know thy face, and if thou goest in broad daylight, thou mayst get thyself into a coil [quarrel] with some of his worship's men-at-arms. Bide thou here till I bring thee money to pay our good Hugh. I warrant he hath no better customers in all Nottinghamshire than we." So saying, Robin left them and entered the forest.

Not far from the trysting tree was a great rock in which a chamber had been hewn, the entrance being barred by a massive oaken door two palms' breadth in thickness, studded about with spikes, and fastened with a great padlock. This was the treasure-house of the band, and thither Robin Hood went, and unlocking the door, entered the chamber, from which he brought forth a bag of gold, which he gave to Little John to pay Hugh Longshanks withal for the cloth of Lincoln green.

Then up got Little John, and, taking the bag of gold, which he thrust into his bosom, he strapped a girdle about his loins, took a stout pikestaff full seven feet long in his hand, and set forth upon his journey.

So he strode whistling along the leafy forest path that led to Fosse Way, turning neither to the right hand nor the left, until at last he came to where the path branched, leading on the one hand onward to Fosse Way, and on the other, as well Little John knew, to the merry Blue Boar Inn. Here Little John suddenly ceased whistling, and stopped in the middle of the path. First he looked up and then he looked down, and then, tilting his cap over one eye, he slowly scratched the back part of his head. For thus it was: at the sight of these two roads, two voices began to alarum within him, the one crying, "There lies the road to the Blue Boar Inn, a can of brown October, and a merry night with sweet companions such as thou mayst find there"; the other, "There lies the way to Ancaster and the duty thou art sent upon."

Now the first of these two voices was far the louder, for Little John had grown passing fond of good living through abiding at the Sheriff's house. Presently, looking up into the blue sky, across which bright clouds were sailing like silver boats, and swallows skimming in circling flight, quoth he, "I fear me it will rain this evening, so I'll e'en stop at the Blue Boar till it passes by, for I know my good master would not have me wet to the skin." So, without more ado, off he strode

down the path that lay the way of his likings. Now there was
no sign of any foul weather, but when one wishes to do a thing,
as Little John did, one finds no lack of reasons for it.

Four merry wags were at the Blue Boar Inn—a butcher, a
beggar, and two barefoot friars. Little John heard them singing from afar as he walked through the hush of the mellow
twilight that was now falling over hill and dale. Right glad
were they to welcome such a merry blade as Little John. Fresh
cans of ale were brought, and with jest and song and merry
tales the hours slipped away on fleeting wings. None thought
of time or tide till the night was so far gone that Little John
put by the thought of setting forth upon his journey again
that night and so bided at the Blue Boar Inn until the morrow.

Now it was an ill piece of luck for Little John that he left
his duty for his pleasure, and he paid a great score for it, as
we are apt to do in the same case, as you shall see.

Up he rose at the dawn of the next day, and, taking his
stout pikestaff in his hand, he set forth upon his journey once
more, as though he would make up for lost time.

In the good town of Blyth there lived a stout tanner, celebrated far and near for feats of strength and many tough
bouts at wrestling and the quarterstaff. For five years he had
held the midcountry champion belt for wrestling, till the
great Adam o' Lincoln cast him in the ring and broke one of
his ribs; but at quarterstaff he had never yet met his match
in all the country about. Besides all this, he dearly loved the
long bow and a sly jaunt in the forest when the moon was full
and the dun deer in season so that the King's rangers kept a
shrewd eye upon him and his doings, for Arthur a Bland's
house was apt to have a plenty of meat in it that was more
like venison than the law allowed.

Now Arthur had been to Nottingham Town the day before

Little John set forth on his errand, there to sell a halfscore of tanned cowhides. At the dawn of the same day that Little John left the inn, he started from Nottingham, homeward for Blyth. His way led, all in the dewy morn, past the verge of Sherwood Forest, where the birds were welcoming the lovely day with a great and merry jubilee. Across the Tanner's shoulders was slung his stout quarterstaff, ever near enough to him to be gripped quickly, and on his head was a cap of doubled cowhide, so tough that it could hardly be cloven even by a broadsword.

"Now," quoth Arthur a Bland to himself, when he had come to that part of the road that cut through a corner of the forest, "no doubt at this time of year the dun deer are coming from the forest depths nigher to the open meadow lands. Mayhap I may chance to catch sight of the dainty brown darlings thus early in the morn." For there was nothing he loved better than to look upon a tripping herd of deer, even when he could not tickle their ribs with a clothyard shaft. Accordingly, quitting the path, he went peeping this way and that through the underbrush, spying now here and now there, with all the wiles of a master of woodcraft, and of one who had more than once donned a doublet of Lincoln green.

Now as Little John stepped blithely along, thinking of nothing but of such things as the sweetness of the hawthorn buds that bedecked the hedgerows, or the crab-trees that stood here and there all covered with fair pink blossoms, or gazing upwards at the lark, that springing from the dewy grass hung aloft on quivering wings in the yellow sunlight, pouring forth its song that fell like a falling star from the sky, his luck led him away from the highway, not far from the spot where Arthur a Bland was peeping this way and that through the leaves of the thickets. Hearing a rustling of the

branches, Little John stopped, and presently caught sight of
the brown cowhide cap of the Tanner moving amongst the
bushes.

"I do much wonder," quoth Little John to himself, "what
yon knave is after, that he should go thus peeping and peering
about. I verily believe that yon scurvy varlet is no better than
a thief, and cometh here after our own and the King's dun
deer." For by much roving in the forest, Little John had come
to look upon all the deer in Sherwood as belonging to Robin
Hood and his band as much as to good King Harry. "Nay,"
quoth he again, after a time, "this matter must e'en be looked
into." Quitting the high-road, he also entered thickets and
began spying around after stout Arthur a Bland.

For a long time they both of them went hunting about,
Little John after the Tanner, and the Tanner after the deer.
At last Little John trod upon a stick, which snapped under
his foot; whereupon, hearing the noise, the Tanner turned
quickly and caught sight of the yeoman. Seeing that the
Tanner had spied him out, Little John put a bold face upon
the matter.

"Hilloa," quoth he, "what art thou doing here, thou naughty
fellow? Who art thou that comest ranging Sherwood's paths?
In very sooth thou hast an evil cast of countenance, and I do
think, truly, that thou art no better than a thief and comest
after our good King's deer."

"Nay," quoth the Tanner boldly—for, though taken by sur-
prise, he was not a man to be frightened by big words—"thou
liest in thy teeth. I am no thief, but an honest craftsman. As
for my countenance, it is what it is; and, for the matter of
that, thine own is none too pretty, thou saucy fellow."

"Ha!" quoth Little John, in a great loud voice, "Wouldst
thou give me back-talk? Now I have a great part of a mind to

crack thy pate for thee. I would have thee know, fellow, that I am, as it were, one of the King's foresters. Leastwise," muttered he to himself, "I and my friends do take good care of our good sovereign's deer."

"I care not who thou art," answered the bold Tanner, "and unless thou hast many more of thy kind by thee, thou canst never make Arthur a Bland cry 'A mercy.' "

"Is it so?" cried Little John, in a rage. "Now, by my faith, thou saucy rogue, thy tongue hath led thee into a pit thou wilt have a sorry time getting out of; for I will give thee such a drubbing as ne'er hast thou had in all thy life before. Take thy staff in thy hand, fellow, for I will not smite an unarmed man."

"Marry come up with a murrain [plague]!" cried the Tanner, for he, too, had talked himself into a fume. "Big words ne'er killed so much as a mouse. Who art thou that talkest so freely of cracking the head of Arthur a Bland? If I do not tan thy hide this day as ne'er I tanned a calf's hide in all my life before, split my staff into skewers for lamb's flesh and call me no more brave man! Now look to thy self, fellow!"

"Stay!" said Little John. "Let us first measure our cudgels. I do reckon my staff longer than thine, and I would not take vantage of thee by even so much as an inch."

"Nay, I pass not for length," answered the Tanner. "My staff is long enough to knock down a calf; so look to thyself, fellow, I say again."

So, without more ado, each gripped his staff in the middle, and, with fell and angry looks, they came slowly together.

Now news had been brought to Robin Hood how that Little John, instead of doing his bidding, had passed by duty for pleasure, and so had stopped over night with merry company at the Blue Boar Inn, instead of going straight to Ancaster.

Being vexed to his heart by this, he set forth at dawn of day to seek Little John at the Blue Boar, or at least to meet the yeoman on the way and ease his heart of what he thought of the matter. As thus he strode along in anger, putting together the words he would use to chide Little John, he heard, of a sudden, loud and angry voices, as of men in a rage, passing fell-words back and forth from one side to the other. At this, Robin Hood stopped and listened. "Surely," quoth he to himself, "that is Little John's voice, and he is talking in anger. Methinks the other is strange to my ears. Now Heaven forfend that my good trusty Little John should have fallen into the hands of the King's rangers. I must see to this matter at once."

Thus spoke Robin Hood to himself, all his anger passing away like a breath from the windowpane, at the thought that perhaps his trusty right-hand man was in some danger of his life. Cautiously he made his way through the thickets whence the voice came, and pushing aside the leaves, peeped into the little open space where the two men, staff in hand, were coming slowly together.

"Ha!" quoth Robin to himself. "Here is merry sport afoot. Now I would give three golden angels [coins] from my own pocket if yon stout fellow would give Little John a right sound drubbing! It would please me to see him well thumped for having failed in my bidding. I fear me, though, there is but poor chance of my seeing such a pleasant sight." So saying, he stretched himself at length upon the ground, that he might not only see the sport better, but that he might enjoy the merry sight at his ease.

As you may have seen two dogs that think to fight, walking slowly round and round each other, neither cur wishing to begin the combat, so those two stout yeomen moved slowly around, each watching for a chance to take the other unaware, and so get in the first blow. At last Little John struck like a flash, and "rap," the Tanner met the blow and turned it aside, and then smote back at Little John, who also turned the blow; and so this mighty battle began. Then up and down and back and forth they trod, the blows falling so thick and fast that, at a distance, one would have thought that half a score of men were fighting. Thus they fought for nigh a half an hour, until the ground was all plowed up with the digging of their heels, and their breathing grew labored like the ox in the furrow. But Little John suffered the most, for he had become unused to such stiff labor, and his joints were not as supple as they had been before he went to dwell with the Sheriff.

All this time Robin Hood lay beneath the bush, rejoicing at such a comely bout of quarterstaff. "By my faith!" quoth he to himself, "never had I thought to see Little John so evenly matched in all my life. Belike, though, he would have overcome yon stout fellow before this had he been in his former trim."

At last Little John saw his chance, and throwing all the strength he felt going from him into one blow that might have felled an ox, he struck at the Tanner with might and main. And now did the Tanner's cowhide cap stand him in good stead, and but for it he might never have held staff in hand again. As it was, the blow he caught beside the head was so shrewd that it sent him staggering across the little glade, so that, if Little John had had the strength to follow up his vantage, it would have been ill for stout Arthur. But he regained himself quickly, and at arm's length struck back a blow at Little John, and this time the stroke reached its mark, and down went Little John at full length, his cudgel flying from his hand as he fell. Then, raising his staff, stout Arthur dealt him another blow upon the ribs.

"Hold!" roared Little John. "Wouldst thou strike a man when he is down?"

"Ay, marry would I," quoth the Tanner, giving him another thwack with his staff.

"Stop!" roared Little John. "Help! Hold, I say! I yield me! I yield me, I say, good fellow!"

"Hast thou had enough?" asked the Tanner grimly, holding his staff aloft.

"Ay, marry, and more than enough."

"And thou dost own that I am the better man of the two?"

"Yea, truly and a murrain [plague] seize thee!" said Little John, the first aloud and the last to his beard.

"Then thou mayst go thy ways; and thank thy patron saint that I am a merciful man," said the Tanner.

"A plague o' such mercy as thine!" said Little John, sitting up and feeling his ribs where the Tanner had cudgeled him. "I make my vow, my ribs feel as though every one of them were broken in twain. I tell thee, good fellow, I did think there was never a man in all Nottinghamshire could do to me what thou hast done this day."

"And so thought I, also," cried Robin Hood, bursting out of the thicket and shouting with laughter till the tears ran down his cheeks. "O man, man!" said he, as well as he could for his mirth. "'A didst go over like a bottle knocked from a wall. I did see the whole merry bout, and never did I think to see thee yield thyself so, hand and foot, to any man in all merry England. I was seeking thee, to chide thee for leaving my bidding undone; but thou hast been paid all I owed thee, full measure, pressed down and overflowing, by this good fellow. Marry, 'a did reach out his arm full length whilst thou stood gaping at him, and with a pretty rap, tumbled thee over as never have I seen one tumbled before." So spoke bold

Robin, and all the time Little John sat upon the ground, looking as though he had sour curds in his mouth.

"What may be thy name, good fellow?" said Robin next, to
the Tanner.

"Men do call me Arthur a Bland," spoke up the Tanner,
boldly, "and now what may be thy name?"

"Ha, Arthur a Bland!" quoth Robin. "I have heard thy
name before, good fellow. Thou didst break the crown of a
friend of mine at the fair at Ely last October. The folk there
call him Jock o' Nottingham; we call him Will Scathelock.
This poor fellow whom thou hast so belabored is counted the
best hand at the quarterstaff in all merry England. His name
is Little John, and mine Robin Hood."

"How!" cried the Tanner. "Art thou indeed the great Robin
Hood, and is this the famous Little John? Marry, had I known
who thou art, I would never have been so bold as to lift my
hand against thee. Let me help thee to thy feet, good Master
Little John, and let me brush the dust from off thy coat."

"Nay," quoth Little John, testily, at the same time rising
carefully, as though his bones had been made of glass. "I can
help myself, good fellow, without thy aid; and, let me tell thee,
had it not been for that vile cowskin cap of thine, it would
have been ill for thee this day."

At this Robin laughed again, and, turning to the Tanner he
said, "Wilt thou join my band, good Arthur? For I make my
vow thou art truly one of the stoutest men that ever mine
eyes beheld."

"Will I join thy band?" cried the Tanner joyfully. "Ay,
marry, will I! Hey for a merry life!" cried he, leaping aloft
and snapping his fingers. "And hey for the life I love! Away
with tanbark and filthy vats and foul cowhides! I will follow
thee to the ends of the earth, good master, and not a herd of

dun deer in all the forest but shall know the sound of the twang of my bowstring."

"As for thee, Little John," said Robin, turning to him and laughing, "thou wilt start once more for Ancaster, and we will go part way with thee, for I will not have thee turn again to either the right or the left till thou hast fairly gotten away from Sherwood. There are other inns that thou knowest yet, hereabouts." Thereupon, leaving the thickets, they took once more to the highway, and departed upon their business.

CHAPTER 7

Robin Hood and Will Scarlet

THUS they traveled along the sunny road, three stout fellows such as you could hardly match anywhere else in all merry England. Many stopped to gaze after them as they strode along, so broad were their shoulders and so sturdy their gait.

Quoth Robin Hood to Little John, "Why didst thou not go straight to Ancaster, yesterday, as I told thee? Thou hadst not gotten thyself into such a coil [mess] hadst thou done as I ordered."

"I feared the rain that threatened," said Little John in a sullen tone, for he was vexed at being so chafed by Robin with what had happened to him.

"The rain!" cried Robin, stopping of a sudden in the middle of the road, and looking at Little John in wonder. "Why, thou great oaf! Not a drop of rain has fallen these three days, neither has any threatened, nor hath there been a sign of foul weather in earth or sky or water."

"Nevertheless," growled Little John, "the holy Saint Swith-

107

in holdeth the waters of the heavens in his pewter pot, and he could have poured them out, had he chosen, even from a clear sky; and wouldst thou have had me wet to the skin?"

At this Robin Hood burst into a roar of laughter. "O Little John!" said he. "What butter wits hast thou in that head of thine! Who could hold anger against such a one as thou art?"

So saying, they all stepped out once more, with the right foot foremost, as the saying is.

After they had traveled some distance, the day being warm and the road dusty, Robin Hood waxed thirsty; so, there being a fountain of water as cold as ice, just behind the hedgerow, they crossed the stile and came to where the water bubbled from beneath a mossy stone. Here, kneeling and making cups of the palms of their hands, they drank their fill, and then, the spot being cool and shady, they stretched their limbs and rested them for a space.

In front of them, over beyond the hedge, the dusty road stretched away across the plain; behind them the meadow lands and bright green fields of tender young corn lay broadly in the sun, and overhead spread the shade of the cool, rustling leaves of the beechen tree. Pleasantly to their nostrils came the tender fragrance of the purple violets and wild thyme that grew within the dewy moisture of the edge of the little fountain, and pleasantly came the soft gurgle of the water; all else was sunny silence, broken only now and then by the crow of a distant cock, borne up to them on the wings of the soft and gentle breeze, or the drowsy drone of the bumblebee burrowing in the clover blossoms that grew in the sun, or the voice of the busy housewife in the nearest farmhouse. All was so pleasant and so full of the gentle joy of the bright Maytime, that for a long time neither of the three cared to speak, but each lay on his back, gazing up through the trembling leaves of the trees to the bright sky overhead. At last, Robin, whose thoughts were not quite so busy wool-gathering as those of the others and who had been gazing around him now and then, broke the silence.

"Heyday!" quoth he. "Yon is a gayly feathered bird, I take my vow."

The others looked and saw a young man walking slowly down the highway. Gay was he, indeed, as Robin had said, and a fine figure he cut, for his doublet was of scarlet silk and his stockings also; a handsome sword hung by his side, the embossed leathern scabbard being picked out with fine threads of gold; his cap was of scarlet velvet, and a broad feather hung down behind and back of one ear. His hair was long and yellow and curled upon his shoulders, and in his hand he bore an early rose, which he smelt daintily now and then.

"By my life!" quoth Robin Hood, laughing. "Saw ye e'er such a pretty, mincing fellow?"

"Truly, his clothes have overmuch prettiness for my taste," quoth Arthur a Bland, "but, ne'ertheless, his shoulders are broad and his loins are narrow, and seest thou, good master, how that his arms hang from his body? They dangle not down like spindles, but hang stiff and bend at the elbow. I take my vow, there be no bread and milk limbs in those fine clothes, but stiff joints and tough thews [muscles]."

"Methinks thou art right, friend Arthur," said Little John. "I do verily think yon is no such rose-leaf and whipped-cream gallant as he would have one take him to be."

"Pah!" quoth Robin Hood. "The sight of such a fellow doth put a nasty taste in my mouth! Look how he doth hold that fair flower betwixt his thumb and finger, as he would say, 'Good rose, I like thee not so ill but I can bear thy odor for a little while.' I take it ye are both wrong and verily believe that were a furious mouse to run across his path, he would cry, 'La!' or 'Alack-a-day!' and fall straightway into a swoon. I wonder who he may be."

"Some great baron's son, I doubt not," answered Little John, "with good and true men's money lining his purse."

"Ay, marry, that is true, I make no doubt," quoth Robin. "What a pity that such men as he, that have no thought but to go abroad in gay clothes, should have good fellows, whose shoes they are not fit to tie, dancing at their bidding. By Saint Dunstan, Saint Alfred, Saint Withold, and all the good men in the Saxon calendar, it doth make me mad to see such gay lordlings from over the sea go stepping on the necks of good Saxons who owned this land before ever their great-grandsires chewed rind of brawn [boar]! By the bright bow of Heaven, I will have their ill-gotten gains from them, even though I hang for it as high as e'er a forest tree in Sherwood!"

"Why, how now, master," quoth Little John, "what heat is this? Thou dost set thy pot a-boiling, and mayhap no bacon to cook! Methinks yon fellow's hair is over light for Norman locks. He may be a good man and true for aught thou knowest."

"Nay," said Robin, "my head against a leaden farthing, he is what I say. Whenever saw ye Saxon mince along like that, as though he feared to muddy the toes of his shoes? At least, I will go forth and stop him, and see whether his purse be free of foul money. If I am wrong, then he may go forward upon his journey without the loss of so much as a groat [small coin]; but if I am right, I will pluck him as close as ever a goose was plucked for live feathers in midsummer. Thou sayst he is a sturdy fellow, Little John. Lie thou here and watch till I show thee how woodland life toughens a man, as easy living, such as thine hath been of late, drags him down. So, lie ye both here, I say, till I show you how I drub this fellow." So

saying, Robin Hood stepped forth from the shade of the beech tree, crossed the stile, and stood in the middle of the road, with his hands on his hips, in the stranger's path.

Meantime the stranger, who had been walking so slowly that all this talk was held before he came opposite the place where they were, neither quickened his pace nor seemed to see that such a man as Robin Hood was in the world. So Robin stood in the middle of the road, waiting while the other walked slowly forward, smelling his rose, and looking this way and that, and everywhere except at Robin.

"Hold!" cried Robin, when at last the other had come close to him. "Hold! Stand where thou art!"

"Wherefore should I hold, good fellow?" said the stranger in soft and gentle voice. "And wherefore should I stand where I am? Ne'ertheless, as thou dost desire that I should stay, I will abide for a short time, that I may hear what thou mayst have to say to me."

"Then," quoth Robin, "as thou dost so fairly do as I tell thee, and dost give me such soft speech, I will also treat thee with all due courtesy. I would have thee know, fair friend, that I am, as it were, a votary at the shrine of Saint Wilfred, who, thou mayst know, took, willy-nilly, all their gold from the heathen, and melted it up into candlesticks. Wherefore, upon such as come hereabout, I levy a certain toll, which I use for a better purpose, I hope, than to make candlesticks withal. Therefore, sweet chuck, I would have thee deliver to me thy purse, that I may look into it, and judge, to the best of my poor powers, whether thou hast more wealth about thee than our law allows. For, as our good Gaffer Swanthold sayeth, 'He who is fat from overliving must needs lose blood.'"

All this time the youth had been sniffing at the rose that he held betwixt his thumb and finger. "Nay," said he with a gentle smile, when Robin Hood had done, "I do love to hear thee talk, thou pretty fellow, and if, haply, thou are not yet done, finish, I beseech thee. I have yet some little time to stay and listen."

"I have said all," quoth Robin, "and now, if thou wilt give me thy purse, I will let thee go thy way without let [obstacle] or hindrance so soon as I shall see what it may hold. I will take none from thee if thou hast but little."

"Alas, it doth grieve me much," said the other, "that I cannot do as thou dost wish! I have nothing to give thee. Let me go my way, I prythee. I have done thee no harm."

"Nay, thou goest not," quoth Robin, "till thou hast shown me thy purse."

"Good friend," said the other, gently, "I have business elsewhere. I have given thee much time and have heard thee patiently. Prythee, let me now depart in peace."

"I have spoken to thee, friend," said Robin sternly, "and I now tell thee again, that thou goest not one step forward till thou hast done as I bid thee." So saying, he raised his quarterstaff above his head in a threatening way.

"Alas," said the stranger, sadly, "it doth grieve me that this thing must be! I fear that I must slay thee, poor fellow!" So saying, he drew his sword.

"Put by thy weapon," quoth Robin. "I would take no vantage of thee. Thy sword cannot stand against an oaken staff such as mine. I could snap it like a barley straw. Yonder is a good oaken thicket by the roadside. Take thee a cudgel thence and defend thyself fairly, if thou hast a taste for a sound drubbing."

First the stranger measured Robin with his eye, and then he measured the oaken staff. "Thou art right, good fellow," said he presently. "Truly, my sword is no match for that cudgel of thine. Bide thee a while till I get me a staff." So saying, he threw aside the rose that he had been holding all this time, thrust his sword back into the scabbard, and with a more hasty step than he had yet used, stepped to the roadside where grew the little clump of ground oaks Robin had spoken of. Choosing among them, he presently found a sapling to his liking. He did not cut it, but, rolling up his sleeves a little way, he laid hold of it, placed his heel against the ground, and, with one mighty pull, plucked the young tree up by the roots from out the very earth. Then he came back, trimming away the roots and tender stems with his sword as quietly as if he had done naught to speak of.

Little John and the Tanner had been watching all that passed, but when they saw the stranger drag the sapling from the earth, and heard the rending and snapping of its roots, the Tanner pursed up his lips together, drawing his breath between them in a long, inward whistle.

"By the breath of my body!" said Little John, as soon as he could gather his wits from their wonder, "sawest thou that, Arthur? Marry, I think our poor master will stand but an ill chance with yon fellow. By Our Lady, he plucked up yon tree as it were a barley straw."

Whatever Robin Hood thought, he stood his ground, and now he and the stranger in scarlet stood face to face.

Well did Robin Hood hold his own that day as a midcountry yeoman. This way and that they fought, and back and forth, Robin's skill against the stranger's strength. The dust of the highway rose up around them like a cloud, so that at times Little John and the Tanner could see nothing, but only hear the rattle of the staves against one another. Thrice Robin Hood struck the stranger; once upon the arm and twice upon the ribs, and yet had he warded all the other's blows, only one of which, had it met its mark, would have laid stout Robin lower in the dust than he had ever gone before. At last the stranger struck Robin's cudgel so fairly in the middle that he could hardly hold his staff in his hand; again he struck, and Robin bent beneath the blow; a third time he struck, and now not only fairly beat down Robin's guard, but gave him such a rap also, that down he tumbled.

"Hold!" cried Robin Hood, when he saw the stranger raising his staff once more. "I yield me!"

"Hold!" cried Little John, bursting from his cover, with the Tanner at his heels. "Hold! Give over, I say!"

"Nay," answered the stranger quietly, "if there be two

more of you, and each as stout as this good fellow, I am like to have my hands full. Nevertheless, come on, and I will strive my best to serve you all."

"Stop!" cried Robin Hood. "We will fight no more. I take my vow, this is an ill day for thee and me, Little John. I do verily believe that my wrist, and eke my arm, are palsied by the jar of the blow that this stranger struck me."

Then Little John turned to Robin Hood. "Why, how now, good master," said he, "alas, thou art in an ill plight! Marry, thy jerkin is all befouled with the dust of the road. Let me help thee to arise."

"A plague on thy aid!" cried Robin, angrily. "I can get to my feet without thy help, good fellow."

"Nay, but let me at least dust thy coat for thee. I fear thy poor bones are mightily sore," quoth Little John, soberly, but with a sly twinkle in his eyes.

"Give over, I say!" quoth Robin in a fume. "My coat hath been dusted enough already, without aid of thine." Then, turning to the stranger, he said, "What may be thy name, good fellow?"

"My name is Gamwell," answered the other.

"Ha!" cried Robin. "Is it even so? I have near kin of that name. Whence camest thou, fair friend?"

"From Maxfield Town I come," answered the stranger. "There was I born and bred, and thence I come to seek my mother's young brother, whom men call Robin Hood. So, if perchance thou mayst direct me"—

"Ha! Will Gamwell!" cried Robin, placing both hands upon the other's shoulders and holding him off at arm's length. "Surely, it can be none other! I might have known thee by that pretty maiden air of thine—that dainty, finicking manner of gait. Dost thou not know me, lad? Look upon me well."

"Now, by the breath of my body!" cried the other. "I do believe from my heart that thou art mine own Uncle Robin. Nay, certain it is so!" and each flung his arms around the other, kissing him upon the cheek. Then once more Robin held his kinsman off at arm's length and scanned him keenly from top to toe. "Why, how now," quoth he, "what change is here? Verily, some eight or ten years ago I left thee a stripling lad, with great joints and ill-hung limbs, and lo, here thou art, as tight a fellow as e'er I set mine eyes upon. Dost thou not remember, lad, how I showed thee the proper way to nip the goose feather betwixt thy fingers and throw out thy bow arm steadily? Thou gavest promise of being a keen archer. And dost thou not mind how I taught thee to fend and parry with the cudgel?"

"Yea," said young Gamwell, "and I did so look up to thee, and thought thee so above all other men that, I make my vow, had I known who thou wert, I would never have dared to lift hand against thee this day. I trust I did thee no great harm."

"No, no," quoth Robin, hastily, and looking sideways at Little John, "thou didst not harm me. But say no more of that, I prythee. Yet I will say, lad, that I hope I may never feel again such a blow as thou didst give me. By'r Lady, my arm doth tingle yet from fingernail to elbow. Truly, I thought that I was palsied for life. I tell thee, coz, that thou art the strongest man that ever I laid mine eyes upon. I take my vow, I felt my stomach quake when I beheld thee pluck up yon green tree as thou didst. But tell me, how camest thou to leave Sir Edward and thy mother?"

"Alas!" answered young Gamwell. "It is an ill story, uncle, that I have to tell thee. My father's steward, who came to us after old Giles Crookleg died, was ever a saucy varlet, and I know not why my father kept him, saving that he did oversee with great judgment. It used to gall me to hear him speak up so boldly to my father, who, thou knowest, was ever a patient man to those about him, and slow to anger and harsh words. Well, one day—and an ill day it was for that saucy fellow—he sought to berate my father, I standing by. I could stand it no longer, good uncle, so, stepping forth, I gave him a box o' the ear, and—wouldst thou believe it?—the fellow straightway died o't. I think they said I broke his neck, or something o' the like. So off they packed me to seek thee and escape the law. I was on my way when thou sawest me, and here I am."

"Well, by the faith of my heart," quoth Robin Hood, "for anyone escaping the law, thou wast taking it the most easily that ever I beheld in all my life. Whenever did anyone in all the world see one who had slain a man and was escaping because of it, tripping along the highway like a dainty court damsel, sniffing at a rose the while?"

"Nay, uncle," answered Will Gamwell, "over haste never churned good butter, as the old saying hath it. Moreover, I do verily believe that this overstrength of my body hath taken the nimbleness out of my heels. Why, thou didst but just now rap me thrice, and I thee never a once, save by overbearing thee by my strength."

"Nay," quoth Robin, "let us say no more on that score. I am right glad to see thee, Will, and thou wilt add great honor and credit to my band of merry fellows. But thou must change thy name, for warrants will be out presently against thee; so, because of thy gay clothes, thou shalt henceforth and for aye be called Will Scarlet."

"Will Scarlet," quoth Little John, stepping forward and reaching out his great palm, which the other took, "Will Scar-

let, the name fitteth thee well. Right glad am I to welcome thee
amongst us. I am called Little John; and this is a new member
who has just joined us, a stout tanner named Arthur a Bland.
Thou are like to achieve fame, Will, let me tell thee, for there
will be many a merry ballad sung about the country, and
many a merry story told in Sherwood of how Robin Hood
taught Little John and Arthur a Bland the proper way to use
the quarterstaff; likewise, how our good master bit off so large
a piece of cake that he choked on it."

"Nay, good Little John," quoth Robin, gently, for he liked ill
to have such a jest told of him, "Why should we speak of this
little matter? Prythee, let us keep this day's doings amongst
ourselves."

"With all my heart," quoth Little John. "But, good master,
I thought that thou didst love a merry story, because thou
hast so often made a jest about a certain increase of fatness
on my joints, of flesh gathered by my abiding with the—"

"Nay, good Little John," said Robin hastily, "I do bethink
me I have said full enough on that score."

"It is well," quoth Little John, "for in truth I myself have
tired of it somewhat. But now I bethink me, thou didst also
seem minded to make a jest of the rain that threatened last
night, so"—

"Nay, then," said Robin Hood, testily, "I was mistaken. I
remember me now it did seem to threaten rain."

"Truly, I did think so myself," quoth Little John. "Therefore, no doubt, thou dost think it was wise of me to abide all
night at the Blue Boar Inn, instead of venturing forth in such
stormy weather, dost thou not?"

"A plague on thee and thy doings!" cried Robin Hood. "If
thou wilt have it so, thou wert right to abide wherever thou
didst choose."

"Once more, it is well," quoth Little John. "As for myself, I have been blind this day. I did not see thee drubbed; I did not see thee tumbled heels over head in the dust; and if any man says that thou wert, I can with a clear conscience rattle his lying tongue betwixt his teeth."

"Come," cried Robin, biting his nether lip, while the others could not forbear laughing, "We will go no farther today, but will return to Sherwood, and thou shalt go to Ancaster another time, Little John."

So said Robin, for now that his bones were sore, he felt as though a long journey would be an ill thing for him. So, turning their backs, they retraced their steps whence they came.

CHAPTER 8

Adventure with Midge the Miller

WHEN the four yeomen had traveled for a long time toward Sherwood again, high noontide being past, they began to wax hungry. Quoth Robin Hood, "I would that I had something to eat. Methinks a good loaf of white bread, with a piece of snow-white cheese, washed down with a draft of humming ale, were a feast for a king."

"Since thou speakest of it," said Will Scarlet, "methinks it would not be amiss myself. There is that within me crieth out, 'Victuals, good friend, victuals!'"

"I know a house near by," said Arthur a Bland, "and, had I but the money, I would bring ye that ye speak of: to wit, a sweet loaf of bread, and a fair cheese, and a skin of humming brown ale."

"For the matter of that, thou knowest I have money by me, good master," quoth Little John.

"Why, so thou hast, Little John," said Robin. "How much money will it take, good Arthur, to buy us meat and drink at this same house?"

"I think that six broad pennies will buy food enow for a dozen men," said the Tanner.

"Then give him six pennies, Little John," quoth Robin, "for methinks food for three men will about fit my need. Now get thee gone, Arthur, with the money, and bring the food here, for there is a sweet shade in that thicket yonder, beside the road, and there we will eat our meal."

So Little John gave Arthur the money, and the others stepped to the thicket, there to await the return of the Tanner and their meal.

After a time he came back, bearing with him a great brown loaf of bread and a fair, round cheese, and a goat-skin full of stout March beer slung over his shoulders. Then Will Scarlet took his sword and divided the loaf and the cheese into four fair portions, and each man helped himself. Then Robin Hood took a deep pull at the beer.

"Aha!" said he, drawing in his breath, "never have I tasted sweeter drink than this."

After this no man spake more, but each munched away at his bread and cheese lustily, with ever and anon a pull at the beer.

At last Will Scarlet looked at a small piece of bread he still held in his hand and quoth he, "Methinks I will give this to the sparrows." So, throwing it from him, he brushed the crumbs from his jerkin.

"I, too," quoth Robin, "have had enough, I think." As for Little John and the Tanner they had by this time eaten every crumb of their bread and cheese.

"Now, sweet friends," quoth Robin, gathering up the skin of beer, that was not yet nearly empty, "I do wish that ye may ever have such happiness as a good stout meal like this bringeth to my heart. Thus pledging you all, I drink to your health, that it may ever remain in the same fair state as it is this day."

So saying, he took a hearty pull at the stout beer. Next Will Scarlet took the skin, then Little John, and, last of all, the stout Tanner. A good full skin of beer, as fat as a town tradesman, began the round; a poor, flabby hide came forth, as weak and limp as an aged man.

"Now," quoth Robin, "I do feel myself another man and would fain enjoy something pleasant before going farther upon our journey. I do bethink me, Will, that thou didst use to have a pretty voice, and one that tuned sweetly upon a song. Prythee, give us one ere we journey farther."

"Truly, I do not mind turning a tune," answered Will Scarlet, "but I would not sing alone."

"Nay, others will follow. Strike up, lad," quoth Robin.

"In that case 'tis well," said Will Scarlet. Then, clearing his throat, he sang lustily.

"Who may yon fellow be coming along the road?" said Robin, breaking into the song.

"I know not," quoth Little John, in a surly voice. "But this I do know, that it is an ill thing to do to check the flow of a good song."

"Nay, Little John," said Robin, "be not vexed, I prythee, but I have been watching him coming along, bent beneath that great bag over his shoulder. Look, Little John, I pray, and see if thou knowest him."

Little John looked whither Robin Hood pointed. "Truly," quoth he, after a time, "I think yon fellow is a certain young Miller I have seen now and then around the edge of Sherwood Forest; a poor wight, methinks, to spoil a right good song about."

"Now thou speakest of him," quoth Robin Hood, "methinks I myself have seen him now and then. Hath he not a mill over beyond Nottingham Town, nigh on to the Salisbury road?"

"Thou art right; that is the man," said Little John.

"A good stout fellow," quoth Robin. "I saw him crack Ned o' Bradford's crown about a fortnight since, and never saw I hair lifted more neatly in all my life before."

By this time the young miller had come so near that they could see him clearly. His clothes were dusted with flour, and over his back he carried a great sack of meal, bending so as to bring the whole weight upon his shoulders, and across the sack was a thick quarterstaff. His limbs were stout and strong, and he strode along the dusty road right sturdily with the heavy sack across his shoulders. His cheeks were ruddy as a winter hip, his hair was flaxen in color, and on his chin was a downy growth of flaxen beard.

"A good honest fellow," quoth Robin Hood, "and such an one as is a credit to English yeomanrie. Now let us have a merry jest with him. We will go forth as though we were common thieves and pretend to rob him of his honest gains. Then we will take him into the forest and give him a feast such as his stomach never held in all his life before. We will flood his throat with good canary and send him home with crowns in his purse for every penny he hath. What say ye, lads?"

"Truly, it is a merry thought," said Will Scarlet.

"It is well planned," quoth Little John, "but all the saints preserve us from any more drubbings this day! Marry, my poor bones ache so that I"—

"Prythee peace, Little John," quoth Robin. "Thy foolish tongue will get us both well laughed at yet."

"My foolish tongue, forsooth," growled Little John to Arthur a Bland. "I would it could keep our master from getting us into another coil [fight] this day."

But now the Miller, plodding along the road, had come opposite to where the yeomen lay hidden, whereupon all four of them ran at him and surrounded him.

"Hold, friend!" cried Robin to the Miller; whereupon he turned slowly, with the weight of the bag upon his shoulder, and looked at each in turn all bewildered, for though a good stout man his wits did not skip with the speed of roasting chestnuts.

"Who bids me stay?" said the Miller in a voice deep and gruff, like the growl of a great dog.

"Marry that do I," quoth Robin, "and let me tell thee, friend, thou hadst best mind my bidding."

"And who art thou, good friend?" said the Miller, throwing the great sack of meal from his shoulder to the ground. "And who are those with thee?"

"We be four good Christian men," quoth Robin, "and would fain help thee by carrying part of thy heavy load for thee. Art thou not fortunate?"

"I give you all thanks," said the Miller, "but my bag is none that heavy that I cannot carry it e'en by myself."

"Nay, thou dost mistake," quoth Robin. "I meant that thou mightest perhaps have some heavy farthings or pence about thee, not to speak of silver and gold. Our good Gaffer Swanthold sayeth that gold is an over-heavy burden for a two-legged ass to carry; so we would e'en lift some of this load from thee."

"Alas!" cried the Miller. "What would ye do to me? I have not about me so much as a clipped groat [very small coin]. Do me no harm, I pray you, but let me depart in peace. Moreover, let me tell you that ye are upon Robin Hood's ground, and should he find you seeking to rob an honest craftsman, he will clip your ears and scourge you even to the walls of Nottingham Town."

"In truth I fear Robin Hood no more than I do myself," quoth jolly Robin. "Thou must this day give up to me every penny thou hast about thee."

The Miller looked toward his quarterstaff, which lay on the ground beside the bag of meal.

"Nay," said Robin, "if thou dost budge an inch, I will rattle this staff about thine ears."

"Nay, smite me not!" cried the Miller, throwing up his elbow as though he feared the blow. "Thou mayst search me if thou wilt, but thou wilt find nothing upon me, pouch, pocket, or skin."

"It is so?" quoth Robin Hood, looking keenly about him. "Now I believe that what thou tellest is no true tale. If I am not much mistook thou hast somewhat in the bottom of that fat sack of meal. Good Arthur, empty the bag upon the ground; I warrant thou wilt find a shilling or two in the flour."

"Alas!" cried the Miller, falling upon his knees. "Spoil not all my good meal! It can better you not, and will ruin me. Spare it, and I will give up the money in the bottom of the bag."

"Ha!" quoth Robin, nudging Will Scarlet. "Is it so? And have I found where thy money lies? Marry, I have a wondrous nose for the blessed image of good King Harry. I thought that I smelt gold and silver beneath the barley meal. Bring it straight forth, Miller."

Then slowly the Miller arose to his feet and slowly and unwillingly he untied the mouth of the bag, and slowly thrust his hands into the meal and began fumbling about with his arms buried to the elbows in the barley flour. The others gathered round him, their heads together, looking and wondering what he would bring forth.

So they stood, all with their heads close together, gazing down into the sack. But while he pretended to be searching for the money, the Miller gathered two great handfuls of the powdery meal.

"Ha," quoth he, "here they are, the beauties." Then, as the others leaned still more forward to see what he had, he suddenly cast the meal into their faces, filling their eyes and noses and mouths with the flour, blinding and half choking them. Arthur a Bland was worse off than any, for his mouth was open, agape with wonder of what was to come, so that a great cloud of flour flew down his throat, setting him a-coughing till he could scarcely stand.

Then, while all four stumbled about, roaring with the smart of the meal in their eyeballs, and while they rubbed their eyes till the tears made great channels on their faces through the meal, the Miller seized another handful of flour and another and another, throwing it in their faces, so that even had they had a glimmering of light before, they were now as blind as ever a beggar in Nottinghamshire, while their hair and beards and clothes were covered with flour and as white as snow.

Then catching up his great crab staff, the Miller began laying about him as though he were clean gone mad. This way and that way skipped the four, like peas on a drumhead, but they could neither see to defend themselves nor could they run away.

Thwack! thwack! thwack! went the Miller's cudgel across their backs, and at every blow, great white clouds of flour rose into the air from their jackets and went drifting away down the breeze.

"Stop!" roared Robin at last. "Give over, good friend, I am Robin Hood!"

"Thou liest, thou knave," cried the Miller, giving him a rap on the ribs that sent up a great cloud of flour like a puff of smoke. "Stout Robin never robbed an honest tradesman. Ha! Thou wouldst have my money, wouldst thou?" And he gave him another blow. "Nay, thou art not getting thy share, thou long-legged knave. Share and share alike." And he smote Little John across the shoulders so that he sent him skipping half across the road. "Nay, fear not, it is thy turn now, black beard." And he gave the Tanner a crack that made him roar for all his coughing. "How now, red coat, let me brush the dust from thee!" cried he, smiting Will Scarlet. And so he gave them merry words and blows until they could scarcely stand, and whenever he saw one like to clear his eyes he threw more flour in his face.

At last Robin Hood found his horn, and clapping it to his lips, blew three loud blasts upon it.

Now it chanced that Will Stutely and a party of Robin's men were in the glade not far from where this merry sport was going forward. Hearing the hubbub of voices, and blows that sounded like the noise of a flail in the barn in winter time, they stopped, listening amazedly, and wondering what was toward.

Quoth Will Stutely, "Now if I mistake not there is some stout battle with cudgels going forward not far hence. I would fain see this pretty sight." So saying, he and the whole party turned their steps whence the noise came. When they had come near where all the tumult sounded they heard the three blasts of Robin's bugle horn.

"Quick!" cried young David of Doncaster. "Our master is in sore need!" So, without stopping a moment, they dashed

forward with might and main and burst forth from the covert into the high-road.

But what a sight was that which they saw. The road was all white with meal, and five men stood there also white with meal from top to toe, for much of the barley flour had fallen back upon the Miller. "What is thy need, master?" cried Will Stutely. "And what doth all this mean?"

"Why," quoth Robin in a mighty passion, "yon traitor fellow hath come as nigh slaying me as e'er a man in all the world. Hadst thou not come quickly, good Stutely, thy master had been dead."

Hereupon, whilst he and the three others rubbed the meal from their eyes, and Will Stutely and his men brushed their clothes clean, he told them all; how that he had meant to pass a jest upon the Miller, which same had turned so grievously upon them.

"Quick, men, seize the vile Miller!" cried Stutely, who was nigh choking with laughter as were the rest; whereupon several ran upon the stout fellow and seizing him bound his arms behind his back with bowstrings.

"Ha!" cried Robin, when they brought the trembling Miller to him. "Wouldst murder me, wouldst thou? By my faith—" Here he stopped and stood glaring upon the Miller with a grim look.

But Robin's anger could not hold, so first his eyes twinkled, and then in spite of all he broke into a laugh.

Now when they saw their master laugh, the yeomen who stood around could contain themselves no longer, and a mighty shout of laughter went up from all. Many could not stand, but rolled upon the ground from pure merriment.

"What is thy name, good fellow?" said Robin at last to the Miller, who stood gaping and as though he were in a maze.

"Alas, sir, I am Midge, the Miller's son," said he in a frightened voice.

"I make my vow," quoth merry Robin, smiting him upon the shoulder, "thou art the mightiest Midge that e'er mine eyes beheld. Now wilt thou leave thy dusty mill and come and join my band? By my faith, thou art too stout a man to spend thy days betwixt the hopper and the till."

"Then truly, if thou dost forgive me for the blows I struck, not knowing who thou wast, I will join with thee right merrily," said the Miller.

"Then have I gained this day," quoth Robin, "the three stoutest yeomen in all Nottinghamshire. We will get us away to the greenwood tree, and there hold a merry feast in honor of our new friends, and mayhap a cup or two of good sack and canary may mellow the soreness of my poor joints and bones, though I warrant it will be many a day before I am again the man I was." So saying, he turned and led the way, the rest following, and so they entered the forest once more and were lost to sight.

So that night all was ablaze with crackling fires in the woodlands, for though Robin and those others spoken of, only excepting Midge, the Miller's son, had many a sore bump and bruise here and there on their bodies, they were still not so sore in the joints that they could not enjoy a jolly feast given all in welcome to the new members of the band. Thus with songs and jesting and laughter that echoed through the deeper and more silent nooks of the forest, the night passed quickly along, as such merry times are wont to do, until at last each man sought his couch and silence fell on all things and all things seemed to sleep.

Thus came about three merry adventures in one day, the one stepping upon the heels of another.

But Little John's tongue was ever one that was not easy of guidance, so that, inch by inch, the whole story of his fight with the Tanner and Robin Hood's fight with Will Scarlet leaked out.

And so have I told it that you may laugh at the merry tale along with me.

CHAPTER 9 • • •

Robin Hood and Allan a Dale

IT HAS just been told how three unlucky adventures fell upon Robin Hood and Little John all in one day, bringing them sore ribs and aching bones. So next we will tell how they made up for those ill happenings by a good action that came about not without some small pain to Robin.

Two days had passed by, and somewhat of the soreness had passed away from Robin Hood's joints, yet still, when he moved of a sudden and without thinking, pain here and there would, as it were, jog him, crying, "Thou hast had a drubbing, good fellow."

The day was bright and jocund, and the morning dew still lay upon the grass. Under the greenwood tree sat Robin Hood; on one side was Will Scarlet, lying at full length upon his back, gazing up into the clear sky, with hands clasped behind his head; upon the other side sat Little John, fashioning a cudgel out of a stout crab-tree limb; elsewhere upon the grass sat or lay many others of the band.

Will Scathelock, who was as full of tales and legends as an

egg is of meat, was telling of the adventures that befell brave
Sir Carodoc of the Shrunken Arm, of King Arthur's time, and
of his love to his one true maid, and of what they dared and
suffered for each other's sake. That noble story you yourself
may read some time, for it has been written and sung in
more than one ancient tale and ballad, both in courtly and
in homely phrase. To this all listened without a word, and
when it was done many drew deep breaths, being carried
away by the tale of knightly daring and noble sacrifice.

"It doth make a man better," quoth Robin Hood, "to hear
of those noble men that lived so long ago. When one doth
list [listen] to such tales, his soul doth say, 'Put by thy poor
little likings and seek to do likewise.' Truly, one may not do as
nobly oneself, but in the striving one is better. I mind me
our good Gaffer Swanthold was wont to say, 'He who jumps
for the moon and gets it not, leaps higher than he who stoops
for a penny in the mud.'"

"Truly," quoth Will Stutely, "it is a fine thought, but, nevertheless, good master, the one gets a penny and the other gets
nought, and without the penny, one is like to go with an
empty stomach. These same stories are well to listen to but
ill to follow, say I."

"By the faith of my heart," quoth merry Robin, "thou
dost ever trip up a lofty thought that gazes in the sky, and
dost bring its nose in the dust. Nevertheless, thou has a
shrewd wit in thy head, good Stutely; and now that thou
bringest me to things of the world, I do bethink me that we
have had no one to dine with us for this long time. Our money
groweth low in the purse, for no one hath come to pay a
reckoning for many a day. Now busk thee, good Stutely, and
choose thee six men, and get thee gone to Fosse Way or thereabouts, and see that thou bringest someone to eat with us this

evening. Meantime we will prepare a grand feast to do whosoever may come the greater honor. And stay, good Stutely. I would have thee take Will Scarlet with thee, for it is meet that he should become acquainted with the ways of the forest."

"Now do I thank thee, good master," quoth Stutely, springing to his feet, "that thou hast chosen me for this adventure. Truly, my limbs do grow slack through abiding idly here. As for two of my six, I will choose Midge the Miller, and Arthur a Bland, for, as well thou knowest, good master, they are stout fists at the quarter staff. Is it not so, Little John?"

At this all laughed but Little John and Robin, who twisted up his face. "I can speak for Midge," said he, "and likewise for my cousin Scarlet. This very blessed morn I looked at my ribs and found them as many colors as a beggar's cloak."

So, having chosen four more stout fellows, Will Stutely and his band set forth to Fosse Way, to find whether they might not come across some rich guest to feast that day in Sherwood with Robin and his band.

For all the livelong day they abided near this highway. Each man had brought with him a good store of cold meat and a bottle of stout March beer to stay his stomach till the home-coming. So when high noontide had come they sat them down upon the soft grass, beneath a green and wide-spreading hawthorn bush, and held a hearty and jovial feast. After this, one kept watch while the others napped, for it was a still and sultry day.

Thus they passed the time pleasantly enow, but no guest such as they desired showed his face in all the time that they lay hidden there. Many passed along the dusty road in the glare of the sun: now it was a bevy of chattering damsels merrily tripping along; now it was a plodding tinker; now a merry shepherd lad; now a sturdy farmer; all gazing ahead

along the road, unconscious of the seven stout fellows that lay
hidden so near them. Such were the travelers along the way;
but fat abbot, rich esquire, or money-laden usurer came there
none.

At last the sun began to sink low in the heavens; the light
grew red and the shadows long. The air grew full of silence,
the birds twittered sleepily, and from afar came, faint and
clear, the musical song of the milkmaid calling the kine [cows]
home to the milking.

Then Stutely arose from where he was lying. "A plague of
such ill luck!" quoth he. "Here have we abided all day, and no
bird worth the shooting, so to speak, hath come within
reach of our bolt. Had I gone forth on an innocent errand,
I had met a dozen stout priests or a score of pursy money-
lenders. But it is ever thus; the dun deer are never so scarce
as when one has a gray goose feather nipped betwixt the
fingers. Come, lads, let us pack up and home again, say I."
Accordingly, the others arose, and coming from out the thicket,
they all turned their toes back again to Sherwood.

After they had gone some distance, Will Stutely, who headed
the party, suddenly stopped. "Hist!" quoth he, for his ears
were as sharp as those of a five-year-old-fox. "Hark, lads!
Methinks I hear a sound." At this all stopped and listened with
bated breath, albeit for a time they could hear nothing, their
ears being duller than Stutely's. At length they heard a faint
and melancholy sound, like someone in lamentation.

"Ha!" quoth Will Scarlet. "This must be looked into. There
is someone in distress nigh to us here."

"I know not," quoth Will Stutely, shaking his head doubt-
fully. "Our master is ever rash about thrusting his finger into
a boiling pot, but, for my part, I see no use in getting ourselves into mischievous coils [troubles]. Yon is a man's voice,

if I mistake not, and a man should be always ready to get himself out from his own pothers [difficulties]." Thus spoke Will Stutely, yet, in truth, only half meant what he said. Nevertheless, since he had escaped so narrowly from out the Sheriff's clutches he had grown somewhat over-cautious.

Then out spake Will Scarlet boldly. "Now out upon thee, to talk in that manner, Stutely! Stay, if thou dost list. I go to see what may be the trouble of this poor creature."

"Nay," quoth Stutely, "thou dost leap so quickly thou'lt tumble into the ditch. Who said I would not go? Come along, say I." Thus saying, he led the way, the others following till, after they had gone a short distance, they came to a little opening in the woodland, whence a brook, after gurgling out from under the tangle of overhanging bushes, spread out into a broad and glassy pebbled pool. By the side of this pool and beneath the branches of a willow, lay a youth upon his face, weeping aloud, the sound of which had first caught the quick ears of Stutely. His golden locks were tangled, his clothes were all awry, and everything about him betokened sorrow and woe. Over his head from the branches of the osier, hung a beautiful harp of polished wood inlaid with gold and silver in fantastic devices. Beside him lay a stout ashen bow and half a score of fair, smooth arrows.

"Halloa!" shouted Will Stutely, when they had come out from the forest into the little open spot. "Who art thou, fellow, that liest there killing all the green grass with salt water?"

Hearing the voice, the stranger sprang to his feet and snatching up his bow and fitting a shaft, held himself in readiness for whatever ill might befall him.

"Truly," said one of the yeomen, when they had seen the young stranger's face, "I do know that lad right well. He is a certain minstrel that I have seen hereabouts more than once. It was only a week ago I saw him skipping across the hill like a yearling doe. A fine sight he was then, with a flower at his ear and a cock's plume stuck in his cap, but now, methinks, our cockerel is shorn of his gay feathers."

"Pah!" cried Will Stutely, coming up to the stranger, "wipe thine eyes, man! I do hate to see a tall, stout fellow sniveling like a girl of fourteen over a dead tomtit. Put down thy bow, man! We mean thee no harm."

But Will Scarlet, seeing how the stranger, who had a young and boyish look, was stung by the words that Stutely had spoken, came to him and put his hand upon the youth's shoulder. "Nay, thou art in trouble, poor boy!" said he, kindly. "Mind not what these fellows have said. They are rough, but they mean thee well. Mayhap they do not understand a lad like thee. Thou shalt come with us, and perchance we may find a certain one that can aid thee in thy perplexities, whatsoever they may be."

"Yea, truly, come along," said Will Stutely, gruffly. "I meant thee no harm and may mean thee some good. Take down thy singing tool from off this fair tree and come away with us."

The youth did as he was bidden, and with bowed head and sorrowful step, accompanied them, walking along beside Will Scarlet.

So they wended their way through the forest. The bright light faded from the sky and a glimmering gray fell over all things. From the deeper recesses of the forest the strange whispering sounds of night-time came to the ear; all else was silent, saving only for the rattling of their footsteps amid the crisp, dry leaves of the last winter. At last a ruddy glow shone before them here and there through the trees; a little

farther and they came to the open glade, now bathed in the pale moonlight. In the center of the open, crackled a great fire, throwing a red glow on all around. At the fire were roasting juicy steaks of venison, pheasants, capons, and fresh fish from the river. All the air was filled with the sweet smell of good things cooking.

The little band made its way across the glade, many yeomen turning with curious looks and gazing after them, but none speaking or questioning them. So, with Will Scarlet upon one side and Will Stutely upon the other, the stranger came to where Robin Hood sat on a seat of moss under the greenwood tree, with Little John standing beside him.

"Good even, fair friend," said Robin Hood, rising as the other drew near. "And hast thou come to feast with me this day?"

"Alas! I know not," said the lad, looking around him with dazed eyes, for he was bewildered with all that he saw. "Truly, I know not whether I be in a dream," said he to himself in a low voice.

"Nay, marry," quoth jolly Robin, laughing, "thou art awake, as thou wilst presently find, for a fine feast is a-cooking for thee. Thou art our honored guest this day."

Still the young stranger looked about him, as though in a dream. Presently he turned to Robin. "Methinks," said he, "I know now where I am and what hath befallen me. Art not thou the great Robin Hood?"

"Thou hast hit the bull's-eye," quoth Robin, clapping him upon the shoulder. "Men hereabouts do call me by that name. Sin' thou knowest me, thou knowest also that he who feasteth with me must pay his reckoning. I trust thou hast a full purse with thee, fair stranger."

"Alas!" said the stranger, "I have no purse nor money either, saving only the half of a sixpence, the other half of which mine own dear love doth carry in her bosom, hung about her neck by a strand of silken thread."

At this speech a great shout of laughter went up from those around, whereat the poor boy looked as he would die of shame; but Robin Hood turned sharply to Will Stutely.

"Why, how now," quoth he, "is this the guest that thou has brought us to fill our purse? Methinks thou has brought but a lean cock to the market."

"Nay, good master," answered Will Stutely, grinning, "he is no guest of mine; it was Will Scarlet that brought him thither. Nevertheless, as thou mayst remember a certain talk this morning of duty and whatnot being better than a penny plucked from the dust, methinks here is a fine chance for practising charity."

Then up spoke Will Scarlet, and told how they had found the lad in sorrow, and how he had brought him to Robin, thinking that he might perchance aid him in his trouble. Then Robin Hood turned to the youth, and placing his hand upon the other's shoulder, held him off at arm's length, scanning his face closely.

"A young face," quoth he in a low voice, half to himself, "a kind face, a good face. 'Tis like a maiden's for purity, and, withal, the fairest that e'er mine eyes did see; but, if I may judge fairly by thy looks, grief cometh to young as well as to old." At these words, spoken so kindly, the poor lad's eyes brimmed up with tears. "Nay, nay," said Robin, hastily, "cheer up, lad. I warrant thy case is not so bad that it cannot be mended. What may be thy name?"

"Allan a Dale is my name, good master."

"Allan a Dale," repeated Robin, musing. "Allan a Dale. It doth seem to me that the name is not altogether strange to mine ears. Yea, surely thou art the minstrel of whom we have been hearing lately, whose voice so charmeth all men. Dost thou not come from the Dale of Rotherstream, over beyond Stavely?"

"Yea, truly," answered Allan, "I do come thence."

"How old art thou, Allan?" said Robin.

"I am but twenty years of age."

"Methinks thou art over young to be perplexed with trouble," quoth Robin, kindly. Then, turning to the others, he cried, "Come, lads, busk ye and get our feast ready; only thou, Will Scarlet, and thou, Little John, stay here with me."

Then, when the others had gone, each man about his business, Robin turned once more to the youth. "Now, lad," said he, "tell us thy troubles, and speak freely. A flow of words doth ever ease the heart of sorrows; it is like opening the waste weir when the mill-dam is over full. Come, sit thou here beside me, and speak at thine ease."

Then straightway the youth told the three yeomen all that was in his heart, at first in broken words and phrases, then freely and with greater ease when he saw that all listened closely to what he said. So he told them how he had come from York to the sweet vale of Rother, traveling the country through as a minstrel, stopping now at castle, now at hall, and now at farmhouse; how he had spent one sweet evening in a certain broad, low farmhouse, where he sang before a stout franklin and a maiden as pure and lovely as the first snowdrop of spring; how he had played and sung to her, and how sweet Ellen o' the Dale had listened to him and had loved him. Then, in a low, sweet voice, scarcely louder than a whisper, he told how he had watched for her and met her now and then when she went abroad, but was all too afraid in her sweet presence to speak to her, until at last, beside the banks of Rother, he had spoken of his love, and she had whispered that which had made his heartstrings quiver with joy. Then they broke a sixpence between them, and vowed to be true to one another forever.

Next he told how her father had discovered what was a-doing and had taken her away from him so that he never saw her again, and his heart was sometimes like to break; how this morn, only one short month and a half from the time that he had seen her last, he had heard and knew it to be so, that she was to marry old Sir Stephen of Trent, two days hence, for Ellen's father thought it would be a grand thing to have his daughter marry so high, albeit [although] she wished it not; nor was it wonder that a knight should wish to marry his own sweet love, who was the most beautiful maiden in all the world.

To all this the yeomen listened in silence, the clatter of many voices, jesting and laughing, sounding around them, and the red light of the fire shining on their faces and in their eyes. So simple were the poor boy's words, and so deep was his sorrow, that even Little John felt a certain knotty lump rise in his throat.

"I wonder not," said Robin, after a moment's silence, "that thy true love loved thee, for thou hast surely a silver cross beneath thy tongue, even like good Saint Francis, that could charm the birds of the air by his speech."

"By the breath of my body," burst forth Little John, seeking to cover his feelings with angry words, "I have a great part of a mind to go straightway and cudgel the nasty life out of the body of that same vile Sir Stephen. Marry, come up, say I—what a plague—does an old weazen think that tender lasses are to be bought like pullets o' a market day? Out upon him!—I—but no matter, only let him look to himself."

Then up spoke Will Scarlet. "Methinks it seemeth but ill

done of the lass that she should so quickly change at others'
bidding, more especially when it cometh to the marrying of a
man as old as this same Sir Stephen. I like it not in her, Allan."

"Nay," said Allan, hotly, "thou dost wrong her. She is as
soft and gentle as a stockdove. I know her better than anyone in all the world. She may do her father's bidding, but if
she married Sir Stephen, her heart will break and she will
die. My own sweet dear, I—" He stopped and shook his head,
for he could say nothing further.

Whilst the others were speaking, Robin Hood had been sunk
in thought. "Methinks I have a plan might fit thy case, Allan,"
said he. "But tell me first, thinkest thou, lad, that thy true
love hath spirit enough to marry thee were ye together in
church, the banns published, and the priest found, even were
her father to say her nay?"

"Ay, marry would she," cried Allan, eagerly.

"Then, if her father be the man that I take him to be, I will
undertake that he shall give you both his blessing as wedded
man and wife, in the place of old Sir Stephen and upon his
wedding morn. But stay, now I bethink me, there is one thing
reckoned not upon—the priest. Truly, those of the cloth do not
love me over-much, and when it comes to doing as I desire in
such a matter, they are as like as not to prove stiff-necked. As
to the lesser clergy, they fear to do me a favor because of
abbot or bishop."

"Nay," quoth Will Scarlet, laughing, "so far as that goeth,
I know of a certain friar that, couldst thou but get on the
soft side of him, would do thy business even though Pope Joan
herself stood forth to ban him. He is known as the Curtal
Friar of Fountain Abbey and dwelleth in Fountain Dale."

"But," quoth Robin, "Fountain Abbey is a good hundred
miles from here. An we would help this lad, we have no time

to go thither and back before his true love will be married. Naught is to be gained there, coz."

"Yea," quoth Will Scarlet, laughing again, "but this Fountain Abbey is not so far away as the one of which thou speakest, uncle. The Fountain Abbey of which I speak is no such rich and proud place as the other, but a simple little cell; yet, withal, as cosy a spot as ever stout anchorite dwelt within. I know the place well, and can guide thee thither, for, though it is a goodly distance, yet methinks a stout pair of legs could carry a man there and back in one day."

"Then give me thy hand, Allan," cried Robin, "and let me tell thee, I swear by the bright hair of Saint Ælfrida that this time two days hence Ellen a Dale shall be thy wife. I will seek this same Friar of Fountain Abbey tomorrow day, and I warrant I will get upon the soft side of him, even if I have to drub one soft."

At this Will Scarlet laughed again. "Be not too sure of that, good uncle," quoth he. "Nevertheless, from what I know of him, I think this curtal friar will gladly join two such fair lovers, more especially if there be good eating and drinking afoot thereafter."

But now one of the band came to say that the feast was spread upon the grass; so, Robin leading the way, the others followed to where the goodly feast was spread. Merry was the meal. Jest and story passed freely, and all laughed till the forest rang again. Allan laughed with the rest, for his cheeks were flushed with the hope that Robin Hood had given him.

At last the feast was done, and Robin Hood turned to Allan, who sat beside him. "Now, Allan," quoth he, "so much has been said of thy singing that we would fain have a taste of thy skill ourselves. Canst thou not give us something?"

"Surely," answered Allan, readily, for he was no third-rate

songster that must be asked again and again, but said "yes" or "no" at the first bidding. Taking up his harp, he ran his fingers lightly over the sweetly-sounding strings, and all was hushed about the cloth. Then, backing his voice with sweet music on his harp, he sang a wedding song.

Not a sound broke the stillness when Allan a Dale had done, but all sat gazing at the handsome singer, for so sweet was his voice and so sweet the music that each man sat with bated breath, lest one drop more should come and he should lose it.

"By my faith and my troth," quoth Robin at last, drawing a deep breath, "lad, thou art—thou must not leave our company, Allan! Wilt thou not stay with us here in the sweet green forest? Truly, I do feel my heart go out toward thee with great love."

Then Allan took Robin's hand and kissed it. "I will stay with thee always, dear master," said he, "for never have I known such kindness as thou hast shown me this day."

Then Will Scarlet stretched forth his hand and shook Allan's in token of fellowship, as did Little John likewise. And thus the famous Allan a Dale became one of Robin's band.

CHAPTER 10

Robin and the Curtal Friar

THE stout yeomen of Sherwood Forest were ever early risers of a morn, more especially when the summer time had come, for then in the freshness of the dawn the dew was always the brightest, and the song of the small birds the sweetest.

Quoth Robin, "Now will I go to seek this same Friar of Fountain Abbey of whom we spake yesternight, and I will take with me four of my good men, and these four shall be Little John, Will Scarlet, David of Doncaster, and Arthur a Bland. Bide the rest of you here, and Will Stutely shall be your chief whilst I am gone."

Then straightway Robin Hood donned a fine steel coat of chain mail, over which he put on a light jacket of Lincoln green. Upon his head he clapped a steel cap, and this he covered by one of soft white leather, in which stood a nodding cock's plume. By his side he hung a good broadsword of tempered steel, the bluish blade marked all over with strange figures of dragons, winged women, and what not. A gallant sight was Robin so arrayed, I wot [believe] the glint of steel showing here and there as the sunlight caught brightly the links of polished mail that showed beneath his green coat.

So, having arrayed himself, he and the four yeomen set forth upon their way, Will Scarlet taking the lead, for he knew better than the others whither to go. Thus, mile after mile, they strode along, now across a brawling stream, now along a sunlit road, now adown some sweet forest path, over which the trees met in green and rustling canopy, and at the end of which a herd of startled deer dashed away, with rattle of leaves and crackle of branches.

Onward they walked, Robin Hood and his four good yeomen, with song and jest and laughter till high noontide was passed, when at last they came to the banks of a wide, glassy, and lily-padded stream. Here a broad beaten path stretched along beside the banks, on which path labored the horses that tugged at the slow moving barges, laden with barley-meal or what not, from the countryside to the many-towered town. But now, in the hot silence of the midday, no horse was seen nor any man beside themselves. Behind them and before them stretched the river, its placid bosom ruffled here and there by the purple dusk of a small breeze. Sweet green osiers bordered the banks, and far away the red-tiled eaves of some tall tower glimmered in the sun, the weather-vane a spark against the blue sky. And now they traveled more easily, for the road was level and hard. Around them and over the surface of the water skimmed and dipped the swallows, gay dragonflies darted hither and thither glistening in the sun, and now and then a solitary heron rose splashing and with startled cry from its hiding place among the reeds and sedges that grew in the shallow margin of the stream.

"Now, good uncle," quoth Will Scarlet at last, when they had

walked for a long time beside this sweet bright river, "just
beyond yon bend ahead of us is a shallow ford which in no place
is deeper than thy mid-thigh, and upon the other side of the
stream is a certain little hermitage hidden amidst the bosky
tangle of the thickets wherein dwelleth the Friar of Fountain
Dale. Thither will I lead thee, for I know the way; albeit it is
not overhard to find."

"Nay," quoth jolly Robin, stopping suddenly, "had I thought
that I should have had to wade water, even were it so crystal
a stream as this, I had donned other clothes than I have upon
me. But no matter now, for after all a wetting will not wash
the skin away, and what must be must. But bide ye here, lads,
for I would enjoy this merry adventure alone. Nevertheless,
listen well, and if ye hear me sound upon my bugle-horn,
come quickly."

"'Tis ever thus," said Little John, half muttering. "Thou
dost always seek these ventures alone, whilst we, whose lives
are but of small worth beside thine, and who would be but
too glad to enter upon them, must sit, as it were, twiddling
our thumbs in idleness."

"Nay, Little John," quoth jolly Robin, "this venture, I wot,
is without danger to me. I know thou art overready to peril
thyself; nevertheless, bide thou here this time as I bid thee."
So saying he turned and left them, and went striding onward
alone.

Robin had walked no farther than where the bend of the
road hid his good men from his view, when he stopped suddenly, for he thought that he heard voices. He stood still and
listened and presently heard words passed back and forth
betwixt what seemed to be two men, and yet the two voices
were wondrously alike. The sound came from over behind
the bank, that here was steep and high, dropping from the

edge of the road a half a score of feet to the sedgy verge of the river.

" 'Tis strange," muttered Robin to himself after a space, when the voices had ceased their talking. "Surely there be two people that spoke the one to the other, and yet methinks their voices are mightily alike. I make my vow that never have I heard the like in all my life before. Truly, if this twain are to be judged by their voices no two peas were ever more alike. I will look into this matter." So saying, he came softly to the river bank and laying him down upon the grass peered over the edge and down below.

All was cool and shady beneath the bank. A stout osier grew, not straight upward, but leaning across the water, shadowing the spot with its soft foliage. All around grew a mass of feathery ferns such as hide and nestle in cool places, and up to Robin's nostrils came the tender odor of the wild thyme, that loves to grow along the moist verges of running streams.

Here, his broad back against the rugged trunk of the willow and half hidden by the soft ferns around him, sat a stout, brawny fellow, but no other man was there. His head was as round as a ball and covered with a mat of close-clipped curly black hair that grew low down on his forehead. But his crown was shorn as smooth as the palm of one's hand, which, together with his loose robe, cowl, and string of beads, showed that which his looks never would have done, that he was a Friar. His cheeks were as red and shining as a winter crab, albeit they were nearly covered with a close curly black beard, as were his chin and upper lip likewise. His neck was thick like that of a north country bull, and his round head closely set upon shoulders that were e'en a match for those of Little John himself.

Beneath his bushy black brows danced a pair of little gray eyes that could not stand still for very drollery of humor. No man could look into his face and not feel his heartstrings tickled by the merriment of their look. By his side lay a steel cap, which he had laid off for the sake of the coolness to his rown. His legs were stretched wide apart, and betwixt his ees he held a great pasty compounded of juicy meats of ers kinds made savory with tender young onions, both eat and onions being mingled with a good rich gravy. In is right fist he held a great piece of brown crust at which he munched sturdily, and every now and then he thrust his left hand into the pie and drew it forth full of meat; anon he would take a mighty pull at a great bottle of Malmsey that lay beside him.

"By my faith," quoth Robin to himself, "I do verily believe that this is the merriest feast, the merriest wight, the merriest place, and the merriest sight in all merry England. Methought there was another here, but it must have been this holy man talking to himself."

So Robin lay watching the Friar, and the Friar, all unknowing that he was so overlooked, ate his meal placidly. At last he was done, and having first wiped his greasy hands upon the ferns and wild thyme (and sweeter napkin ne'er had king in all the world) he took up his flask and began talking to himself as though he were another man, and answering himself as though he were somebody else.

"Dear lad, thou art the sweetest fellow in all the world, I do love thee as a lover loveth his lass. La, thou dost make me shamed to speak so to me in this solitary place, no one being by, and yet if thou wilt have me say so, I do love thee as thou lovest me. Nay then, wilt thou not take a drink of good Malmsey? After thee, lad, after thee. Nay, I beseech thee, sweeten the draft with thy lips." Here he passed the flask from his right hand to his left. "An thou wilt force it on me so I must needs do thy bidding, yet with the more pleasure do I so as I drink thy very great health." Here he took a long, deep draft. "And now, sweet lad, 'tis thy turn next." Here he passed the bottle from his left hand back again to the right. "I take sweet chuck, and here's wishing thee as much good as th wishest me." Saying this he took another draft, and truly drank enough for two.

All this time merry Robin lay upon the bank and listene while his stomach so quaked with laughter that he was force to press his palm across his mouth to keep it from bursting forth; for, truly, he would not have spoiled such a goodly jest for the half of Nottinghamshire.

Having gotten his breath from his last draft, the Friar began talking again in this wise: "Now, sweet lad, canst thou not sing me a song? La, I know not, I am but in an ill voice this day; prythee ask me not; dost thou not hear how I croak like a frog? Nay, nay, thy voice is as sweet as any bullfinch; come, sing, I prythee, I would rather hear thee sing than eat a fair feast. Alas, I would fain not sing before one that can pipe so well and hath heard so many goodly songs and ballads; ne'ertheless, an thou wilt have it so, I will do my best. But now methinks that thou and I might sing some fair song together. Then dost thou not think that thou couldst take the lass's part if I take the lad's? I know not but I will try; begin thou with the lad and I will follow with the lass." Then, singing first with a voice deep and gruff, and anon in one that was high and squeaking, he blithely trolled the merry catch.

Here Robin could contain himself no longer but burst forth into a mighty roar of laughter; then the holy Friar keeping

on with the song, he joined in the chorus, and together they
sang, or, as one might say, bellow‍ , for the stout Friar did
not seem to have heard Robin's l‍ hter; neither did he seem
to know that the yeoman had jo‍ n with the song, but, with
eyes half closed, looking str‍ ‍efore him and wagging
his round head from side to‍ ‍ime to the music, he kept
on bravely to the end, ‍ ‍obin finishing up with a
mighty roar that might‍ ‍ heard a mile.

But no sooner had ‍ ‍ord been sung than the holy
man seized his steel ‍ ‍ed it on his head, and springing
to his feet cried i‍ ‍at voice, "What spy have we here?
Come forth, thou limb of evil, and I will carve thee into as
fine pudding-meat as e'er a wife in Yorkshire cooked of a
Sunday." Hereupon he drew from beneath his robes a great
broadsword full as stout as was Robin's.

"Nay, put up thy pinking iron, friend," quoth Robin, standing up with the tears of laughter still on his cheeks. "Folk who
have sung so sweetly together should not fight thereafter."
Hereupon he came leaping down the bank to where the other
stood.

"I tell thee, friend," said he, "my throat is parched with
that song as e'er a barley stubble in October. Hast thou haply
any Malmsey left in that stout pottle [two-quart measure]?"

"Truly," said the Friar in a glum voice, "thou dost ask
thyself freely where thou art not bidden. Yet I trust I am too
good a Christian to refuse any man drink that is athirst.
Such as there is o't thou art welcome to a drink of the same."
And he held the pottle out to Robin.

Robin took it without more ado and putting it to his lips
tilted his head back, while that which was within said "glug!
glug! glug!" for more than three winks, I wot. The stout
Friar watched Robin anxiously the while, and when he was

done took the bottle quickly. He shook it, held it betwixt his
eyes and the light, looked reproachfully at the yeoman, and
straightway placed it at his own lips. When it came away
again there was naught within it.

"Dost thou know the country hereabouts, thou good and
holy man?" asked Robin, laughing.

"Yea, somewhat," answered the other, dryly.

"And dost thou know of a certain spot called Fountain
Abbey?"

"Yea, somewhat."

"Then perchange thou knowest also of a certain one who
goeth by the name of the Curtal Friar of Fountain Abbey."

"Yea, somewhat."

"Well, then, good fellow, holy father, or whatever thou art,"
quoth Robin, "I would know whether this same Friar is to be
found upon this side of the river or the other."

"Truly, the river hath no side but the other," said the Friar.

"How dost thou prove that?" asked Robin.

"Why, thus," said the Friar, noting the points upon his
fingers. "The other side of the river is the other, thou
grantest?"

"Yea, truly."

"Yet the other side is but one side, thou dost mark?"

"No man could gainsay that," said Robin.

"Then if the other side is on one side, this side is the other
side. But the other side is the other side, therefore both sides
of the river are the other side. Q. E. D."

" 'Tis well and pleasantly argued," quoth Robin. "Yet I am
still in the dark as to whether this same Curtal Friar is upon
the side of the river on which we stand or upon the side of the
river on which we do not stand."

"That," quoth the Friar, "is a practical question upon

which the cunning rules appertaining to logic touch not. I do advise thee to find that out by the air of thine own five senses —sight, feeling, and what not."

"I do wish much," quoth Robin, looking thoughtfully at the stout priest, "to cross yon ford and strive to find this same good Friar."

"Truly," said the other, piously, "it is a goodly wish on the part of one so young. Far be it from me to check thee in so holy a quest. Friend, the river is free to all."

"Yea, good father," said Robin, "but thou seest that my clothes are of the finest and I fain would not get them wet. Methinks thy shoulders are stout and broad. Couldst thou not find it in thy heart to carry me across?"

"Now, by the white hand of the holy Lady of the Fountain!" burst forth the Friar in a mighty rage. "Dost thou, thou poor puny stripling, thou kiss-my-lady-la poppenjay; thou— thou—What shall I call thee? Dost thou ask me, the holy Tuck, to carry thee? Now I swear—" Here he paused suddenly, then slowly the anger passed from his face, and his little eyes twinkled once more. "But why should I not?" quoth he, piously. "Did not the holy Saint Christopher ever carry the stranger across the river? And should I, poor sinner that I am, be ashamed to do likewise? Come with me, stranger, and I will do thy bidding in an humble frame of mind." So saying he clambered up the bank, closely followed by Robin, and led the way to the shallow pebbly ford, chuckling to himself the while as though he were enjoying some goodly jest within himself.

Having come to the ford, he girded up his robes about his loins, tucked his good broadsword beneath his arm, and stooped his back to take Robin upon it. Suddenly he straightened up. "Methinks," quoth he, "thou'lt get thy weapon wet. Let me tuck it beneath mine arm along with mine own."

"Nay, good father," said Robin, "I would not burden thee with aught of mine but myself."

"Dost thou think," said the Friar, mildly, "that the good Saint Christopher would ha' sought his own ease so? Nay, give me thy tool as I bid thee, for I would carry it as a penance to my pride."

Upon this, without more ado, Robin Hood unbuckled his sword from his side and handed it to the other, who thrust it with his own beneath his arm. Then once more the Friar bent his back, and Robin having mounted upon it, he stepped sturdily into the water, and so strode onward, splashing in the shoal, and breaking all the smooth surface into ever-widening rings. At last he reached the other side and Robin leaped lightly from his back.

"Many thanks, good father," quoth he. "Thou are indeed a good and holy man. Prythee give me my sword and let me away, for I am in haste."

At this the stout Friar looked upon Robin for a long time, his head on one side and with a most waggish twist to his face; then he slowly winked his right eye. "Nay, good youth," said he gently, "I doubt not that thou art in haste with thine affairs, yet thou dost think nothing of mine. Thine are of a carnal nature; mine are of a spiritual nature, a holy work, so to speak; moreover, mine affairs do lie upon the other side of this stream. I see by thy quest of this same holy recluse that thou art a good young man and most reverent to the cloth. I did get wet coming hither and am sadly afraid that should I wade the water again I might get certain cricks and pains i' the joints that would mar my devotions for many a day to come. I know that since I have so humbly done thy bidding thou wilt carry me back again. Thou seest how Saint Godrick, that holy hermit whose natal day this is, hath placed in my hands two swords and in thine never a one. Therefore be persuaded, good youth, and carry me back to the other side."

Robin Hood looked up and he looked down, biting his nether lip. Quoth he, "Thou cunning Friar, thou hast me fair and fast enow [enough]. Let me tell thee that not one of thy cloth hath so hoodwinked me in all my life before. I might have known from thy looks that thou wert no such holy man as thou didst pretend to be."

"Nay," interrupted the Friar, "I bid thee speak not so scurrilously neither, lest thou mayst perchance feel the prick of an inch or so of blue steel."

"Tut, tut," said Robin, "speak not so, Friar; the loser hath ever the right to use his tongue as he doth list. Give me my sword. I do promise to carry thee back straightway. Nay, I will not lift the weapon against thee."

"Marry, come up," quoth the Friar, "I fear thee not, fellow. Here is thy skewer; and get thyself presently ready, for I would hasten back."

So Robin took his sword again and buckled it at his side; then he bent his stout back and took the Friar upon it.

Now I wot Robin Hood had a heavier load to carry in the Friar than the Friar had in him. Moreover he did not know the ford, so he went stumbling among the stones, now stepping into a deep hole, and now nearly tripping over a boulder, while the sweat ran down his face in beads from the hardness of his journey and the heaviness of his load. Meantime, the Friar kept digging his heels into Robin's sides and bidding him hasten, calling him many ill names the while. To all this Robin answered never a word, but having softly felt around till he found the buckle of the belt that held the Friar's sword, he worked slyly at the fastenings, seeking to loosen them. Thus it came about that by the time he had reached the other bank with his load, the Friar's sword-belt was loose albeit he knew it not. When Robin stood on dryland and the Friar leaped from his back, the yeoman gripped hold of the sword so that blade, sheath, and strap came away from the holy man, leaving him without a weapon.

"Now, then," quoth merry Robin, panting as he spake and wiping the sweat from his brow, "I have thee, fellow. This time that same Saint of whom thou didst speak but now hath delivered two swords into my hand and hath stripped thine away from thee. Now if thou dost not carry me back, and that speedily, I swear I will prick thy skin till it is as full of holes as a slashed doublet."

The good Friar said not a word for a while, but he looked at Robin with a grim look. "Now," said he at last, "I did think that thy wits were of the heavy sort and knew not that thou wert so cunning. Truly, thou hast me upon self-defense; also I promise to do thy bidding and take thee upon my back and carry thee."

So jolly Robin gave him his sword again, which the Friar buckled to his side, and this time looked to it that it was more secure in its fastenings; then tucking up his robes once more, he took Robin Hood upon his back and without a word stepped into the water, and so waded on in silence while Robin sat laughing upon his back. At last he reached the middle of the ford where the water was deepest. Here he stopped for a moment, and then, with a sudden lift of his hand and heave of his shoulders, fairly shot Robin over his head as though he were a sack of grain.

Down went Robin into the water with a mighty splash. "There," quoth the holy man, calmly turning back again to shore, "let that cool thy hot spirit, if it may."

Meantime, after much splashing, Robin had gotten to his feet and stood gazing about him all bewildered, the water running from him in pretty little rills. At last he shot the water out of his ears and spat some out of his mouth, and gathering his scattered wits together, saw the stout Friar standing on the bank laughing.

Then, I wot, was Robin Hood a mad man.

"Stay, thou villain!" roared he. "I am after thee straight, and if I do not carve thy brawn for thee this day, may I never lift finger again!" So saying, he dashed, splashing, to the bank.

"Thou needst not hasten thyself unduly," quoth the stout Friar. "Fear not; I will abide here, and if thou dost not cry 'Alack-a-day' ere long time is gone, may I never more peep through the brake at a fallow deer."

And now Robin having reached the bank, began without more ado to roll up his sleeves above his wrists. The Friar, also, tucked his robes more about him, showing a great, stout arm on which the muscles stood out like humps of an aged tree. Then Robin saw, what he had not wotted of before, that the Friar had also a coat of mail beneath his gown.

"Look to thyself," cried Robin, drawing his good sword.

"Ay, marry," quoth the Friar, who held his already in his hand. So, without more ado, they came together, and there-upon began a fierce and mighty battle. Right and left, up and down, and back and forth they fought. The swords flashed in the sun and then met with a clash that sounded far and near. I wot this was no playful bout at quarterstaff, but a grim and serious fight of real earnest. Thus they strove for an hour or more, pausing every now and then to rest, at which times each looked at the other with wonder, and thought that never had he seen so stout a fellow; then once again they would go at it more fiercely than ever. Yet in all this time neither had harmed the other nor caused his blood to flow. At last merry Robin cried, "Hold thy hand, good friend!" Whereupon both lowered their swords.

"Now I crave a boon ere we begin again," quoth Robin, wiping the sweat from his brow; for they had striven so long that he began to think that it would be an ill-done thing either to be smitten himself or to smite so stout and brave a fellow as this Friar.

"What wouldst thou have of me?" asked the Friar.

"Only this," quoth Robin, "that thou wilt let me blow thrice upon my bugle horn."

The Friar bent his brows and looked shrewdly at Robin Hood. "Now I do verily think that thou hast some cunning trick in this," quoth he. "Ne'ertheless, I fear thee not and will let thee have thy wish, providing thou wilt also let me blow thrice upon this little whistle."

"With all my heart," quoth Robin, "so, here goes for one." So saying, he raised his silver horn to his lips and blew thrice upon it, clear and high.

Meantime, the Friar stood watching keenly for what might come to pass, holding in his fingers the while a pretty silver whistle, such as knights use for calling their hawks back to their wrists, which whistle always hung at his girdle along with his rosary.

Scarcely had the echo of the last note of Robin's bugle come winding back from across the river, when four tall men in Lincoln green came running around the bend of the road, each with a bow in his hand and an arrow ready nocked upon the string.

"Ha! It is thus, thou traitor knave!" cried the Friar. "Then, marry, look to thyself!" So saying, he straightway clapped the hawk's whistle to his lips and blew a blast that was both loud and shrill. And now there came a crackling of the bushes that lined the other side of the road, and presently forth from the covert burst four great, shaggy hounds.

"At 'em, Sweet Lips! At 'em, Bell Throat! At 'em, Beauty! At 'em, Fangs!" cried the Friar, pointing at Robin.

And now it was well for that yeoman that a tree stood nigh him beside the road, else had he had ill chance of it. Ere one could say "Gaffer Downthedale" the hounds were upon him, and he had only time to drop his sword and leap lightly into the tree, around which the hounds gathered, looking up at him as though he were a cat on the eaves. But the Friar quickly called off his dogs. "At 'em!" cried he, pointing down the road to where the yeomen were standing stock still with wonder of what they saw. As the hawk darts down upon its quarry, so sped the four dogs at the yeomen; but when the four men saw the hounds so coming, all with one accord, saving only Will Scarlet, drew each man his goose feather to his ear and let fly his shaft.

And now the old ballad telleth of a wondrous thing that happened, for thus it says, that each dog so shot at leaped lightly aside, and as the arrow passed him whistling, caught it in his mouth and bit it in twain. Now it would have been an ill day for these four good fellows had not Will Scarlet stepped before the others and met the hounds as they came rushing. "Why, how now, Fangs!" cried he, sternly. "Down, Beauty! Down, sirrah! What means this?"

At the sound of his voice each dog shrank back quickly, and then straightway came to him and licked his hands and fawned upon him, as is the wont of dogs when they meet someone they know.

Then the four yeomen came forward, the hounds leaping

around Will Scarlet joyously. "Why, how now!" cried the stout Friar. "What means this? Art thou wizard to turn those wolves into lambs? Ha!" cried he, when they had come still nearer. "Can I trust mine eyes? What means it that I see young Master William Gamwell in such company?"

"Nay, Tuck," said the young man, as the four came forward to where Robin was now clambering down from the tree in which he had been roosting, he having seen that all danger was over for the time, "nay, Tuck, my name is no longer Will Gamwell, but Will Scarlet. And this is my good uncle, Robin Hood, with whom I am abiding just now."

"Truly, good master," said the Friar, looking somewhat abashed and reaching out his great palm to Robin, "I ha' oft heard thy name both sung and spoken of, but I never thought to meet thee in battle. I crave thy forgiveness and do wonder not that I found so stout a man against me."

"Truly, most holy father," said Little John, "I am more thankful than e'er I was in all my life before that our good friend Scarlet knew thee and thy dogs. I tell thee seriously that I felt my heart crumble away from me when I saw my shaft so miss its aim, and those great beasts of thine coming straight at me."

"Thou mayst indeed be thankful, friend," said the Friar, gravely. "But, Master Will, how cometh it that thou dost now abide in Sherwood?"

"Why, Tuck, dost thou not know of my ill happening with my father's steward?" answered Scarlet.

"Yea, truly, yet I knew not that thou wert in hiding because of it. Marry, the times are all awry when a gentleman must lie hidden for so small a thing."

"But we are losing time," quoth Robin, "and I have yet to find that same curtal Friar."

"Why, uncle, thou hast not far to go," said Will Scarlet, pointing to the Friar, "for there he stands beside thee."

"How?" quoth Robin. "Art thou the man that I have been at such pains to seek all day and have got such a ducking for?"

"Why, truly," said the Friar, demurely, "some do call me the curtal Friar of Fountain Abbey; others again call me in jest the Abbot of Fountain Abbey; others still again call me simple Friar Tuck."

"I like the last name best," quoth Robin, "for it doth slip more glibly off the tongue. But why didst thou not tell me thou wert he I sought, instead of sending me searching for black moonbeams?"

"Why, truly, thou didst not ask me, good master," quoth stout Tuck. "But what didst thou desire of me?"

"Nay," quoth Robin, "the day groweth late, and we cannot stand longer talking here. Come back with us to Sherwood, and I will unfold all to thee as we travel along."

So, without tarrying longer, they all departed, with the stout dogs at their heels, and wended their way back to Sherwood again; but it was long past nightfall ere they reached the greenwood tree.

Now Robin Hood was able, aided by the merry Friar Tuck of Fountain Dale, to compass the happiness of two young lovers. Friar Tuck performed the ceremony uniting fair Ellen to Allan a Dale in marriage, and when it was done Robin Hood gathered his men together, and with Allan and his young bride in their midst, they all turned their footsteps toward the woodlands. On the way thither Friar Tuck came close to Robin and plucked him by the sleeve. "Thou dost lead a merry life, good master," quoth he, "but dost thou not think that it would be for the welfare of all your souls to have a good stout chaplain, such as I, to oversee holy matters? Truly,

I do love this life mightily." At this merry Robin laughed again, and bade him stay and become one of their band if he wished.

That night there was such a feast held in the greenwood as Nottinghamshire never saw before. Thus ends the merry story of Allan a Dale, and how Robin Hood and Friar Tuck benefited him.

CHAPTER 11

Robin Hood Aideth a Sorrowful Knight

SO PASSED the gentle springtime away in budding beauty, its silver showers and sunshine, its green meadows and its flowers. So likewise, passed the summer with its yellow sunlight, its quivering heat and deep, bosky foliage, its long twilights and its mellow nights, through which the frogs croaked and fairy folk were said to be out on the hillsides.

All this passed by, and the time of fall came, bringing with it its own pleasures and joyousness; for now, when the harvest was gathered home, merry bands of gleaners roamed the country about, singing along the roads in the daytime and sleeping beneath the hedgerows and the hay-ricks at night. Now the hips burned red in the tangled thickets and the haws waxed black in the hedgerows, the stubble lay all crisp and naked to the sky, and the green leaves were fast turning russet and brown. Also, at this merry season, good things of the year are gathered in great store. Brown ale lies ripening in the cellar, hams and bacon hang in the smoke-shed, and crabs are stowed away in the straw for roasting in the winter

166

time, when the north wind piles the snow in drifts around the gables and the fire crackles warm upon the hearth.

So passed the seasons then, so they pass now, and so they will pass in time to come, whilst we come and go like leaves of the tree that fall and are soon forgotten.

Quoth Robin Hood, snuffing the air, "Here is a fair day, Little John, and one that we can ill waste in idleness. Choose such men as thou dost need, and go thou east while I will wend to the west, and see that each of us bringeth back some goodly guest to dine this day beneath the greenwood tree."

"Marry," cried Little John, clapping his palms together for joy, "thy bidding fitteth my liking like haft to blade. I'll bring thee back a likely guest this day, or come not back mine own self."

Then they each chose such of the band as they wished, and so went forth by different paths from the forest.

Now, you and I cannot go two ways at the same time whilst we join in these merry doings; so we will e'en let Little John follow his own path while we tuck up our skirts and trudge after Robin Hood. And here is good company, too: Robin Hood, Will Scarlet, Allan a Dale, Will Scathelock, Midge, the Miller's son, and others. A score or more of stout fellows had abided in the forest, with Friar Tuck, to make ready for the home-coming, but all the rest were gone either with Robin Hood or Little John.

They traveled onward, Robin following his fancy and the others following Robin. Now they wended their way through open dale with cottage and farm lying therein, and now again they entered woodlands once more. Passing by fair Mansfield Town, with its towers and battlements and spires all smiling in the sun, they came at last out of the forest lands. Onward they journeyed, through highway and byway, through vil-

lages where good wives and merry lasses peeped through the
casements at the fine show of young men, until at last they
came over beyond Alverton in Derbyshire. By this time high
noon-tide had come, yet they had met no guest such as was
worth their while to take back to Sherwood. Coming at last
to a certain spot where a shrine stood at the crossing of two
roads, Robin called upon them to stop, for here on either side
was shelter of high hedgerows, behind which was good hiding,
whence they could watch the roads at their ease, whilst they
ate their midday meal.

Quoth merry Robin, "Here, methinks, is good lodging, where
peaceful folk, such as we be, can eat in quietness; therefore
we will rest here, and see what may, perchance, fall into our
luck-pot."

So thy crossed a stile and came behind a hedgerow where
the mellow sunlight was bright and warm, and where the
grass was soft, and there sat them down. Then each man
drew from the pouch that hung beside him that which he had
brought to eat, for a merry walk such as this had been
sharpens the appetite till it is as keen as a March wind. No
more words were spoken, but each man saved his teeth for
better use—munching at brown crust and cold meat right
lustily.

In front of them, one of the high-roads crawled up the steep
hill and then dipped suddenly over its crest, sharp-cut with
hedgerow and shaggy grass against the sky. Over the top of
the windy hill peeped the eaves of a few houses of the village
that fell back into the valley behind; there, also, showed the
top of a windmill, the sails slowly rising and dipping from
behind the hill against the clear blue sky, as the light wind
moved them with creaking and labored swing.

So the yeomen lay behind the hedge and finished their

midday meal, but still the time slipped along, and no one came. At last, a man came slowly riding over the hill, and down the stony road toward the spot where Robin and his band lay hidden. He was a good stout knight, but sorrowful of face and downcast of mien. His clothes were plain and rich, but no chain of gold, such as folk of his stand in life wore at most times, hung around his neck, and no jewel was about him; yet no one could mistake him for aught but one of proud and noble blood. His head was bowed upon his breast and his hands drooped limp on either side; and so he came slowly riding, as though sunk in sad thoughts, whilst even his horse, the reins loose upon his neck, walked with hanging head, as though he shared his master's grief.

Quoth Robin Hood, "Yon is verily a sorry-looking gallant and doth seem to have donned ill-content with his jerkin this morning; nevertheless, I will out and talk with him, for there may be some pickings here for a hungry daw. Methinks his dress is rich, though he himself is so downcast. Bide ye here till I look into this matter." So saying, he arose and left them, crossed the road to the shrine, and there stood, waiting for the sorrowful Knight to come near him.

Presently, when the Knight came riding slowly along, jolly Robin stepped forward and laid his hand upon the bridle rein. "Hold, Sir Knight," quoth he. "I prythee tarry for a short time, for I have a few words to say to thee."

"What art thou, friend, who dost stop a traveler in this manner upon his most gracious Majesty's highway?" said the Knight.

"Marry," quoth Robin, "that is a question hard to answer. One man calleth me kind, another calleth me cruel; this one calleth me good, honest fellow, and that one vile thief. Truly, the world hath as many eyes to look upon a man withal as there are spots on a toad; so, with what pair of eyes thou regardeth me lieth entirely with thine own self. My name is Robin Hood."

"Truly, good Robin," said the Knight, a smile twitching at the corners of his mouth, "thou hast a quaint conceit. As for the pair of eyes with which I regard thee, I would say that they are as favorable as may be, for I hear much good of thee and little ill. What is thy will of me?"

"Now, I make my vow, Sir Knight," quoth Robin, "thou hast surely learned thy wisdom of good Gaffer Swanthold, for he sayeth, 'Fair words are as easy spoke as foul, and bring good will in the stead of blows.' Now I will show thee the truth of this saying; for, if thou wilt go with me this day to Sherwood Forest, I will give thee as merry a feast as ever thou hadst in all thy life."

"Thou art indeed kind," said the Knight, "but methinks thou wilt find me but an ill-seeming and sorrowful guest. Thou hadst best let me pass on my way in peace."

"Nay," quoth Robin, "thou mightst go thine own way but for one thing, and that I will tell thee. We keep an inn, as it were, in the very depths of Sherwood, but so far from highroads and beaten paths that guests do not often come nigh; so I and my friends set off merrily and seek them when we grow dull of ourselves. Thus the matter stands, Sir Knight; yet I will furthermore tell thee that we count upon our guest paying a reckoning."

"I take thy meaning, friend," said the Knight, gravely, "but I am not thy man, for I have no money by me."

"Is it sooth?" said Robin, looking at the Knight keenly. "I can scarce choose but believe thee; yet, Sir Knight, there be those of thy order whose word is not to be trusted as much as they would have others believe. Thou wilt think no ill if I look for myself in this matter." Then, still holding the horse by the bridle rein, he put his fingers to his lips and blew a shrill whistle, whereupon fourscore yeomen came leaping over the stile and ran to where the Knight and Robin stood. "These," said Robin, looking upon them proudly, "are some of my merry men. They share and share alike with me all joys and troubles, gains and losses. Sir Knight, I prythee tell me what money thou hast about thee."

For a time the Knight said not a word, but a slow red arose into his cheeks. At last he looked Robin in the face and said: "I know not why I should be ashamed, for it should be no shame to me; but, my friend, I tell thee the truth, when I say that in my purse are ten shillings, and that that is every groat that Sir Richard of the Lea hath in all the wide world."

When Sir Richard ended a silence fell, until at last Robin said, "And dost thou pledge me thy knightly word that this is all thou hast with thee?"

"Yea," answered Sir Richard, "I do pledge thee my most solemn word, as a true knight, that it is all the money I have in the world. Nay, here is my purse. Ye may find for yourselves the truth of what I say." And he held his purse out to Robin.

"Put up thy purse, Sir Richard," quoth Robin. "Far be it from me to doubt the word of so gentle a knight. The proud I strive to bring low, but those that walk in sorrow I would aid if I could. Come, Sir Richard, cheer up thy heart and go with us into the greenwood. Even I may perchance aid thee, for thou surely knowest how the good Athelstane was saved by the little blind mole that digged a trench over which he that sought the king's life stumbled."

"Truly, friend," said Sir Richard, "methinks thou meanest kindness in thine own way; nevertheless my troubles are such that it is not likely that thou canst cure them. But I will go with thee this day into Sherwood." Hereupon he turned his horse's head, and they all wended their way to the woodlands, Robin walking on one side of the Knight and Will Scarlet on the other, whilst the rest of the band trudged behind.

After they had traveled thus for a time Robin Hood spake. "Sir Knight," said he, "I would not trouble thee with idle questions; but dost thou find it in thy heart to tell me thy sorrows?"

"Truly, Robin," quoth the Knight, "I see no reason why I should not do so. Thus it is: My castle and my lands are in pawn for a debt that I owe. Three days hence the money must be paid or else all mine estate is lost forever, for then it falls into the hands of the Priory of Emmet, and what they swallow they never give forth again."

Quoth Robin, "I understand not why those of thy kind live in such manner that all their wealth passeth from them like snow beneath the springtide sun."

"Thou wrongest me, Robin," said the Knight, "for listen: I have a son but twenty winters old; nevertheless he has won his spurs as knight. Last year, on a certain evil day, the jousts were held at Chester, and thither my son went, as did I and my lady wife. I wot it was a proud time for us, for he unhorsed each knight that he tilted against. At last he ran a course with a certain knight, Sir Walter of Lancaster; yet, though my son was so youthful, he kept his seat, albeit both spears were shivered to the haft. But it happened that a splinter of my boy's lance ran through the visor of Sir Walter's helmet, and pierced through his eye into his brain, so that he died ere his esquire could unlace his helm. Now, Robin, Sir Walter had great friends at court; therefore his kinsmen stirred up things against my son so that, to save him from prison, I had to pay a ransom of six hundred pounds in gold. All might have gone well even yet, only that, by ins and outs and crookedness of laws, I was shorn like a sheep that is clipped to the quick. So it came that I had to pawn my lands to the Priory of Emmet for more money, and a hard bargain they drove with me in my hour of need. Yet I would have thee understand I grieve so only because of my dear lady wife."

"But where is thy son now?" asked Robin, who had listened closely to all the Knight had said.

"In Palestine," said Sir Richard, "battling like a brave Christian soldier for the cross and the holy sepulchre. Truly, England was an ill place for him because of Sir Walter's death, and the hate of the Lancastrian's kinsmen."

"Truly," said Robin, much moved, "thine is a hard lot. But tell me, what is owing to Emmet for thine estates?"

"Only four hundred pounds," said Sir Richard.

At this Robin smote his thigh in anger. "O the bloodsuckers!" cried he. "A noble estate to be forfeit for four hundred pounds! But what will befall thee if thou dost lose thy lands, Sir Richard?"

"It is not mine own lot that doth trouble me in that case," said the Knight, "but my dear lady's; for should I lose my land she will have to betake herself to some kinsman and there abide in charity, which, methinks, would break her proud heart. As for me, I will over the salt sea, and so to Palestine to join my son in fight for the holy sepulchre."

Then up spake Will Scarlet. "But hast thou no friend that will help thee in thy dire need?"

"Never a man," said Sir Richard. "Whilst I was rich enow [enough] at home and had friends, they blew great boasts of how they loved me. But when the oak falls in the forest the swine run from beneath it lest they should be smitten down also. So my friends have left me; for not only am I poor but I have great enemies."

Then Robin said, "Thou sayst thou hast no friends, Sir Richard. I make no boast, but many have found Robin Hood a friend in their troubles. Cheer up, Sir Knight, I may help thee yet."

The Knight shook his head with a faint smile, but for all that Robin's words made him more blithe of heart; for in truth hope, be it never so faint, bringeth a gleam into darkness, like a little rushlight that costeth but a groat.

The day was well-nigh gone when they came near to the greenwood tree. Even at a distance they saw by the number of men that Little John had come back with some guest, but when they came near enough, who should they find but the Lord Bishop of Hereford. The good Bishop was in a fine stew, I wot. Up and down he walked beneath the tree like a fox caught in a hencoop. Behind him were three black friars standing close together in a frightened group, like three black sheep in a tempest. Hitched to the branches of the trees close at hand were six horses, one of them a barb with gay trappings upon which the Bishop was wont to ride, and the others laden with packs of divers shapes and kinds, one of which made Robin's eyes glisten, for it was a box not over large, but heavily bound with bands and ribs of iron.

When the Bishop saw Robin and those with him come into the open he made as though he would have run toward the yeoman, but the fellow that guarded the Bishop and the three friars thrust his quarterstaff in front, so that his lordship was fain to stand back, with frowning brow and angry speech.

"Stay, my Lord Bishop," cried jolly Robin, in a loud voice, when he saw what had passed. "I will come to thee with all

speed, for I would rather see thee than any man in merry England." So saying, he quickened his steps, and soon came to where the Bishop stood fuming.

"Now, now," quoth the Bishop in a loud and angry voice, when Robin had so come to him, "is this the way that thou and thy band treat one so high in the church as I am? I and these brethren were passing peacefully along the high-road with our packhorses, and a half score of men to guard them, when up comes a great strapping fellow full seven feet high, with fourscore or more men back of him, and calls upon me to stop—me, the Lord Bishop of Hereford, mark thou! Whereupon my armed guards—beshrew them for cowards!—straight ran away. But look ye; not only did this fellow stop me, but he threatened me, saying that Robin Hood would strip me as bare as a winter's hedge. Then, beside all this, he called me such vile names as 'fat priest,' 'man-eating bishop,' 'money-gorging usurer,' and what not, as though I were no more than a strolling beggar or tinker. Moreover, when I came here I found a great fat man, a mock priest, that slapped me upon the shoulder as though I were a pot-house fellow."

"Marry come up with a wanion! [May you be plagued!]" cried Friar Tuck, bustling forward and thrusting himself in front of the Bishop. "Marry come up, I say!" He snapped his fingers under the Bishop's nose, whereat the other started back as though the snap were a clap of thunder. "Mock priest, thou callest me, forsooth! Look ye now, Bishop, I wot I am as holy a man as thou art, and might have been a bishop mine own self, had I not been born under a hedge. I am as learned, too, as thou art, albeit I could never master that vile Latin, my tongue being only shaped for good stout English; yet I tell thee, I can say my 'Paters' and 'Aves' with no more a slip o' the tongue than thou, thou fat man!"

At this the Bishop glared upon the stout Friar like an angry cat, whilst even Sir Richard laughed; only Robin kept a grave face. "Stand back, Tuck," said he. "Thou shouldst not beard his lordship's reverence in this wise. Alas, my lord, that thou hast been so ill-treated by my band! I tell thee truly that we greatly reverence thy cloth. Little John, stand forth."

At these words Little John came forward, twisting his face into a whimsical look, as though he would say, "Ha' mercy upon me, good master." Then Robin turned to the Bishop of Hereford and said, "Was this the man who spake so boldly?"

"Ay, truly it was the same," said the Bishop, "a naughty fellow, I wot."

"And didst thou, Little John," said Robin in a sad voice, "call his lordship a fat priest?"

"Ay," said Little John, sorrowfully.

"And man-eating bishop?"

"Ay," said Little John, more sorrowfully than before.

"And a money-gorging usurer?"

"Ay," said Little John, in so sorrowful a voice that it might have drawn tears from the Dragon of Wentley.

"Alas, that these things should be!" said jolly Robin, turning to the Bishop. "For I have ever found Little John a truthful man."

At this a roar of laughter went up, whereat the blood rushed into the Bishop's face till it was cherry red from crown to chin; but he said nothing and only swallowed his words, though they well-nigh choked him.

"Nay, my Lord Bishop," said Robin, "we are rough fellows, but I trust not such ill men as thou thinkest, after all. There is not a man here that would harm a hair of thy reverence's head. I know thou art galled by our jesting, but we are all equal here in the greenwood, for there are no bishops nor barons nor earls among us, but only men, so thou must share our life with us whilst thou dost abide here. Come, busk ye, my merry men, and get the feast ready. Meantime we will show our guests our woodland sports."

So, whilst some went to kindle the fires for roasting meats, others ran leaping to get their cudgels and long bows. Then Robin brought Sir Richard o' the Lea. "My Lord Bishop," said he, "here is another guest that we have with us this day. I wish that thou mightst know him better, for I and all my men will strive to honor you both at this merrymaking."

"Sir Richard," said the Bishop, in a reproachful tone, "methinks thou and I are companions and fellow sufferers in this den of—" He was about to say "thieves," but stopped suddenly and looked askance at Robin Hood.

"Speak out, Bishop," quoth Robin, laughing. "We of Sherwood check not an easy flow of words. 'Den of thieves' thou was about to say."

Quoth the Bishop, "Mayhap that was what I meant to say, Sir Richard; but this I will say, that I saw thee just now laugh at the scurrilous jests of these fellows. It would have been more becoming of thee, methinks, to have checked them with frowns instead of spurring them on by laughter."

"I meant no harm to thee," said Sir Richard, "but a merry jest is a merry jest, and I may truly say I would have laughed at it had it been against mine own self."

But now Robin Hood called upon certain ones of his band who spread soft moss upon the ground and laid deer skins thereon. Then Robin made his guests be seated, and so they all three sat down, some of the chief men, such as Little John, Will Scarlet, Allan a Dale, and others, stretching themselves upon the ground near by. Then a garland was set up at the far end of the glade, and thereat the bowmen shot, and such shooting was done that day as it would have made one's heart leap to see. And all the while Robin talked so quaintly to the Bishop and the Knight that, the one forgetting his vexation and the other his troubles, they both laughed aloud again and again.

Then men shot three rounds of arrows each, and although the garland was but three palms' breadth width, and was full sevenscore yards distant, only two arrows went without the ring. "By Our Lady, good friend," said the Bishop to Robin, "never did I see such shooting in all my life as these men of thine do. But I have heard so oft of thy skill, canst thou not show us a touch of it?"

"Why," quoth Robin, "the light groweth somewhat dim, and things begin to glimmer, ne'ertheless I will try what I can do." So saying he arose from where he sat, then, drawing his dagger, he cut a hazel wand a little greater in girth than a man's thumb, and peeling the bark therefrom, he walked with measured steps fourscore yards distance. There he thrust the staff into the ground and came back to where the others sat, and Allan a Dale handed him his good stout yew bow, which Robin forthwith strung. Then emptying his quiver upon the ground, he searched among the arrows carefully till he had chosen one to his liking. Having so done, he nocked the arrow and stood in position, and all around was so hushed that you might have heard the falling of a leaf. Then he drew the string quickly to his ear, and straightened his bow arm, and ere you could draw a breath loosed the string with a twang. So swift flew the arrow that the eye could not follow it, but a great shout went up from the yeomen when it had sped, and Will Scathelock ran leaping and brought the wand, and lo, the arrow was sticking in the wood which it had cleft. Then all the yeomen shouted again till those about the fires came running, for they were proud of their master's skill, which none could hope to match.

But meantime Robin had set him down again between his guests; then, without giving them time for word of praise, he called those of his band who were the most deft at quarterstaff. So they sat and watched the game till the shades of evening fell.

Then Allan a Dale came forth and tuned his harp, and all was hushed around, and he sang in his wondrous voice songs of love, of war, of glory, and of sadness, and all listened without a movement or a sound. So Allan sang till the great round silver moon gleamed with its clear white light amid the upper tangle of the mazy branches of the trees.

At last two fellows came to say that the feast was ready spread, so Robin, leading his guests with either hand, brought them to where great smoking dishes, that sent savory smells far and near, stood along the white linen cloth spread upon the grass. All around was a glare of torches that lit everything up with a red light. Then, straightway sitting down, all fell to with noise and hubbub, the rattling of platters blending with the sound of loud talking and laughter. A long time the feast lasted, but at last all was over, and the bright wine and humming ale passed briskly. Then Robin Hood called aloud for silence, and all was hushed till he spoke.

"I have a story to tell you all, so listen to what I have to say," quoth he; whereupon, without more ado, he told them all about Sir Richard, and how his lands were in pawn. But, as he went on, the Bishop's face, that had erst [at first] been smiling and ruddy with merriment, waxed serious, and he put aside the horn of wine he held in his hands for he knew the story of Sir Richard, and his heart sank within him with grim forebodings. Then, when Robin Hood had done, he turned to the Bishop of Hereford. "Now, my Lord Bishop," said he, "dost thou not think this ill done of anyone, much more of a churchman, who should live in humbleness and charity?"

To this the Bishop answered not a word, but looked upon the ground with moody eyes.

Quoth Robin, "Now, thou art the richest bishop in all England. Canst thou not help this needy brother?" But still the Bishop answered not a word.

Then Robin turned to Little John and quoth he, "Go thou and Will Stutely and bring forth those five pack-horses yonder." Whereupon the two yeomen did as they were bidden, those about the cloth making room on the green, where the light was brightest, for the five horses which Little John and Will Stutely presently led forward.

"Who hath the score of the goods?" asked Robin Hood, looking at the Black Friars.

Then up spake the smallest of all, in a trembling voice— an old man he was, with a gentle, wrinkled face. "That have I, but, I pray thee, harm me not."

"Nay," quoth Robin, "I have never harmed harmless man yet; but give it to me, good father." So the old man did as he was bidden and handed Robin the tablet on which was marked down the account of the various packages upon the horses. This Robin handed to Will Scarlet, bidding him to read the same. So Will Scarlet began:

"Three bales of silk to Quentin, the mercer [textile dealer] at Ancaster."

"That we touch not," quoth Robin, "for this Quentin is an honest fellow, who hath risen by his own thrift." So the bales of silk were laid aside without being opened.

"One bale of silk velvet for the Abbey of Beaumont."

"What do these priests want of silk velvet?" quoth Robin.

"Nevertheless, though they need it not, I will not take all from them. Measure it off into three lots, one to be sold for charity, one for us, and one for the abbey." So this, too, was done as Robin Hood bade.

"Twoscore wax candles for the Chapel of Saint Thomas."

"That belongeth fairly to the chapel," quoth Robin, "so lay it to one side. Far be it from us to take from the blessed Saint Thomas that which belongeth to him." So this, also, was done according to Robin's bidding, and the candles were laid to one side, along with honest Quentin's unopened bales of silk. So the list was gone through with, and the goods adjudged according to what Robin thought most fit. Some things were laid aside untouched, and many were opened and divided into three equal parts, for charity, for themselves, and for the owners. And now all the ground in the torchlight was covered over with silks and velvets and cloths of gold and cases of rich wines, and so they came to the last line upon the tablet:

"A box belonging to the Lord Bishop of Hereford."

At these words the Bishop shook as with a chill, and the box was set upon the ground.

"My Lord Bishop, hast thou the key of this box?" asked Robin.

The Bishop shook his head.

"Go, Will Scarlet," said Robin, "thou art the strongest man here, bring a sword straightway, and cut this box open, if thou canst."

Then up rose Will Scarlet and left them, coming back in a short time, bearing a great two-handed sword. Thrice he smote that strong, iron-bound box, and at the third blow it burst open and a great heap of gold come rolling forth, gleaming red in the light of the torches. At this sight a murmur

went all around among the band, like the sound of the wind in distant trees; but no man came forward nor touched the money.

Quoth Robin, "Thou, Will Scarlet, thou, Allan a Dale, and thou, Little John, count it over."

A long time it took to count all the money, and when it had been duly scored up, Will Scarlet called out that there were fifteen hundred golden pounds in all. But in among the gold they found a paper, and this Will Scarlet read in a loud voice, and all heard that this money was the rental and fines and forfeits from certain estates belonging to the Bishopric of Hereford.

"My Lord Bishop," said Robin Hood, "I will not strip thee, as Little John said, like a winter hedge, for thou shalt take back one third of thy money. One third of it thou canst well spare to us for thy entertainment and that of thy train, for thou art very rich; one third of it thou canst better spare for charity, for Bishop, I hear that thou art a hard master to those beneath thee and a close hoarder of gains that thou couldst better and with more credit to thyself give to charity than spend upon thy own likings."

At this the Bishop looked up, but he could say never a word; yet he was thankful to be allowed to keep at least a part of his wealth.

Then Robin turned to Sir Richard of the Lea, and quoth he, "Now, Sir Richard, the church seemed like to despoil thee, therefore some of the overplus of church gains may well be used in aiding thee. Thou shalt take that five hundred pounds laid aside for people more in need than the Bishop is, and shalt pay thy debts to Emmet therewith."

Sir Richard looked at Robin until something arose in his eyes that made all the lights and the faces blur together. At last he said, "I thank thee, friend, from my heart, for what thou doest for me; yet, think not ill if I cannot take thy gift freely.

"But this I can and will do: I will take the money and pay my debts, and in a year and a day hence will return it safe either to thee or to the Lord Bishop of Hereford. For this I pledge my most solemn knightly word. I feel free to borrow, for I know no man that should be more proud to aid me than one so high in that church that hath driven such a hard bargain with me."

"Truly, Sir Knight," quoth Robin. "I do not understand those fine scruples that weigh with those of thy kind; but, nevertheless, it shall all be as thou dost wish. But thou hadst best bring the money to me at the end of the year, for mayhap we in Sherwood Forest may make better use of it than the Bishop."

Turning to those near, he gave his orders, and five hundred pounds were counted out and tied up in a leathern bag for Sir Richard.

The rest of the treasure was divided, and part taken to the treasure-house of the band, and part put by with the other things for the Bishop.

Then Sir Richard arose. "I cannot stay later, good friends," said he, "for my lady will wax anxious if I come not home; so I crave leave to depart."

Then Robin Hood and all his merry men arose, and Robin said, "Forsooth, we cannot let thee go home unattended, Sir Richard."

Then up spake Little John: "Good master, let me choose a score of stout fellows from the band, and let us arm ourselves in a seemly manner, and so serve as retainers to Sir Richard till he can get others in our stead."

"Thou hast spoken well, Little John, and it shall be done," said Robin.

Then up spake Will Scarlet: "Let us give him a golden chain to hang about his neck, such as befits one of his blood, and also golden spurs to wear at his heels."

Then Robin Hood said, "Thou hast spoken well, Will Scarlet, and it shall be done."

Then up spake Will Stutely: "Let us give him yon bale of rich velvet and yon roll of cloth of gold to take home to his noble lady wife as a present from Robin Hood and his merry men all."

At this all clapped their hands for joy, and Robin said, "Thou hast well spoken, Will Stutely, and it shall be done."

Then Sir Richard o' the Lea looked all around and strove to speak, but could scarcely do so for the feelings that choked him; at last he said in a husky, trembling voice, "Ye shall all see, good friends, that Sir Richard o' the Lea will ever remember your kindness this day. And if ye be at any time in dire need or trouble, come to me and my lady, and the walls of Castle Lea shall be battered down ere harm shall befall you. I—" He could say no further, but turned hastily away.

But now Little John and nineteen stout fellows, whom he had chosen for his band, came forth all ready for the journey. Each man wore upon his breast a coat of linked mail, and on his head a cap of steel, and at his side a good stout sword. A gallant show they made as they stood all in a row. Then Robin came and threw a chain of gold about Sir Richard's neck, and Will Scarlet knelt and buckled the golden spurs upon his heel; and now Little John led forward Sir Richard's horse, and the Knight mounted. He looked down at Robin for a little time, then of a sudden stooped and kissed his cheek. All the forest glades rang with the shout that went up as the Knight and the yeomen marched off through the woodland with glare of torches and gleam of steel, and so were gone.

Then up spake the Bishop of Hereford in a mournful voice, "I, too, must be jogging, good fellow, for the night waxes late."

But Robin laid his hand upon the Bishop's arm and stayed him firmly.

"Be not so hasty, my Lord Bishop," said he. "Three days hence Sir Richard must pay his debts to Emmet; until that time thou must be content to abide with me lest thou breed trouble for the Knight. I promise thee that thou shalt have great sport, for I know that thou art fond of hunting the dun deer. Lay by thy mantle of melancholy and strive to lead a joyous yeoman life for three stout days. I promise thee thou shalt be sorry to go when the time has come."

So the Bishop and his train abided with Robin for three days, and much sport his lordship had in that time, so that, as Robin had said, when the time had come for him to go he was sorry to leave the greenwood. At the end of three days Robin set him free and sent him forth from the forest with a guard of yeomen to keep freebooters from taking what was left of the packs and bundles.

But, as the Bishop rode away, he vowed within himself that he would sometime make Robin rue the day that he stopped him in Sherwood.

But now a twelvemonth and a day passed, and Sir Richard o' the Lea, having prospered with his lands after paying his debts at Emmet Priory, rode forth on a bright and merry morn to pay his debt to Robin Hood.

Robin Hood stood in the merry greenwood with Little John and most of his stout yeomen around him, awaiting Sir Richard's coming. At last a glint of steel was seen through the brown forest leaves, and forth from the covert into the open rode Sir Richard at the head of his men. He came straight forward to Robin Hood, and leaping from off his horse clasped the yeoman in his arms.

"Why, how now," said Robin, after a time, holding Sir Richard off and looking at him from top to toe, "methinks thou art a gayer bird than when I saw thee last."

"Yes, thanks to thee, Robin," said the Knight, laying his hand upon the yeoman's shoulder. "But for thee I would have been wandering in misery in a far country by this time. But I have kept my word, Robin, and have brought back the money that thou didst lend me, and which I have doubled four times over again, and so become rich once more. Along with this money I have brought a little gift to thee and thy brave men from my dear lady and myself." Then, turning to his men, he called aloud, "Bring forth the packhorses."

But Robin stopped them. "Nay, Sir Richard," said he, "think it not bold of me to cross thy bidding, but we of Sherwood do no business till after we have eaten and drunk." Whereupon, taking Sir Richard by the hand, he led him to the seat beneath the greenwood tree, whilst others of the chief men of the band came and seated themselves around their master.

So they talked until after a while one came forward to say that the feast was spread; whereupon all arose and went thereto. When at last it was done, the Knight called upon his men to bring the packhorses forward, which they did according to his bidding. Then one of the men brought the Knight a strong box, which he opened and took from it a bag and counted out five hundred pounds, the sum of the money he had gotten from Robin.

"Sir Richard," quoth Robin, "thou wilt pleasure us all if

thou wilt keep that money as a gift from us of Sherwood. Is it not so, my lads?"

Then all shouted "Ay" with a mighty voice.

"I thank you all deeply," said the Knight, earnestly, "but think it not ill of me if I cannot take it. Gladly have I borrowed it from you, but it may not be that I can take it as a gift."

Then Robin Hood said no more, but gave the money to Little John to put away in the treasury, for he had shrewdness enough to know that nought breeds ill-will and heart-bitterness like gifts forced upon one that cannot choose but take them.

Then Sir Richard had the packs laid upon the ground and opened, whereupon a great shout went up that made the forest ring again, for lo, there were tenscore bows of finest Spanish yew, all burnished till they shone again, and each bow inlaid with fanciful figures in silver, yet not inlaid so as to mar their strength. Beside these were tenscore quivers of leather embroidered with golden thread, and in each quiver were a score of shafts with burnished heads that shone like silver; each shaft also was feathered with peacock's plumes and innocked [notched] with silver.

Sir Richard gave to each yeoman a bow and a quiver of arrows, but to Robin he gave a stout bow inlaid with the cunningest workmanship in gold, whilst each arrow in his quiver was innocked with gold.

Then all shouted again for joy of the fair gift, and all swore among themselves that they would die if need be for Sir Richard and his lady.

At last the time came when Sir Richard must go, whereupon Robin Hood called his band around him, and each man of the yeomen took a torch in his hand to light the way through the woodlands. So they came to the edge of Sherwood, and there the Knight kissed Robin upon the cheeks and left him and was gone.

Thus Robin Hood helped a noble knight out of his dire misfortunes, that else would have smothered the happiness from his life.

CHAPTER 12 • • •

Robin Shoots Before the Queen

THE high-road stretched white and dusty in the hot summer afternoon sun, and the trees stood motionless along the roadside. All across the meadow lands the hot air danced and quivered, and in the limpid waters of the lowland brook, spanned by a little stone bridge, the fish hung motionless above the yellow gravel, and the dragonfly sat quite still, perched upon the sharp tip of a spike of the rushes, with its wings glistening in the sun.

Along the road a youth came riding upon a fair milk-white barb, and the folk that he passed stopped and turned and looked after him, for never had so lovely a lad or one so gayly clad been seen in Nottingham before. He could not have been more than sixteen years of age and was as fair as any maiden. His long yellow hair flowed behind him as he rode along, all clad in silk and velvet, with jewels flashing and dagger jingling against the pommel of the saddle. Thus came the Queen's Page, young Richard Partington, from famous London Town down into Nottinghamshire, upon her

191

majesty's bidding, to seek one Robin Hood who abideth in Sherwood Forest.

The road was hot and dusty and his journey had been long, for that day he had come all the way from Leicester Town, a good twenty miles and more; wherefore young Partington was right glad when he saw before him a sweet inn, all shady and cool beneath the trees, in front of the door of which a sign hung pendant, bearing the picture of a Blue Boar. Here he drew rein and called loudly for a pottle of Rhenish wine to be brought him, for stout country ale was too coarse a drink for this young gentleman. Five lusty fellows sat upon the bench beneath the pleasant shade of the wide-spreading oak in front of the inn door, drinking ale and beer, and all stared amain at this fair and gallant lad. Two of the stoutest of them were clothed in Lincoln green, and a great heavy oaken staff leaned against the gnarled oak tree trunk beside each fellow.

The landlord came and brought a pottle of wine and a long narrow glass upon a salver, which he held up to the Page as he sat upon his horse. Young Partington poured forth the bright yellow wine, and holding the glass aloft, cried, "Here is to the health and long happiness of my royal mistress the noble Queen Eleanor; and may my journey and her desirings soon have end, and I find a certain stout yeoman, Robin Hood."

At these words all stared, but presently the two stout yeomen in Lincoln green began whispering together. Then one of the two, whom Partington thought to be the tallest and stoutest fellow he had ever beheld, spoke up and said, "What seekest thou of Robin Hood, Sir Page? And what does our good Queen Eleanor wish of him? I ask this of thee, not foolishly, but with reason, for I know somewhat of this stout yeoman."

"An thou knowest aught of him, good fellow," said young Partington, "thou wilt do great service to him and great pleasure to our royal Queen by aiding me to find him."

Then up spake the other yeoman, who was a handsome fellow with sunburnt face and nut-brown, curling hair, "Thou hast an honest look, Sir Page, and our Queen is kind and true to all stout yeomen. Methinks I and my friend here might safely guide thee to Robin Hood, for we know where he may be found. Yet I tell thee plainly, we would not for all merry England have aught of harm befall him."

"Set thy mind at ease; I bring nought of ill wind with me," quoth Richard Partington. "I bring a kind message to him from our Queen; therefore an ye know where he is to be found, I pray you to guide me thither."

Then the two yeomen looked at one another again, and the tall man said, "Surely it were safe to do this thing, Will," whereat the other nodded. Thereupon both arose, and the tall yeoman said, "We think thou art true, Sir Page, and meanest no harm, therefore we will guide thee to Robin Hood as thou dost wish."

Then Partington paid his score, and the yeomen coming forward, they straightway departed upon their way.

Under the greenwood tree, in the cool shade that spread all around upon the sward, with flickering lights here and there, Robin Hood and many of his band lay upon the soft green grass, whilst Allan a Dale sang and played upon his sweetly sounding harp. All listened in silence, for young Allan's singing was one of the greatest joys in all the world to them; but as they so listened there came of a sudden a sound of horse's feet, and presently Little John and Will Stutely came forth from the forest path into the open glade, young Richard Partington riding between them upon his milk-white horse. The three came toward where Robin Hood sat, all the band staring with might and main, for never had they seen so gay a sight as this young Page, nor one so richly clad in silks and velvets and gold and jewels.

Then Robin Hood arose and stepped forth to meet him, and Partington leaped from his horse and doffing his cap of crimson velvet, met Robin as he came.

"Now, welcome!" cried Robin. "Now, welcome, fair youth, and tell me, I prythee, what bringeth one of so fair a presence and clad in such noble garb to our poor forest of Sherwood?"

Then young Partington said: "If I err not, thou art the famous Robin Hood, and these thy stout band of outlawed yeomen. To thee I bring greeting from our noble Queen Eleanor. Oft hath she heard thee spoken of and thy merry doings hereabouts, and fain would she behold thy face; therefore she bids me tell thee that if thou wilt presently come to London Town, she will do all in her power to guard thee against harm, and will send thee back safe to Sherwood Forest again. Four days hence, in Finsbury Fields, our good King Henry, of great renown, holdeth a grand shooting match, and all the most famous archers of merry England will be thereat. Our Queen would fain see thee strive with these, knowing that if thou wilt come thou wilt, with little doubt, carry off the prize. Therefore she hath sent me with this greeting, and furthermore sends thee, as a sign of great good will, this golden ring from off her own fair thumb, which I give herewith into thy hands."

Then Robin Hood bowed his head, and taking the ring, kissed it right royally, and then slipped it upon his little finger. Quoth he, "Sooner would I lose my life than this ring, and ere it departs from me, my hand shall be cold in death or stricken off at the wrist. Fair Sir Page, I will do our Queen's bidding and will presently hie with thee to London; but, ere we go, I will feast thee here in the woodlands with the very best we have."

"It may not be," said the Page. "We have no time to tarry; therefore get thyself ready straightway; and if there be any of thy band that thou wouldst take with thee, our Queen bids me say that she will make them right welcome likewise."

"Truly, thou art right," quoth Robin, "and we have but short time to stay; therefore I will get me ready presently. I will choose three of my men, only, to go with me, and these three shall be Little John, mine own true right-hand man, Will Scarlet, my cousin, and Allan a Dale, my minstrel. Go, lads, and get ye ready straightway, and we will presently off with all speed that we may. Thou, Will Stutely, shalt be the chief of the band while I am gone."

Then Little John and Will Scarlet and Allan a Dale ran leaping, full of joy, to make themselves ready, whilst Robin also prepared himself for the journey. After a while they all four came forth, and a right fair sight they made, for Robin was clad in blue from head to foot, and Little John and Will Scarlet in good Lincoln green, and as for Allan a Dale, he was dressed in scarlet from the crown of his head to the toes of his pointed shoes. Each man wore beneath his cap a little head covering of burnished steel set with rivets of gold, and underneath his jerkin a coat of linked mail, as fine as carded wool, yet so tough that no arrow could pierce it. Then, seeing all were ready, young Partington mounted his horse again, and the yeomen having shaken hands all around, the five departed upon their way.

That night they took up their inn in Melton Mowbray, in Leicestershire; and the next night they lodged at Kettering, in Northamptonshire; and the next at Bedford Town; and the next at St. Albans, in Hertfordshire. This place they left not long after the middle of the night, and traveling fast through the tender dawning of the summer day, when the dews lay shining on the meadows and faint mists hung in the dales, when the birds sang their sweetest and the cobwebs beneath the hedges glimmered like fairy cloth of silver, they came at last to the towers and walls of famous London Town, whilst the morn was still young and all golden toward the east.

Queen Eleanor sat in her royal bower, through the open casements of which poured the sweet yellow sunshine in great floods of golden light. All about her stood her ladies in waiting chatting in low voices, whilst she herself sat dreamily where the mild air came softly drifting into the room laden with the fresh perfumes of the sweet red roses that bloomed in the great garden beneath the wall. To her came one who said that her page, Richard Partington, and four stout yeomen waited her pleasure in the court below. Then Queen Eleanor arose joyously and bade them all be straightway shown into her presence.

Thus Robin Hood and Little John and Will Scarlet and Allan a Dale came before the Queen into her own royal bower. Then Robin kneeled before the Queen with his hands folded upon his breast, saying, in simple phrase, "Here am I, Robin Hood. Thou didst bid me come, and lo, I do thy bidding. I give myself to thee as thy true servant, and will do thy commanding, even if it be to the shedding of the last drop of my life's blood."

But good Queen Eleanor smiled pleasantly upon him, bidding him to arise; then she made them all be seated to rest themselves after their long journey. Rich food was brought them and noble wines, and she had her own pages to wait upon the wants of the yeomen. At last, after they had eaten

all they could, she began questioning them of their merry adventures. Then they told her all of the lusty doings herein spoken of, and among others that concerning the Bishop of Hereford and Sir Richard of the Lea, and how the Bishop had abided three days in Sherwood Forest.

At this the Queen and the ladies about her laughed again and again, for they pictured to themselves the stout Bishop abiding in the forest and ranging the woods in lusty sport with Robin and his band. Then, when they had told all that they could bring to mind, the Queen asked Allan to sing to her, for his fame as a minstrel had reached even to the court at London Town. So straightway Allan took his harp in his hand, and without more asking, touched the strings lightly till they all rang sweetly and sang, and as he sang all eyes dwelt upon him and not a sound broke the stillness, and even after he had done, the silence hung for a short space. So the time passed till the hour drew nigh for the holding of the great archery match in Finsbury Fields.

A gay sight were famous Finsbury Fields on that bright and sunny morning of lusty summer time. Along the end of the meadow stood the booths for the different bands of archers, for the King's yeomen were divided into companies of fourscore men, and each company had a captain over it; on the bright greensward stood ten booths of striped canvas, a booth for each band of the royal archers, and at the peak of each fluttered a flag in the mellow air, and the flag was the color that belonged to the captain of each band. From the center booth hung the yellow flag of Tepus, the famous bow-bearer of the King; next to it, on one hand, was the blue flag of Gilbert of the White Hand, and on the other the blood-red pennant of stout young Clifton of Buckinghamshire. The seven other archer captains were also men of great renown;

among them were Egbert of Kent and William of Southampton; but those first named were most famous of all. The noise of many voices in talk and laughter came from within the booths, and in and out ran the attendants like ants about an anthill. Some bore ale and beer, and some bundles of bowstrings or sheaves of arrows.

On each side of the archery range were rows upon rows of seats reaching high aloft, and in the center of the north side was a raised dais for the King and Queen, shaded by canvas of gay colors, and hung about with streaming silken pennants of red and blue and green and white. As yet the King and Queen had not come, but all the other benches were full of people, rising head above head high aloft till it made the eye dizzy to look upon them. Eightscore yards distant from the mark from which the archers were to shoot stood ten fair targets, each target marked by a flag of the color belonging to the band that was to shoot thereat. So all was ready and all waited for the coming of the King and Queen.

At last a great blast of bugles sounded, and into the meadow came riding six trumpeters with silver trumpets, from which hung velvet banners heavy with rich workings of silver and gold thread. Behind these came stout King Henry upon a dapple-gray stallion, with his Queen beside him upon a milk-white palfrey. On either side of them walked the yeomen of the guard, the bright sunlight flashing from the polished blades of the steel halberds they carried. Behind these came the Court in a great crowd, so that presently all the lawn was alive with bright colors, with silk and velvet, with waving plumes and gleaming gold, with flashing jewels and sword hilts, a gallant sight on that bright summer day.

Then all the people arose and shouted, so that their voices sounded like the storm upon the Cornish coast, when the dark waves run upon the shore and leap and break, surging amid the rocks; so, amid the roaring and the surging of the people, and the waving of scarfs and kerchiefs, the King and Queen came to their place, and, getting down from their horses, mounted the broad stairs that led to the raised platform, and there took their seats on two thrones that were right royally bedecked with purple silks and cloths of silver and gold.

When all was quiet a bugle sounded, and straightway the archers came marching in order from their tents. Fortyscore they were in all, as stalwart a band of yeomen as could be found in all the wide world. So they came in orderly fashion and stood in front of the dais where King Henry and his Queen sat. King Henry looked up and down their ranks right proudly, for his heart warmed within him at the sight of such a gallant band of yeomen. Then he bade his herald, Sir Hugh de Mowbray, stand forth and proclaim the rules governing the game. Sir Hugh stepped to the edge of the platform and spoke in a loud clear voice, so that they could hear him even to the ends of the range, and these were the rules he proclaimed:

That each man should shoot seven arrows at the target that belonged to his band, and of the fourscore yeomen of each band, the three that shot the best should be chosen. These three should shoot three arrows apiece, and the one that shot the best should again be chosen. Then each of these should again shoot three arrows apiece, and the one that shot the best should have the first prize, the one that shot the next best should have the second, and the one that shot next best should have the third prize. Each of the others should have fourscore silver pennies for his shooting. The first prize was to be twoscore and ten golden pounds, a silver bugle horn inlaid

with gold, and a quiver with ten white arrows tipped with
gold and feathered with white swan's wing therein. The
second prize was to be fivescore of the fattest bucks that run
on Dallen Lea, to be shot when the yeoman that won them
chose. The third prize was to be two tuns of good Rhenish
wine.

So Sir Hugh spoke, and when he had done all the archers
waved their bows aloft and shouted. Then each band turned
and marched in order back to its place.

And now the shooting began, the captains first taking stand
and speeding their shafts and then making room for the
men who shot, each in turn after them. Two hundred and
eightyscore shafts were shot in all, and so deftly were they
sped that when the shooting was done each target looked
like the back of a hedgehog when the farm dog snuffs at it.
A long time was taken in this shooting, and when it was over
the judges came forward, looked carefully at the targets, and
proclaimed in a loud voice which three had shot the best from
the separate band. Then a great hubbub of voices arose, each
man among the crowd that looked on calling for his favorite
archer. Then ten fresh targets were brought forward, and
every sound was hushed as the archers took their places once
more and prepared to shoot.

This time the shooting was more speedily done, for only
nine shafts were shot by each band. Not an arrow missed the
targets, but in that of Gilbert of the White Hand five arrows
were in the small white spot that marked the center; of these
five three were sped by Gilbert. Then the judges came forward
again, and looking at the targets, called aloud the names of the
archer chosen as the best bowman of each band. Of these
Gilbert of the White Hand led, for six of the ten arrows he
had shot had lodged in the center; but stout Tepus and young

Clifton trod close upon his heels; yet the others stood a fair chance for the second or third place.

And now, amid the roaring of the crowd, those ten stout fellows that were left went back to their tents to rest for a while and change their bowstrings for nought must fail at this next round, and no hand must tremble or eye grow dim because of weariness.

Then whilst the deep buzz and hum of talking sounded all around like the noise of the wind in the leafy forest, Queen Eleanor turned to the King and quoth she, "Thinkest thou that these yeomen so chosen are the very best archers in all merry England?"

"Yea, truly," said the King, smiling, for he was well pleased with the sport that he had seen, "and I tell thee, that not only are they the best archers in all merry England, but in all the wide world beside."

"But what wouldst thou say," quoth Queen Eleanor, "if I were to find three archers to match the best three yeomen of all thy guard?"

"I would say thou hast done what I could not do," said the King, laughing, "for I tell thee there lives not in all the world three archers to match Tepus and Gilbert and Clifton of Buckinghamshire."

"Now," said the Queen, "I know of three yeomen, and in truth I have seen them not long since, that I would not fear to match against any three that thou canst choose from among all thy fortyscore archers; and, moreover, I will match them here this very day. But I will only match them with thy archers providing that thou wilt grant a free pardon to all that may come in my behalf."

At this the King laughed loud and long. "Truly," said he, "thou art taking up with strange matters for a queen. If

thou wilt bring those three fellows that thou speakest of I
will promise faithfully to give them free pardon for forty
days, to come or to go wheresoever they please, nor will I harm
a hair of their heads in all that time. Moreover, if these that
thou bringest shoot better than my yeomen, man for man, they
shall have the prizes for themselves according to their shooting. But as thou hast so taken up of a sudden with sports of
this kind, hast thou a mind for a wager?"

"Why, in sooth," said Queen Eleanor, laughing, "I know
nought of such matters, but if thou hast a mind to do somewhat in that way, I will strive to pleasure thee. What wilt thou
wager upon thy men?"

Then the merry King laughed again, for he dearly loved a
goodly jest; so he said, amidst his laughter, "I will wager
thee ten tuns of Rhenish wine, ten tuns of the stoutest ale,
and tenscore bows of tempered Spanish yew, with quivers
and arrows to match."

All that stood around smiled at this, for it seemed a merry
wager for a king to give to a queen, but Queen Eleanor bowed
her head quietly. "I will take thy wager," said she, "for I
know right well where to place those things that thou hast
spoken of. Now, who will be on my side in this matter?"
And she looked around upon them that stood about; but no
one spake or cared to wager upon the Queen's side against
such archers as Tepus and Gilbert and Clifton.

Then the Queen spoke again.

"Now, who will back me in this wager? Wilt thou, my Lord
Bishop of Hereford?"

"Nay," quoth the Bishop, hastily, "it ill befits one of my
cloth to deal in such matters. Moreover, there are no such
archers as his majesty's in all the world; therefore I would
but lose my money."

"Methinks the thought of thy gold weigheth more heavily with thee than the wrong to thy cloth," said the Queen, smiling; and at this a ripple of laughter went around, for everyone knew how fond the Bishop was of his money. Then the Queen turned to a knight who stood near, whose name was Sir Robert Lee. "Wilt thou back me in this matter?" said she. "Thou art surely rich enough to risk so much for the sake of a lady."

"To pleasure my Queen I will do it," said Sir Robert Lee, "but for the sake of no other in all the world would I wager a groat, for no man can stand against Tepus and Gilbert and Clifton."

Then turning to the King, Queen Eleanor said, "I want no such aid as Sir Robert giveth me; but against thy wine and beer and stout bows of yew I wager this girdle all set with jewels from around my waist, and surely that is worth more than thine."

"Now, I take thy wager," quoth the King. "Send for thy archers straightway. But here come forth the others. Let them shoot, and then I will match those that win against all the world."

"So be it," said the Queen. Thereupon, beckoning to young Richard Partington, she whispered something in his ear, and straightway the Page bowed and left the place, crossing the meadow to the other side of the range where he was presently lost in the crowd. At this all that stood around whispered to one another, wondering what it all meant, and what three men the Queen was about to set against those famous archers of the King's guard.

And now the ten archers of the King's guard took their stand again, and all the crowd was hushed to the stillness of death. Slowly and carefully each man shot his shafts, and so

deep was the silence that you could hear every arrow
rap against the target as it struck it. Then, when the last shaft
had sped, a great roar went up, and the shooting, I wot, was
well worthy of the sound. Once again Gilbert had lodged
three arrows in the white; Tepus came second with two in the
white and one in the black ring next to it; but stout Clifton
had gone down and Hubert of Suffolk had taken the third
place, for, while both of those good yeomen had lodged two in
the white, Clifton had lost one shot upon the fourth ring, and
Hubert came in with one in the third.

All the archers around Gilbert's booth shouted for joy till
their throats were hoarse, tossing their caps aloft and shaking hands with one another.

In the midst of all this noise and hubbub five men came
walking across the lawn toward the King's pavilion. The first
was Richard Partington and was known to most folk there,
but the others were strange to everybody. Beside young Partington walked a yeoman clad in blue, and behind came three
others, two in Lincoln green and one in scarlet. This last
yeoman carried three stout bows of yew tree, two fancifully
inlaid with silver and one with gold.

Whilst these five men came walking across the meadow,
attracting all eyes to themselves, a messenger came running
from the King's booth and summoned Gilbert and Tepus and
Hubert to go with him. And now the shouting quickly ceased,
for all saw that something unwonted was toward, so the folk
stood up in their places and leaned forward to see what was
the ado.

When Partington and the others came before the spot where
the King and Queen sat, the four yeomen bent their knees
and doffed their caps unto her. King Henry leaned far forward and stared at them closely, but the Bishop of Hereford,

when he saw their faces, started as though stung by a wasp. He opened his mouth as though about to speak, but, looking up, he saw the Queen gazing at him with a smile upon her lips, so he said nothing, but bit his nether lip whilst his face was as red as a cherry.

Then the Queen leaned forward and spake in a clear voice. "Locksley," said she, "I have laid a wager with the King that thou and two of thy men can outshoot any three that he can send against you. Wilt thou do thy best for my sake?"

"Yea," quoth Robin Hood, to whom she spake, "I will do my best for thy sake, and, if I fail, I make my vow never to finger bowstring more."

Now, although Little John had been somewhat abashed in the Queen's bower, he felt himself the sturdy fellow he was when the soles of his feet pressed green grass again; so he said boldly,"Now, blessings on thy sweet face, say I. An there lived a man that would not do his best for thee—I will say nought, only I would like to have the cracking of his knave's pate!"

"Peace, Little John!" said Robin Hood, hastily, in a low voice, but good Queen Eleanor laughed aloud, and a ripple of merriment sounded all over the booth.

The Bishop of Hereford did not laugh; neither did the King, but he turned to the Queen, and quoth he, "Who are these men that thou hast brought before us?"

Then up spoke the Bishop, hastily, for he could hold his peace no longer. "Your majesty," quoth he, "yon fellow in blue is a certain outlawed thief of the midcountry, named Robin Hood; yon tall strapping villain goeth by the name of Little John; the other fellow in green is a certain backsliding gentleman, known as Will Scarlet; the man in red is a rogue of a northern minstrel, named Allan a Dale."

At this speech the King's brows drew together blackly, and he turned to the Queen. "Is it true?" said he, sternly.

"Yea," said the Queen, smiling, "the Bishop hath told the truth; and truly he should know them well, for he and two of his friars spent three days in merry sport with Robin Hood in Sherwood Forest. I did little think that the good Bishop would so betray his friends. But bear in mind that thou hast pledged thy promise for the safety of these good yeomen for forty days."

"I will keep my promise," said the King, in a deep voice that showed the anger in his heart; "but when these forty days are gone let this outlaw look to himself, for mayhap things will not go so smoothly with him as he would like." Then he turned to his archers, who stood near the Sherwood yeomen, listening and wondering at all that passed. Quoth he, "Gilbert, and thou, Tepus, and thou, Hubert, I have pledged myself that ye shall shoot against these three fellows. If ye outshoot the knaves I will fill your caps with silver pennies; if ye fail ye shall lose your prizes that ye have won so fairly, and they go to them that shoot against you, man to man. Do your best, lads, and if ye win this bout ye shall be glad of it to the last days of your life.

"Go, now, and get you gone to the butts."

Then the three archers of the King turned and went back to their booths, and Robin and his men went to their places at the mark from which they were to shoot. Then they strung their bows and made themselves ready, looking over their quivers of arrows, and picking out the roundest and the best feathered.

But when the King's archers went to their tents, they told their friends all that had passed, and how that these four men were the famous Robin Hood and three of his band, to wit,

Little John, Will Scarlet, and Allan a Dale. The news of this buzzed around among the archers in the booths, for there was not a man there that had not heard of these great midcountry yeomen. From the archers the news was taken up by the crowd that looked on at the shooting, so that at last everybody stood up, craning their necks to catch sight of the famous outlaws.

Six fresh targets were now set up, one for each man that was to shoot; whereupon Gilbert and Tepus and Hubert came straightway forth from the booths. Then Robin Hood and Gilbert of the White Hand tossed a farthing aloft to see who should lead in the shooting, and the lot fell to Gilbert's side; thereupon he called upon Hubert of Suffolk to lead.

Hubert took his place, planted his foot firmly, and fitted a fair, smooth arrow; then, breathing upon his fingertips, he drew the string slowly and carefully. The arrow sped true, and lodged in the white; again he shot, and again he hit the clout; a third shaft he sped, but this time failed of the center, and but struck the black, yet not more than a finger's breadth from the white. At this a shout went up, for it was the best shooting that Hubert had yet done that day.

Merry Robin laughed and quoth he, "Thou wilt have an ill time bettering that round, Will, for it is thy turn next. Brace thy thews, lad, and bring not shame upon Sherwood."

Then Will Scarlet took his place; but, because of over-caution, he spoiled his target with the very first arrow that he sped, for he hit the next ring to the black, the second from the center. At this Robin bit his lips. "Lad, lad," quoth he, "hold not the string so long! Have I not often told thee what Gaffer Swanthold sayeth, that 'over-caution spilleth the milk?'" To this Will Scarlet took heed, so the next arrow he shot lodged fairly in the center ring; again he shot, and again he smote the center; but, for all that, stout Hubert had outshot him, and showed the better target. Then all those that looked on clapped their hands for joy because that Hubert had overcome the stranger.

Quoth the King, grimly, to the Queen, "If thy archers shoot no better than that, thou art like to lose thy wager, lady." But Queen Eleanor smiled, for she looked for better things from Robin Hood and Little John.

And now Tepus took his place to shoot. He, also, took overheed to what he was about, and so he fell into Will Scarlet's error. The first arrow he struck into the center ring, but the second missed its mark, and smote the black; the last arrow was tipped with luck, for it smote the very center of the clout, upon the black spot that marked it. Quoth Robin Hood, "That is the sweetest shot that hath been sped this day; but, nevertheless, friend Tepus, thy cake is burned, methinks. Little John, it is thy turn next."

So Little John took his place as bidden, and shot his three arrows quickly. He never lowered his bow arm in all the shooting, but fitted each shaft with his long bow raised; yet all three of his arrows smote the center within easy distance of the black. At this no sound of shouting was heard, for, although it was the best shooting that had been done that day, the folk of London Town did not like to see the stout Tepus overcome by a fellow from the countryside, even were he as famous as Little John.

And now stout Gilbert of the White Hand took his place and shot with the greatest care; and again, for the third time in one day, he struck all three shafts into the clout.

"Well done, Gilbert!" quoth Robin Hood, smiting him upon the shoulder. "I make my vow, thou art one of the best archers that ever mine eyes beheld. Thou shouldst be a free and merry ranger like us, lad, for thou art better fitted for the greenwood than for the cobble-stones and gray walls of London Town." So saying, he took his place, and drew a fair, round arrow from his quiver, which he turned over and over ere he fitted it to his bowstring.

Then the King muttered in his beard, "Now, blessed Saint Hubert, if thou wilt but jog that rogue's elbow so as to make him smite even the second ring, I will give eightscore waxen candles three fingers' breadth in thickness to thy chapel nigh Matching." But it may be Saint Hubert's ears were stuffed with tow, for he seemed not to hear the King's prayer this day.

Having gotten three shafts to his liking, merry Robin looked carefully to his bowstring ere he shot. "Yea," quoth he to Gilbert, who stood nigh him to watch his shooting, "thou shouldst pay us a visit at merry Sherwood." Here he drew the bowstring to his ear. "In London"—here he loosed his shaft— "thou canst find nought to shoot at but rooks and daws; there one can tickle the ribs of the noblest stags in England." So he shot even whilst he talked, yet the shaft lodged not more than an inch from the very center.

"By my soul!" cried Gilbert. "Art thou the devil in blue, to shoot in that wise?"

"Nay," quoth Robin, laughing, "not quite so ill as that, I trust." And he took up another shaft and fitted it to the string. Again he shot, and again he smote his arrow close beside the center; a third time he loosed his bowstring, and dropped his arrow just betwixt the other two and into the very center, so that the feathers of all three were ruffled together, seeming from a distance to be one thick shaft.

And now a low murmur ran all among that great crowd, for never before had London seen such shooting as this, and never again would it see it after Robin Hood's day had gone.

All saw that the King's archers were fairly beaten, and stout
Gilbert clapped his palm to Robin's, owning that he could
never hope to draw such a bowstring as Robin Hood or Little
John. But the King, full of wrath, would not have it so, though
he knew in his mind that his men could not stand against
those fellows. "Nay!" cried he, clenching his hands upon the
arms of his seat, "Gilbert is not yet beaten! Did he not strike
the clout thrice? Although I have lost my wager, he hath not
yet lost the first prize. They shall shoot again, and still again,
till either he or that knave Robin Hood cometh off the best.
Go thou, Sir Hugh, and bid them shoot another round, and
another, until one or the other is overcome." Then Sir Hugh,
seeing how wroth the King was, said never a word, but went
straightway to do his bidding; so he came to where Robin
Hood and the other stood, and told them what the King had
said.

"With all my heart," quoth merry Robin, "I will shoot from
this time till tomorrow day if it can pleasure my most gracious
lord and king. Take thy place, Gilbert lad, and shoot."

So Gilbert took his place once more, but this time he failed,
for, a sudden little wind arising, his shaft missed the center
ring, but by not more than the breadth of a barley straw.

"Thy eggs are cracked, Gilbert," quoth Robin, laughing,
and straightway he loosed a shaft and once more smote the
white circle of the center.

Then the King arose from his place, and not a word said
he, but he looked around with a baleful look, and it would
have been an ill day for anyone that he saw with a joyous or
a merry look upon his face. Then he and his Queen and all
the court left the place, but the King's heart was brimming
full of wrath within him.

After the King had gone, all the yeomen of the archer guard

came crowding around Robin, and Little John, and Will, and
Allan, to snatch a look at these famous fellows from the midcountry, and with them came many that had been onlookers
at the sport, for the same purpose. Thus it happened presently
that the yeomen, to whom Gilbert stood talking, were all
surrounded by a crowd of people that formed a ring about
them. "Marry," quoth Little John to Will Scarlet, "one
would think that these poor fellows had never seen a stout
yeoman ranger in all their lives before, or that we were some
curious spectacle, like the Cumberland Giant, or the Welsh
Dwarf, that we saw last month at the fair at Norwich."

After a while the three judges that had the giving away of
the prizes came forward, and the chief of them all spake to
Robin and said: "According to agreement, the first prize belongeth rightly to thee; so here I give thee the silver bugle,
here the quiver of ten golden arrows, and here a purse of twoscore and ten golden pounds." And as he spake he handed
those things to Robin, and then turned to Little John. "To
thee," he said, "belongeth the second prize, to wit, fivescore
of the finest harts that run on Dallen Lea. Thou mayest
shoot them whensoever thou dost list." Last of all he turned
to stout Hubert. "Thou," said he, "hast held thine own against
the yeoman with whom thou didst shoot, and so thou hast
kept the prize duly thine, to wit, two tuns of good Rhenish
wine. These shall be delivered to thee whensoever thou dost
list." Then he called upon the other seven of the King's archers
who had last shot, and gave each one of them fourscore silver
pennies.

Then up spake Robin and quoth he, "This silver bugle I
keep in honor of this shooting match, but thou, Gilbert, art
the best archer of all the King's guard, and to thee I freely
give this purse of gold. Take it, man, and would it were ten

times as much, for thou art a right yeoman, good and true as my very own.

"Further, to each of the ten that last shot I give one of these golden shafts apiece. Keep them always by you, so that ye may tell your grandchildren, an ye are ever blessed with them, that ye are the very stoutest yeomen in all the wide world." At this all shouted aloud, for it pleased them to hear Robin speak so of them.

Then up spake Little John. "Good friend Tepus," said he, "I want not those harts of Dallen Lea that yon stout judge spoke of but now, for in truth we have enow [enough] and more than enow in our own country. Twoscore and ten I give to thee for thine own shooting, and five I give to each band for their pleasure."

At this another great shout went up, and many tossed their caps aloft and swore among themselves that no better fellows ever walked the sod than Robin Hood and his stout yeomen from Sherwood Forest.

Whilst they so shouted with loud voices, a tall burly yeoman of the King's guard came forward and plucked Robin by the sleeve. "Good master," quoth he, "I have somewhat to tell thee in thine ear, a silly thing, I wot, for one stout yeoman to tell another; but a young peacock of a page, one Richard Partington, was seeking thee without avail in the crowd, and, not being able to find thee, told me that he bore a message to thee from a certain lady that thou wottest of. This message he bade me tell thee privily, word for word, and thus it was. Let me see—I trust I have forgot it not—yea, thus it was: 'The lion growls. Beware thy head.'"

"Is it so?" quoth Robin, staring, for he knew right well that it was the Queen sent the message, and that she spake of the King's wrath. "Now, I thank thee, good fellow, for thou hast done me greater service than thou knowest of this day." Then he called his three yeomen together, and told them privately that they had best be jogging, as it was like to be ill for them so nigh merry London Town. So, without tarrying longer, they made their way through the crowd until they had come out from the press. Then, without stopping, they left London Town, and started northward.

CHAPTER 13 • • •

The Chase of Robin Hood

SO ROBIN Hood and the others left the archery range at Finsbury Fields, and, tarrying not, set forth straightway upon their homeward journey. It was well for them that they did so, for they had not gone more than three or four miles upon their way when six of the yeomen of the King's guard came bustling amongst the crowd that still lingered, seeking for Robin and his men, to seize them and make them prisoners. Truly, it was an ill-done thing in the King to break his promise, but it all came about through the Bishop of Hereford's doing, for thus it happened:

After the King left the archery ground, he went straightway to his cabinet, and with him went the Bishop of Hereford and Sir Robert Lee; but the King said never a word to these two, but sat gnawing his nether lip, for his heart was galled within him by what had happened.

At last the Bishop of Hereford spoke, in a low, sorrowful voice: "It is a sad thing, your majesty," quoth he, "that this knavish outlaw should be let to escape in this wise; for, let him but get back to Sherwood Forest safe and sound, and he may snap his fingers at King and King's men."

At these words the King raised his eyes and looked grimly upon the Bishop. "Sayst thou so?" quoth he. "Now, I will show thee, in good time, how much thou dost err, for, when the forty days are past and gone, I will seize upon this thieving outlaw, if I have to tear down all of Sherwood to find him. Thinkest thou that the laws of the King of England are to be so evaded by one poor knave without friend or money?"

Then the Bishop spoke again, in his soft, smooth voice: "Forgive my boldness, your majesty, and believe that I have naught but the good of England and your majesty's desirings at heart; but what would it boot though my gracious lord did root up every tree of Sherwood? Are there not other places for Robin Hood's hiding? Cannock Chase is not far from Sherwood, and the great Forest of Arden is not far from Cannock Chase. Beside these are many other woodlands in Nottingham and Derby, Lincoln and York, amid day of which your majesty might as well think to seize upon Robin Hood as to lay finger upon a rat among the dust and broken things of a garret. Nay, my gracious lord, if he doth once plant foot in the woodland, he is lost to the law forever."

At these words the King tapped his finger-tips upon the table beside him with vexation. "What wouldst thou have me do, Bishop?" quoth he. "Didst thou not hear me pledge my word to the Queen? Thy talk is as barren as the wind from the bellows upon dead coals."

"Far be it from me," said the cunning Bishop, "to point the way to one so clear-sighted as your majesty, but, were I the King of England, I should look upon the matter in this wise: I have promised my Queen, let us say, that for forty days the cunningest rogue in all England shall have freedom to come and go; but, lo! I find this outlaw in my grasp. Shall I, then, foolishly cling to a promise so hastily given? Suppose that I had promised to do her majesty's bidding, whereupon she bade me to slay myself. Should I, then, shut mine eyes and run blindly upon my sword? Thus would I argue within myself. Moreover, I would say unto myself, a woman knoweth nought of the great things appertaining to state government; and, likewise, I know a woman is ever prone to take up a fancy, even as she would pluck a daisy from the roadside, and then throw it away when the savor is gone; therefore, though she hath taken a fancy to this outlaw, it will soon wane away and be forgotten. As for me, I have the greatest villain in all England in my grasp. Shall I, then, open my hand and let him slip betwixt my fingers? Thus, your majesty, would I say to myself, were I the King of England." So the Bishop talked, and the King bent his ear to his evil counsel, until after a while he turned to Sir Robert Lee and bade him send six of the yeomen of the guard to take Robin Hood and his three men prisoners.

Now Sir Robert Lee was a gentle and noble knight, and he felt grieved to the heart to see the King so break his promise; nevertheless, he said nothing, for he saw how bitterly the King was set against Robin Hood; but he did not send the yeomen of the guard at once, but went first to the Queen and told her all that had passed and bade her send word to Robin of his danger. This he did not for the well-being of Robin Hood, but because he would save his lord's honor if he could. Thus it came about that when, after a while the yeomen of the guard went to the archery field, they found not Robin and the others and so got no cakes at that fair.

The afternoon was already well-nigh gone when Robin Hood, Little John, Will, and Allan set forth upon their homeward way, trudging along merrily through the yellow slanting light, which speedily changed to rosy red as the sun sank low in the heavens. The shadows grew long and finally merged into the grayness of the mellow twilight. The dusty highway lay all white betwixt the dark hedgerows, and along it walked the four fellows like four shadows, the pat of their feet sounding loud, and their voices, as they talked, ringing clear upon the silence of the air. The great round moon was floating breathlessly up in the eastern sky when they saw before them the twinkling lights of Barnet Town, some ten or twelve miles from London. Down they walked through the stony streets and past the cozy houses with overhanging gables, before the doors of which sat the burghers and craftsmen in the mellow moonlight, with their families about them, and so came at last, on the other side of the hamlet, to a little inn, all shaded with roses and woodbines. Before this inn Robin Hood stopped, for the spot pleased him well. Quoth he, "Here will we take up our inn and rest for the night, for we are well away from London Town and our King's wrath. What say ye, lads?"

"In sooth, good master," quoth Little John, "thy bidding and my doing ever fit together like cakes and ale. Let us in, say I also."

Then up spake Will Scarlet: "I am ever ready to do what thou sayest, uncle, yet I could wish that we were farther upon our way ere we rest for the night. Nevertheless, if thou thinkest best, let us in for the night, say I also."

So in they went and called for the best that the place afforded. Then a right good feast was set before them, with two stout bottles of old sack to wash it down withal. These things were served by as plump and buxom a lass as you could find in all the land, so that Little John, who always had an eye for a fair lass, even when meat and drink were by, stuck his arms akimbo and fixed his eyes upon her, winking sweetly whenever he saw her looking toward him. Then you should have seen how the lass twittered with laughter and how she looked at Little John out of the corners of her eyes, a dimple coming in either cheek; for the fellow had always a taking way with the women-folk.

"Come, come, Little John," quoth Robin, "leave the lass in peace, and fall to thy victuals, or thou wilt belike go with an empty stomach. Eat first and woo afterward is as good a saying as one can open ears to."

"Nay," quoth Little John, boldly, "it is an ill saying for me, for who would turn to victuals and drink and let so fair a lass go, without paying heed to the sweet looks that the blessed saints have bestowed upon her? Come hither, thou dainty little duck, and pour forth some wine for me, that I may drink to thy good health and pray the good Saint Withold that he send thee what is meet, to wit, a lord or an earl for a husband. By my soul, I would rather drink water that thou hadst poured into my cup than rich Muscat after any other she in all England!"

At this speech the other yeomen roared with laughter, and the lass looked down, blushing, and thought that Little John was as nice a lad as she had seen in all her life.

So the feast passed merrily, and never had an inn seen such lusty feeders as these four stout fellows; but at last they were done their eating, though it seemed as though they never would have ended, and sat loitering over the sack. As they so sat, the landlord came in of a sudden, and said that there was one at the door, a certain esquire, Richard Partington, of the Queen's household, who wished to see the lad in blue and speak with him, without loss of time. So Robin arose quickly, and bidding the landlord not to follow him, left the others gazing at one another and wondering what was about to happen.

When Robin came out of the inn, he found young Richard Partington sitting upon his horse in the white moonlight, awaiting his coming.

"What news bearest thou, Sir Page?" said Robin. "I trust that it is not of an ill nature."

"Why," said young Partington, "for the matter of that, it is ill enow [enough]. The King hath been bitterly stirred up against thee by that vile Bishop of Hereford. He sent to arrest thee at the archery butts at Finsbury Fields, but not finding thee there, he hath gathered together his armed men, fifty-score and more, and is sending them in haste along this very road to Sherwood, either to take thee on the way or to prevent thy getting back to the woodlands again. He hath given the Bishop of Hereford command over all these men, and thou knowest what thou hast to expect of the Bishop of Hereford— short shrift and a long rope. Two bands of horsemen are already upon the road, not far behind me, so thou hadst best get thee gone from this place straightway, for, if thou tarriest longer, thou art like to sleep this night in a cold dungeon. This word the Queen hath bidden me to bring to thee."

"Now, Richard Partington," quoth Robin, "this is the second time that thou hast saved my life, and if the proper time ever cometh I will show thee that Robin Hood never forgets these things. As for the Bishop of Hereford, if I ever catch him nigh to Sherwood again, things will be like to go ill with him. Thou mayst tell the good Queen that I will leave this place without delay and will let the landlord think that we are going to St. Albans; but when we are upon the high-road again, I will go one way through the country and will send my men the other, so that if one falleth into the King's hands the others may haply escape. We will go by devious ways and so, I hope, will reach Sherwood in safety. And now, Sir Page, I wish thee farewell."

"Farewell, thou bold yeoman," said young Partington, "and mayst thou reach thy hiding in safety." So each shook the other's hand, and the lad, turning his horse's head, rode back toward London, whilst Robin entered the inn once more.

There he found his yeomen sitting in silence, waiting his coming; likewise the landlord was there, for he was curious to know what Master Partington had to do with the fellow in blue. "Up, my merry men!" quoth Robin, "this is no place for us, for those are after us with whom we will stand but an ill chance an we fall into their hands. So we will go forward once more, nor will we stop this night till we reach Saint Albans." Hereupon, taking out his purse, he paid the landlord his score, and so they left the inn.

When they had come to the high-road without the town, Robin stopped and told them all that had passed between young Partington and himself, and how that the King's men were after them with hot heels. Then he told them that here they should part company, they three going to the eastward and he to the westward, and so, skirting the main high-roads, would come by devious paths to Sherwood. "So, be ye wily," said Robin Hood, "and keep well away from the northward roads till ye have gotten well to the eastward. And thou, Will Scarlet, take the lead of the others, for thou hast a cunning turn to thy wits." Then Robin kissed the three upon the cheeks, and they kissed him, and so they parted company.

Not long after this, a score or more of the King's men came clattering up to the door of the inn at Barnet Town. Here they leaped from their horses and quickly surrounded the place, the leader of the band and four others entering the room where the yeoman had been. But they found that their birds had flown again, and that the King had been balked a second time.

"Methought that they were naughty fellows," said the host, when he heard who the men-at-arms sought. "But I heard that blue-clad knave say that they would go straight forward to Saint Albans; so, an ye hurry forward, ye may, perchance, catch them on the high-road betwixt here and there." For this news the leader of the band thanked mine host right heartily, and calling his men together, mounted and set forth again, galloping forward to Saint Albans upon a wild-goose chase.

After Little John and Will Scarlet and Allan a Dale had left the highway near Barnet, they traveled toward the eastward, without stopping, as long as their legs could carry them, until they came to Chelmsford, in Essex. Thence they turned northward, and came through Cambridge and Lincolnshire, to the good town of Gainsborough.

Then, striking to the westward and the south, they came at last to the northern borders of Sherwood Forest, without in all that time having met so much as a single band of the King's men. Eight days they journeyed thus ere they reached the woodlands in safety, but when they got to the greenwood glade, they found that Robin had not yet returned.

After having left the great northern road, he turned his face to the westward and so came past Aylesbury, to fair Woodstock, in Oxfordshire. Thence he turned his footsteps northward, traveling for a great distance by way of Warwick Town, till he came to Dudley, in Staffordshire. Seven days it took him to journey thus far, and then he thought he had gotten far enough to the north, so, turning toward the eastward, shunning the main roads, and choosing byways and grassy lanes, he went, by way of Litchfield and Ashby de la Zouch, toward Sherwood, until he came to a place called Stanton. And now Robin's heart began to laugh aloud, for he thought that his danger had gone by, and that his nostrils would soon snuff the spicy air of the woodlands once again. But there is many a slip betwixt the cup and the lip, and this Robin was to find. For thus it was:

When the King's men found themselves foiled at Saint Albans, and that Robin and his men were not to be found high nor low, they knew not what to do. Presently another band of horsemen came, and another, until all the moonlit streets were full of armed men. Betwixt midnight and dawn, another band came to the town, and with them came the Bishop of Hereford.

Now, when he heard that Robin Hood and his men had once more slipped out of the trap, he stayed not a minute, but, gathering his bands together, he pushed forward to the northward with speed, leaving orders for all the troops that came to Saint Albans to follow after him without tarrying. On the evening of the fourth day he reached Nottingham Town, and there straightway divided his men into bands of six or seven, and sent them all through the countryside, blocking every highway and byway to the eastward and the southward and the westward of Sherwood. The Sheriff of Nottingham called forth all his men likewise and joined with the Bishop, for he saw that this was the best chance that had ever befallen of paying back his score in full to Robin Hood. Will Scarlet and Little John and Allan a Dale had just missed the King's men to the eastward, for the very next day after they had passed the line and entered Sherwood the roads through which they had traveled were blocked, so that, had they tarried in their journeying, they would surely have fallen into the Bishop's hands.

But of all this Robin knew not a whit; so he whistled merrily as he trudged along the road beyond Stanton, with his heart as free from care as the yolk of an egg is from cobwebs. At last he came to where a little stream spread across the road in a shallow sheet, tinkling and sparkling as it fretted over its bed of golden gravel. Here Robin stopped, being athirst, and kneeling down, he made a cup of the palms of his hands and began to drink. On either side of the road, for a long distance, stood tangled thickets of bushes and young trees, and it pleased Robin's heart to hear the little birds singing therein, for it made him think of Sherwood, and it seemed a lifetime since he had breathed the air of the woodlands.

But of a sudden, as he thus stooped, drinking from his hands, something hissed past his ear, and struck with a splash into the gravel and water beside him. Quick as a wink Robin sprang to his feet, and at one bound crossed the stream and the roadside and plunged headlong into the thicket, without looking around, for he knew right well that that which had hissed so venomously beside his ear was a gray goose shaft, and that to tarry so much as a moment meant death. Even as he leaped into the thicket six more arrows rattled among the branches after him, one of which pierced his doublet, and would have struck deeply into his side but for the tough coat of steel that he wore. Then up the road came riding some of the King's men at headlong speed. They leaped from their horses and plunged straightway into the thicket after Robin.

But Robin knew the ground better than they, so crawling here, stooping there, and anon running across some little open, he soon left them far behind, coming out, at last, upon another road about eight hundred paces distant from the one he had left. Here he stood for a moment, listening to the distant shouts of the seven men as they beat up and down in the thickets like hounds that had lost the scent of the quarry. Then, buckling his belt more tightly around his waist, he ran fleetly down the road toward the eastward and Sherwood.

But Robin had not gone more than three furlongs in that direction when he came suddenly to the brow of a hill, and saw beneath him another band of the King's men seated in the shade along the roadside in the valley beneath. Then he paused not a moment, but seeing that they had not caught sight of him, he turned and ran back whence he had come, knowing that it was better to run the chance of escaping those fellows that were yet in the thickets than to rush into the arms of those in the valley. So back he ran with all speed, and had gotten safely past the thickets, when the seven men came forth into the open road. They raised a great shout when they saw him, such as the hunter gives when the deer breaks cover, but Robin was then a quarter of a mile and more away from them, coursing over the ground like a greyhound. He never slackened his pace, but ran along, mile after mile, till he had come nigh to Mackworth, over beyond the Derwent River, nigh to Derby Town. Here, seeing that he was out of present danger, he slackened in his running, and at last sat him down beneath a hedge where the grass was the longest and the shade coolest, to rest and catch his wind.

"By my soul, Robin," quoth he to himself, "that was the narrowest miss that e'er thou hadst in all thy life. I do say most solemnly that the feather of that wicked shaft tickled mine ear as it whizzed past. This same running hath given me a most craving appetite for victuals and drink. Now I pray Saint Dunstan that he send me speedily some meat and beer."

It seemed as though Saint Dunstan was like to answer his

prayer, for along the road came plodding a certain cobbler, one Quince, of Derby, who had been to take a pair of shoes to a farmer nigh Kirk Langly, and was now coming back home again, with a fair boiled capon in his pouch and a stout pottle of beer by his side, which same the farmer had given him for joy of such a stout pair of shoon [shoes]. Good Quince was an honest fellow, but his wits were somewhat of the heavy sort, like unbaked dough, so that the only thing that was in his mind was, "Three shillings sixpence ha'penny for thy shoon, good Quince,—three shillings sixpence ha'penny for thy shoon," and this traveled round and round inside of his head, without another thought getting into his noodle, as a pea rolls round and round inside an empty quart pot.

"Halloa, good friend," quoth Robin, from beneath the hedge, when the other had come near, "whither away so merrily?"

Hearing himself so called upon, the Cobbler stopped, and seeing a well-clad stranger in blue, he spoke to him in seemly wise. "Give ye good den, fair sir, and I would say that I come from Kirk Langly, where I ha' sold my shoon and got three shillings six-pence ha'penny for them in as sweet money as ever thou sawest and honestly earned too, I would ha' thee know. But, an I may be so bold, thou pretty fellow, what dost thou there beneath the hedge?"

"Marry," quoth merry Robin, "I sit beneath the hedge here to drop salt on the tails of golden birds; but in sooth thou art the first chick of any worth I ha' seen this blessed day."

At these words the Cobbler's eyes opened big and wide, and his mouth grew round with wonder, like a knot-hole in a board fence. "Alack-a-day," quoth he, "look ye, now! I ha' never seen those same golden birds. And dost thou in sooth find them in these hedges, good fellow? Prythee, tell me, are there many of them? I would fain find them mine ownself."

"Ay, truly," quoth Robin, "they are as thick here as fresh herring in Cannock Chase."

"Look ye, now!" said the Cobbler, all drowned in wonder. "And dost thou in sooth catch them by dropping salt on their pretty tails?"

"Yea," quoth Robin, "but this salt is of an odd kind, let me tell thee, for it can only be gotten by boiling down a quart of moonbeams in a wooden platter, and then one hath but a pinch. But tell me, now, thou witty man, what hast thou gotten there in that pouch by thy side and in that pottle?"

At these words the Cobbler looked down at those things of which merry Robin spoke, for the thoughts of the golden bird had driven them from his mind, and it took him some time to scrape the memory of them back again. "Why," said he at last, "in the one is good March beer, and in the other is a fat capon. Truly, Quince the Cobbler will ha' a fine feast this day an I mistake not."

"But tell me, good Quince," said Robin, "hast thou a mind to sell those things to me? For the hearing of them sounds sweet in mine ears. I will give thee these gay clothes of blue that I have upon my body and ten shillings to boot for thy clothes and thy leather apron and thy beer and thy capon. What sayst thou, bully boy?"

"Nay, thou dost jest with me," said the Cobbler, "for my clothes are coarse and patched, and thine are of fine stuff and very pretty."

"Never a jest do I speak," quoth Robin. "Come, strip thy jacket off and I will show thee, for I tell thee I like thy clothes well. Moreover, I will be kind to thee, for I will feast straightway upon the good things thou hast with thee, and thou shalt be bidden to the eating." At these words he began slipping off his doublet, and the Cobbler, seeing him so in earnest, began peeling off his clothes also, for Robin Hood's garb tickled his eye. So each put on the other fellow's clothes, and Robin gave the honest Cobbler ten bright new shillings. Quoth merry Robin, "I ha' been a many things in my life before, but never have I been an honest cobbler. Come, friend, let us fall to and eat, for something within me cackles aloud for that good fat capon." So both sat down and began to feast right lustily, so that when they were done the bones of the capon were picked as bare as charity. Then Robin stretched his legs out with a sweet feeling of comfort within him.

Of a sudden six horsemen burst upon them where they sat, and seized roughly upon the honest craftsman, hauling him to his feet, and very nearly plucking the clothes from him as they did so.

"Ha!" roared the leader of the band in a great big voice of joy, "have we then caught thee at last, thou blue-clad knave? Now, blessed be the name of Saint Hubert, for we are four-score pounds richer this minute than we were before, for the good Bishop of Hereford hath promised that much to the band that shall bring thee to him. Oho! Thou cunning rascal! Thou wouldst look so innocent, forsooth! We know thee, thou old fox. But off thou goest with us to have thy brush clipped forthwith." At these words the poor Cobbler gazed all around him with his great blue eyes as round as those of a dead fish, while his mouth gaped as though he had swallowed all his words and so lost his speech.

Robin also gaped and stared in a wondering way, just as the Cobbler would have done in his place. "Alack-a-daisy, me," quoth he. "I know not whether I be sitting here or in no-man's land! What meaneth all this stir i' th' pot, dear good gentlemen? Surely this is a sweet, honest fellow, and you mean another when you call him knave?"

" 'Honest fellow,' sayst thou, clown?" quoth one of the men. "Why, I tell thee that this is that same rogue that men call Robin Hood."

At this speech the Cobbler stared and gaped more than ever, for there was such a threshing of thoughts going on within his poor head that his wits were all befogged with the dust and chaff thereof. Moreover, as he looked at Robin Hood and saw the yeoman look so like what he knew himself to be, he began to doubt and to think that mayhap he was the great outlaw in real sooth. Said he in a slow, wondering voice, "Am I in very truth that fellow?—Now I had thought—but nay, Quince, thou art mistook—yet—am I?—Nay, I must indeed be Robin Hood! Yet, truly, I had never thought to pass from an honest craftsman to such a great yeoman."

"Alas!" quoth Robin Hood. "Look ye there, now! See how your ill-treatment hath curdled the wits of this poor lad and turned them all sour! I, myself, am Quince, the Cobbler of Derby Town."

"Is it so?" said Quince. "Then, indeed, I am somebody else, and can be none other than Robin Hood. Take me, fellows; but let me tell you that ye ha' laid hand upon the stoutest yeoman that ever trod the woodlands."

"Thou wilt play madman, wilt thou?" said the leader of the band. "Here, Giles, fetch a cord and bind this knave's hands behind him. I warrant we will bring his wits back to him again when we get him safe before our good Bishop at Tutbury Town." Thereupon they tied the Cobbler's hands behind him, and led him off with a rope, as the farmer leads off the calf he hath brought from the fair. Robin stood looking after them, and when they were gone he laughed till the tears rolled down his cheeks; for he knew that no harm would befall the honest fellow, and he pictured to himself the Bishop's face

when good Quince was brought before him as Robin Hood. Then, turning his steps once more to the eastward, he stepped out right foot foremost toward Nottinghamshire and Sherwood Forest.

But Robin Hood had gone through more than he wotted of [realized]. His journey from London had been hard and long, and in a se'ennight he had traveled sevenscore and more of miles. He thought now to travel on without stopping until he had come to Sherwood, but ere he had gone a half score of miles he felt his strength giving way beneath him like a river bank which the waters have undermined. He sat him down and rested, but he knew within himself that he could go no farther that day, for his feet felt like lumps of lead, so heavy were they with weariness. Once more he arose and went forward, but after traveling a couple of miles he was fain to give the matter up, so, coming to an inn just then, he entered, and calling the landlord bade him show him to a room, although the sun was only then just sinking in the western sky. There were but three bedrooms in the place, and to the meanest of these the landlord showed Robin Hood, but little Robin cared for the looks of the place, for he could have slept that night upon a bed of broken stones. Stripping off his clothes without more ado, he rolled into the bed and was asleep almost ere his head touched the pillow.

Not long after Robin had gone to his rest a great cloud peeped blackly over the hills to the westward. Higher and higher it arose until it piled up into the night like a mountain of darkness. All around beneath it came ever and anon a dull red flash, and presently a short grim mutter of the coming thunder was heard. Then up rode four stout burghers of Nottingham Town, for this was the only inn within five miles' distance, and they did not care to be caught in such a thunderstorm as this that was coming upon them. Leaving their nags to the stableman, they entered the best room of the inn, where fresh green rushes lay all spread upon the floor, and there called for the goodliest fare that the place afforded. After having eaten heartily they bade the landlord show them their rooms, for they were aweary, having ridden all the way from Dronfield that day. So off they went, grumbling at having to sleep two in a bed, but their troubles on this score, as well as all others, were soon lost in the quietness of sleep.

And now came the first gust of wind, rushing past the place, clapping and banging the doors and shutters, smelling of the coming rain, and all wrapped in a cloud of dust and leaves. As though the wind had brought a guest along with it, the door opened of a sudden and in came a friar of Emmet Priory, and one in high degree, as was shown by the softness and sleekness of his robes and the richness of his rosary. He called the landlord, and bade him first have his mule well fed and bedded in the stable, and then bring him the very best there was in the house. So presently a savory stew of tripe and onions, with sweet little fat dumplings, was set before him, likewise a good stout pottle of Malmsey, and straightway the holy friar fell to with great courage and heartiness, so that in a short time nought was left but a little pool of gravy in the center of the platter, not large enow to keep the life of a starving mouse.

In the meantime the storm broke. Another gust of wind went rushing by, and with it fell a few heavy drops of rain, which presently came rattling down in showers, beating against the casements like a hundred little hands. Bright flashes of lightning lit up every raindrop, and with them came cracks of thunder that went away rumbling and bumping as though Saint Swithin were busy rolling great casks of water across rough ground overhead. The womenfolks screamed, and the merry wags in the tap room put their arms around their waists to soothe them into quietness.

At last the holy friar bade the landlord show him to his room, but when he heard that he was to bed with a cobbler, he was as ill contented a fellow as you could find in all England; nevertheless there was nothing for it, and he must sleep there or nowhere, so taking up his candle, he went off, grumbling like the now distant thunder. When he came to the room where he was to sleep he held the light over Robin and looked at him from top to toe; then he felt better pleased, for instead of a rough, dirty-bearded fellow, he beheld as fresh and clean a lad as one could find in a week of Sundays; so slipping off his clothes, he also huddled into the bed, where Robin, grunting and grumbling in his sleep, made room for him. Robin was more sound asleep, I wot, than he had been for many a day, else he would never have rested so quietly with one of the friar's sort so close beside him. As for the friar, had he known whom Robin Hood was, you may well believe he would almost as soon have slept with an adder as with the man he had for a bedfellow.

So the night passed comfortably enough, but at the first dawn of day Robin opened his eyes and turned his head upon the pillow. Then how he gaped and how he stared, for there beside him lay one all shaven and shorn, so that he knew it must be a fellow in holy orders. He pinched himself sharply, but, finding he was awake, sat up in bed, whilst the other slumbered as peacefully as though he were safe and sound at home in Emmet Priory.

"Now," quoth Robin to himself, "I wonder how this thing hath dropped into my bed during the night." So saying he arose softly, so as not to waken the other, and looking about the room he espied the Friar's clothes lying upon a bench near the wall. First he looked at the clothes, with his head on one side, and then he looked at the Friar and slowly winked one eye. Quoth he, "Good brother, What-e'er-thy-name-may-be, as thou hast borrowed my bed so freely I'll e'en borrow thy clothes in return." So saying, he straightway donned the holy man's garb, but kindly left the cobbler's clothes in the place of it.

Then he went forth into the freshness of the morning, and the stableman that was up and about the stables opened his eyes as though he saw a green mouse before him, for such men as the friar of Emmet were not wont to be early risers; but the man bottled his thoughts and only asked Robin whether he wanted his mule brought from the stable.

"Yea, my son," quoth Robin—albeit he knew nought of the mule—"and bring it forth quickly, I prythee, for I am late and must be jogging." So presently the stableman brought forth the mule, and Robin mounted it and went on his way rejoicing.

As for the holy friar, when he arose he was in as pretty a stew as any man in all the world, for his rich, soft robes were gone, likewise his purse with ten golden pounds in it and nought was left but patched clothes and a leathern apron. He raged and swore like any layman, but as his swearing mended nothing and the landlord could not aid him, and as, more-over, he was forced to be at Emmet Priory that very morning upon matters of business, he was fain either to don the cobbler's clothes or travel the road in nakedness. So he put on the clothes, and still raging and swearing vengeance against all the cobblers in Derbyshire, he set forth upon his way afoot; but his ills had not yet done with him, for he had not gone far ere he fell into the hands of the King's men, who

marched him off, willy nilly, to Tutbury Town and the
Bishop of Hereford.

In vain he swore he was a holy man, and showed his shaven
crown; off he must go, for nothing would do but that he was
none other than Robin Hood.

Meanwhile merry Robin rode along contentedly, passing
safely by two bands of the King's men, until his heart began
to dance within him because of the nearness of Sherwood;
so he traveled ever on to the eastward, till, of a sudden, he
met a noble knight in a shady lane. Then Robin checked his
mule quickly, and leaped from off its back. "Now, well met,
Sir Richard of the Lea," cried he, "for rather than any other
man in England would I see thy good face this day!" Then he
told Sir Richard all the happenings that had befallen him,
and that now at last he felt himself safe, being so nigh to
Sherwood again.

But when Robin had finished the story, Sir Richard shook
his head sadly. "Thou art in greater danger now, Robin, than
thou hast yet been," said he, "for before thee lie bands of the
Sheriff's men blocking every road and letting none pass
through the lines without examining them closely. I myself
know this, having passed them but now. Before thee lie the
Sheriff's men and behind thee the King's men, and thou
canst not hope to pass either way. By this time they will know
of thy disguise, and will be in waiting to seize upon thee. My
castle and everything within it are thine, but nought could
be gained there, for I could not hope to hold it against such a
force as is now in Nottingham of the King's guard and the
Sheriff's men."

Having so spoken, Sir Richard bent his head in thought,
and Robin felt his heart sink within him like that of the fox
that hears the hounds at his heels, and finds his den blocked

with earth so that there is no hiding for him. But presently
Sir Richard spoke again, saying, "One thing thou canst do,
Robin, and only one. Go back to London and throw thyself
upon the mercy of our good Queen Eleanor. Come with me
straightway to my castle. Doff these clothes and put on such
as my retainers wear. Then I will hie me to London Town
with a troop of men behind me, and thou shalt mingle with
them, and thus will I bring thee to where thou mayst see and
speak with the Queen. Thy only hope is to get to Sherwood,
for there none can reach thee, and thou wilt never get to Sherwood but in this way."

So Robin went with Sir Richard of the Lea, and did as he
said, for he saw the wisdom of that which the knight advised,
and that this was his only chance of safety.

Queen Eleanor walked in her royal garden, amid the roses
that bloomed sweetly, and with her walked six of her ladies-
in-waiting, chattering blithely together. Of a sudden a man
leaped up to the top of the wall from the other side, and then,
hanging for a moment, dropped lightly upon the grass within.
All the ladies-in-waiting shrieked at the suddenness of his
coming, but the man ran to the Queen and kneeled at her
feet, and she saw it was Robin Hood.

"Why, how now, Robin!" cried she. "Dost thou dare to
come into the very jaws of the raging lion? Alas, poor fellow!
Thou art lost indeed if the King finds thee here. Dost thou
not know that he is seeking thee through all the land?"

"Yea," quoth Robin, "I do know right well that the King
seeks me, and therefore I have come; for, surely, no ill can
befall me when he hath pledged his royal word to your majesty
for my safety. Moreover, I know your majesty's kindness and
gentleness of heart, and so I lay my life freely in your
gracious hands."

"I take thy meaning, Robin Hood," said the Queen, "and that thou dost convey reproach to me, as well thou mayst, for I know that I have not done by thee as I ought to have done. I know right well that thou must have been hard pressed by peril to leap so boldly into one danger to escape another. Once more I promise thee mine aid and will do all I can to send thee back in safety to Sherwood Forest. Bide thou here till I return." So saying, she left Robin in the garden of roses and was gone a long time.

When she came back Sir Robert Lee was with her, and the Queen's cheeks were hot and the Queen's eyes were bright, as though she had been talking with high words. Then Sir Robert came straight forward to where Robin Hood stood, and he spoke to the yeoman in a cold, stern voice. Quoth he, "Our gracious Sovereign the King hath mitigated his wrath toward thee, fellow, and hath once more promised that thou shalt depart in peace and safety. Not only hath he promised this, but in three days he will send one of his pages to go with thee and see that none arrest thy journey back again. Thou mayst thank thy patron saint that thou hast such a good friend in our noble Queen for, but for her persuasion and arguments, thou hadst been a dead man, I can tell thee.

"Let this peril that thou hast passed through teach thee two lessons:

"First, be thou more honest.

"Second, be thou not so bold in thy comings and goings. A man that walketh in the darkness as thou dost may escape for a time, but in the end he will surely fall into the pit. Thou hast put thy head in the angry lion's mouth, and yet thou hast escaped by a miracle. Try it not again." So saying, he turned and left Robin and was gone.

For three days Robin abided in London in the Queen's

household, and at the end of that time the King's head page, Edward Cunningham, came, and taking Robin with him, departed northward upon his way to Sherwood. Now and then they passed bands of the King's men coming back again to London, but none of those bands stopped them, and so, at last, they reached the sweet, leafy woodlands.

CHAPTER 14 • • •

Robin Hood and Guy of Gisbourne

A LONG time passed after the great shooting-match, and during that time Robin followed one part of the advice of Sir Robert Lee, to wit, that of being less bold in his comings and his goings; for though mayhap he may not have been more honest (as most folks regard honesty) he took good care not to travel so far from Sherwood that he could not reach it again both easily and quickly.

Great changes had fallen in this time; for King Henry had died and King Richard had come to the crown that fitted him so well through many hard trials and through adventures as stirring as any that ever befell Robin Hood. But though great changes came, they did not reach to Sherwood's shades, for there Robin Hood and his men dwelt as merrily as they had ever done, with hunting and feasting and singing and blithe woodlands sports; for it was little outside striving of the world troubled them.

The dawning of a summer's day was fresh and bright, and the birds sang sweetly in a great tumult of sound. So loud was their singing that it awakened Robin Hood where he lay sleeping, so that he stirred, and turned, and arose. Up rose Little John also, and all the merry men; then, after they had broken their fast, they set forth hither and thither upon the doings of the day.

Robin Hood and Little John walked down a forest path where all around the leaves danced and twinkled as the breeze trembled through them and the sunlight came flickering down. Quoth Robin Hood, "I make my vow, Little John, my blood tickles my veins as it flows through them this gay morn. What sayst thou to our seeking adventures, each one upon his own account?"

"With all my heart," said Little John. "We have had more than one pleasant doing in that way, good master. Here are two paths. Take thou the one to the right hand, and I will take the one to the left, and then let us each walk straight ahead till he tumble into some merry doing or other."

"I like thy plan," quoth Robin, "therefore we will part here. But look thee, Little John, keep thyself out of mischief, for I would not have ill befall thee for all the world."

"Marry come up [Heavens above]," quoth Little John, "how thou talkest! Methinks thou art wont to get thyself into tighter coils than I am like to do."

At this Robin Hood laughed. "Why, in sooth, Little John," said he, "thou hast a blundering hard-headed way that seemeth to bring the right side uppermost in all thy troubles; but let us see who cometh out best this day." So saying, he clapped his palm to Little John's and each departed upon his way, the trees shutting the one from the other's sight.

Robin Hood strolled onward till he came to where a broad woodland road stretched before him. Overhead the branches of the trees laced together in flickering foliage, all golden

where it grew thin to the sunlight; beneath his feet the ground
was soft and moist from the sheltering shade. Here in this
pleasant spot the sharpest adventure that ever befell Robin
Hood came upon him; as he walked down the woodland
path thinking of nought but the songs of the birds, he came
of a sudden to where a man was seated upon the mossy roots
beneath the shade of a broad-spreading oak tree. Robin Hood
saw that the stranger had not caught sight of him, so he
stopped and stood quite still, looking at the other a long time
before he came forward. And the stranger, I wot, was well
worth looking at, for never had Robin seen a figure like that
sitting beneath the tree. From his head to his feet he was clad
in a horse's hide, dressed with the hair upon it. Upon his
head was a cowl that hid his face from sight, and which was
made of the horse's skin, the ears whereof stuck up like those of
a rabbit. His body was clad in a jacket made of the hide,
and his legs were covered with the hairy skin likewise. By
his side was a heavy broadsword and a sharp, double-edged
dagger. A quiver of smooth round arrows hung across his
shoulders, and his stout bow of yew leaned against the tree
beside him.

"Halloa, friend," cried Robin, coming forward at last,
"who art thou that sittest there? And what is that that thou
hast upon thy body? I make my vow I ha' never seen such a
sight in all my life before. Had I done an evil thing, or did my
conscience trouble me, I would be afraid of thee, thinking that
thou wast some one from down below bringing a message
bidding me come straightway to King Nicholas."

To this speech the other answered not a word, but he pushed
the cowl from his head and showed a knit brow, a hooked
nose, and a pair of fierce, restless, black eyes, which altogether made Robin think of a hawk as he looked on his face.

But beside this there was something about the lines on the stranger's face, and his thin cruel mouth, and the hard glare of his eyes, that made one's flesh creep to look upon.

"Who art thou, rascal?" said he at last, in a loud, harsh voice.

"Tut, tut," quoth merry Robin, "speak not so sourly, brother. Has thou fed upon vinegar and nettles this morning that thy speech is so stinging?"

"An thou likest not my words," said the other, fiercely, "thou hadst best be jogging, for I tell thee plainly, my deeds match them."

"Nay, but I do like thy words, thou sweet, pretty thing," quoth Robin, squatting down upon the grass in front of the other. "Moreover, I tell thee thy speech is witty and gamesome as any I ever heard in all my life."

The other said not a word, but he glared upon Robin with a wicked and baleful look, such as a fierce dog bestows upon man ere it springs at his throat. Robin returned the gaze with one of wide-eyed innocence, not a shadow of a smile twinkling in his eyes or twitching at the corners of his mouth. So they sat staring at one another for a long time, until the stranger broke the silence suddenly. "What is thy name, fellow?" said he.

"Now," quoth Robin, "I am right glad to hear thee speak, for I began to fear the sight of me had stricken thee dumb. As for my name, it may be this or it may be that; but methinks it is more meet for thee to tell me thine, seeing that thou art the greater stranger in these parts. Prythee, tell me sweet chuck, why wearest thou that dainty garb upon thy pretty body?"

At these words the other broke into a short, harsh roar of laughter. "By the bones of the Daemon Odin," said he, "thou art the boldest spoken man that ever I have seen in all my life. I know not why I do not smite thee down where thou sittest, for only two days ago I skewered a man over back of Nottingham Town for saying not half so much to me as thou hast done. I wear this garb, thou fool, to keep my body warm; likewise it is near as good as a coat of steel against a common sword-thrust. As for my name, I care not who knoweth it. It is Guy of Gisbourne, and thou mayst have heard it before. I come from the woodlands over in Herefordshire, upon the lands of the Bishop of that [the same] ilk. I am an outlaw, and get my living by hook and by crook in a manner it boots not now to tell of. Not long since the Bishop sent for me, and said that if I would do a certain thing that the Sheriff of Nottingham would ask of me, he would get me a free pardon and give me tenscore pounds to boot. So straightway I came to Nottingham Town and found my sweet Sheriff, and what thinkest thou he wanted of me? Why, forsooth, to come here to Sherwood to hunt up one Robin Hood, also an outlaw, and to take him alive or dead. It seemeth that they have no one here to face that bold fellow, and so sent all the way to Herefordshire, and to me, for thou knowest the old saying, 'Set a thief to catch a thief.' As for the slaying of this fellow, it galleth me not a whit, for I would shed the blood of my own brother for the half of two hundred pounds."

To all this Robin listened, and as he listened his gorge rose. Well he knew of this Guy of Gisbourne, and of all the bloody and murderous deeds that he had done in Herefordshire, for his doings were famous throughout all the land. Yet, although he loathed the very presence of the man, he held his peace, for he had an end to serve. "Truly," quoth he, "I have heard of thy gentle doings. Methinks there is no one in all the world that Robin Hood would rather meet than thee."

At this Guy of Gisbourne gave another harsh laugh. "Why,"

quoth he, "it is a merry thing to think of one stout outlaw like Robin Hood meeting another stout outlaw like Guy of Gisbourne. Only in this case it will be an ill happening for Robin Hood, for the day he meets Guy of Gisbourne he shall die."

"But thou gentle, merry spirit," quoth Robin, "dost thou not think that mayhap this same Robin Hood may be the better man of the two? I know him right well, and many think that he is one of the stoutest men hereabouts."

"He may be the stoutest of men hereabouts," quoth Guy of Gisbourne, "yet, I tell thee, fellow, this sty of yours is not the wide world. I lay my life upon it I am the better man of the two. He an outlaw, forsooth! Why, I hear that he hath never let blood in all his life, saving when he first came to the forest. Some call him a great archer; marry, I would not be afraid to stand against him all the days of the year with a bow in my hand."

"Why, truly, some folk do call him a great archer," said Robin Hood, "but we of Nottinghamshire are famous hands with the long bow. Even I, though but a simple hand at the craft, would not fear to try a bout with thee."

At these words Guy of Gisbourne looked upon Robin with wondering eyes and then gave another roar of laughter till the woods rang. "Now," quoth he, "thou art a bold fellow to talk to me in this way. I like thy spirit in so speaking up to me, for few men have dared to do so. Put up a garland, lad, and I will try a bout with thee."

"Tut, tut," quoth Robin, "only babes shoot at garlands hereabouts. I will put up a good Nottingham mark for thee." So saying he arose, and going to a hazel thicket not far off, he cut a wand about twice the thickness of a man's thumb. From this he peeled the bark and sharpening the point, stuck it up in the ground in front of a great oak tree. Thence he

measured off fourscore paces, which brought him beside the
tree where the other sat. "There," quoth he, "is the kind of
mark that Nottingham yeomen shoot at. Now let me see thee
split that wand if thou art an archer."

Then Guy of Gisbourne arose. "Now out upon it!" cried
he. "The Devil himself could not hit such a mark as that."

"Mayhap he could and mayhap he could not," quoth merry
Robin, "but that we shall never know till thou hast shot
thereat."

At these words Guy of Gisbourne looked upon Robin with
knit brows, but, as the yeoman still looked innocent of any
ill meaning, he bottled his words and strung his bow in silence. Twice he shot, but neither time did he hit the wand,
missing it the first time by a span and the second time by a
good palm's breadth. Robin laughed and laughed. "I see now,"
quoth he, "that the Devil himself could not hit that mark.
Good fellow, if thou art no better with the broadsword than
thou art with the bow and arrow, thou wilt never overcome
Robin Hood."

At these words Guy of Gisbourne glared savagely upon
Robin. Quoth he, "Thou hast a merry tongue, thou villain;
but take care that thou makest not too free with it, or I may
cut it out from thy throat for thee."

Robin Hood strung his bow and took his place with never
a word, albeit his heartstrings quivered with anger and
loathing. Twice he shot, the first time hitting within an
inch of the wand, the second time splitting it fairly in the
middle. Then, without giving the other a chance for speech, he
flung his bow upon the ground. "There, thou bloody villain!"
cried he, fiercely, "let that show thee how little thou knowest
of manly sports. And now look thy last upon the daylight, for
the good earth hath been befouled long enough by thee, thou

vile beast! This day, Our Lady willing, thou diest—I am Robin Hood." So saying, he flashed forth his bright sword in the sunlight.

For a time Guy of Gisbourne stared upon Robin as though bereft of his wits, but his wonder quickly passed to a wild rage. "Art thou indeed Robin Hood?" cried he. "Now I am glad to meet thee, thou poor wretch! Shrive thyself, for thou wilt have no time for shriving when I am done with thee." So saying, he also drew his sword.

And now came the fiercest fight that ever Sherwood saw; for each man knew that either he or the other must die, and that no mercy was to be had in this battle. Up and down they fought, till all the sweet green grass was crushed and ground beneath the trampling of their heels. More than once the point of Robin Hood's sword felt the softness of flesh, and presently the ground began to be sprinkled with bright red drops, albeit not one of them came from Robin's veins. At last Guy Gisbourne made a fierce and deadly thrust at Robin Hood, from which he leaped back lightly, but in so leaping he caught his heel in a root, and fell heavily upon his back. "Now, Holy Mary aid me!" muttered he, as the other leaped at him, with a grin of rage upon his face. Fiercely Guy of Gisbourne stabbed at the other with his great sword; but Robin caught the blade in his naked hand, and though it cut his palm, he turned the point away so that it plunged deep into the ground close beside him; then, ere a blow could be struck again, he leaped to his feet, with his good sword in his hand. And now despair fell upon Guy of Gisbourne's heart in a black cloud, and he looked around him wildly, like a wounded hawk. Seeing that his strength was going from him, Robin leaped forward, and, quick as a flash, struck a back-handed blow beneath the sword arm. Down fell the sword from Guy of Gis-

bourne's grasp, and back he staggered at the stroke, and ere he could regain himself, Robin's sword passed through and through his body. Round he spun upon his heel, and flinging his hands aloft with a shrill, wild cry, fell prone upon his face upon the green sod.

Then Robin Hood wiped his sword and thrust it back into the scabbard, and, coming to where Guy of Gisbourne lay, he stood over him with folded arms, talking to himself the while. "This is the first man I have slain since I shot the King's forester in the hot days of my youth. I ofttimes think bitterly, even yet, of that first life I took, but of this I am as glad as though I had slain a wild boar that lay waste a fair country. Since the Sheriff of Nottingham hath sent such a one as this against me, I will put on the fellow's garb and go forth to see whether I may not find his worship and perchance pay him back some of the debt I owe him upon this score."

So saying, Robin Hood stripped the hairy garments off the dead man, and put them on himself, all bloody as they were. Then, strapping the other's sword and dagger around his body and carrying his own in his hand, together with the two bows of yew, he drew the cowl of horse's hide over his face, so that none could tell who he was, and set forth from the forest, turning his steps toward the eastward and Nottingham Town. As he strode along the country roads, men, women, and children hid away from him, for the terror of Guy of Gisbourne's name and of his doings had spread far and near.

And now let us see what befell Little John while these things were happening.

Little John walked on his way through the forest paths until he had come to the outskirts of the woodlands where, here and there, fields of barley, corn, or green meadow lands lay

smiling in the sun. So he came to the high-road and to where
a little thatched cottage stood back of a cluster of twisted
crab-trees, with flowers in front of it. Here he stopped of a
sudden, for he thought that he heard the sound of some one in
sorrow. He listened, and found that it came from the cottage;
so, turning his footsteps thither, he pushed open the wicket
and entered the place. There he saw a gray-haired dame sitting
beside a cold hearthstone, rocking herself to and fro and
weeping bitterly.

Now Little John had a tender heart for the sorrows of other
folk, so coming to the old woman and patting her kindly upon
the shoulder, he spoke comforting words to her, bidding her
cheer up and tell him her troubles, for that mayhap he might
do something to ease them. At all this the good dame shook
her head; but all the same his kind words did soothe her
somewhat, so after a while she told him all that bore upon
her mind. That morning she had three as fair, tall sons beside
her as one could find in all Nottinghamshire, but they were
now taken from her, and were like to be hanged straightway.
Want having come upon them, her eldest boy had gone out,
the night before into the forest, and had slain a hind in the
moonlight; the King's rangers had followed the blood upon the
grass until they had come to her cottage, and had there
found the deer's meat in the cupboard. As neither of the
younger sons would betray their brother, the foresters had
taken all three away, in spite of the oldest saying that he
alone had slain the deer. As they went, she had heard the
rangers talking among themselves, saying that the Sheriff
had sworn that he would put a check upon the great slaughter
of deer that had been going on of late by hanging the very
first rogue caught thereat upon the nearest tree; and that
they would take the three youths to the King's Head Inn,

near Nottingham Town, where the Sheriff was abiding that day, there to await the return of a certain fellow he had sent into Sherwood to seek for Robin Hood.

To all this Little John listened, shaking his head sadly now and then. "Alas," quoth he, when the good dame had finished her speech, "this is indeed an ill case. But who is this that goeth into Sherwood after Robin Hood, and why doth he go to seek him? But no matter of that now; only that I would that Robin Hood were here to advise us. Nevertheless, no time may be lost in sending for him at this hour, if we would save the lives of thy three sons. Tell me, hast thou any clothes hereabouts that I may put on in place of these of Lincoln green? Marry, if our stout Sheriff catcheth me without disguise, I am like to be run up more quickly than thy sons, let me tell thee, dame."

Then the old woman told him that she had in the house some of the clothes of her good husband, who had died only two years before. These she brought to Little John, who, doffing his garb of Lincoln green, put them on in its stead. Then, making a wig and false beard of uncarded wool, he covered his own brown hair and beard, and, putting on a great, tall hat that had belonged to the old peasant, he took his staff in one hand and his bow in the other, and set forth with all speed to where the Sheriff had taken up his inn.

A mile or more from Nottingham Town, and not far from the southern borders of Sherwood Forest, stood the cozy inn bearing the sign of the King's Head. Here was a great bustle and stir on this bright morning, for the Sheriff and a score of his men had come to stop there and await Guy of Gisbourne's return from the forest. Great hiss and fuss of cooking was going on in the kitchen, and great rapping and tapping of wine kegs and beer barrels was going on in the cellar. The

Sheriff sat within, feasting merrily of the best the place
afforded, and the Sheriff's men sat upon the bench before
the door, quaffing ale, or lay beneath the shade of the broad-
spreading oak trees, talking and jesting and laughing. All
around stood the horses of the band, with a great noise of
stamping feet and a great switching of tails. To this inn came
the King's rangers, driving the widow's three sons before
them. The hands of the three youths were tied tightly behind
their backs, and a cord from neck to neck fastened them all
together. So they were marched to the room where the
Sheriff sat at meat and stood trembling before him as he
scowled sternly upon them.

"So," quoth he, in a great, loud, angry voice, "ye have been
poaching upon the King's deer, have you? Now I will make
short work of you this day, for I will hang up all three of you
as a farmer would hang up three crows to scare others of the
kind from the field. Our fair county of Nottingham hath
been too long a breeding-place for such naughty [wicked]
knaves as ye are. I have put up with these things for many
years, but now I will stamp them out once for all, and with you
I will begin."

Then one of the fellows opened his mouth to speak, but the
Sheriff roared at him in a loud voice to be silent, and bade
the rangers to take them away till he had done his eating
and could attend to the matters concerning them. So the three
poor youths were marched outside, where they stood with
bowed heads and despairing hearts, till after a while the
Sheriff came forth. Then he called his men about him, and
quoth he, "These three villains shall be hanged straightway,
but not here, lest they breed ill-luck to this goodly inn. We
will take them over yonder to that belt of woodlands, for
I would fain hang them upon the very trees of Sherwood it-

self, to show those vile outlaws therein what they may expect of me if I ever lay my hands upon them."

So saying he mounted his horse, as did his men-at-arms likewise, and altogether they set forth for the belt of woodlands he had spoken of, the poor youths walking in their midst guarded by the rangers. So they came at last to the spot, and here nooses were fastened around the necks of the three, and the ends of the cords flung over the branch of a great oak tree that stood there. Then the three youths fell upon their knees and loudly besought mercy of the Sheriff, but the Sheriff of Nottingham laughed scornfully.

"Now," quoth he, "I would that I had a priest here to shrive you; but, as none is nigh, you must e'en travel your road with all your sins packed upon your backs, and trust to Saint Peter to let you in through the gates of Paradise like three peddlers into the town."

In the meantime, whilst all this had been going forward, an old man had drawn near and stood leaning on his staff, looking on. His hair and beard were all curly and white, and across his back was a bow of yew that looked much too strong for him to draw. As the Sheriff looked around ere he ordered his men to string the youths up to the oak tree, his eyes fell upon this strange old man. Then his worship beckoned to him, saying, "Come hither, father, I have a few words to say to thee." Little John, for it was none other than he, came forward, and the Sheriff looked upon him thinking that there was something strangely familiar in the face before him. "How, now," said he, "methinks I have seen thee before. What may thy name be, father?"

"Please your worship," said Little John, in a cracked voice like that of an old man, "my name is Giles Hobble, at your worship's service."

"Giles Hobble, Giles Hobble," muttered the Sheriff to himself, turning over the names that he had in his mind to try to find one to fit this. "I remember not thy name," said he at last, "but it matters not. Hast thou a mind to earn sixpence this bright morn?"

"Ay, marry [indeed]," quoth Little John, "for money is not so plenty with me that I should cast sixpence away an I could earn it by an honest turn. What is it your worship would have me do?"

"Why, this," said the Sheriff. "Here are three men that need hanging as badly as any e'er I saw. If thou wilt string them up I will pay thee twopence apiece for them. I like not that my men-at-arms should turn hangmen. Wilt thou try thy hand?"

"In sooth," said Little John, still in the old man's voice. "I ha' never done such a thing before; but an a sixpence is to be earned so easily I might as well ha' it as anybody. But, your worship, are these naughty [wicked] fellows shrived?"

"Nay," said the Sheriff, laughing, "never a whit; but thou mayst turn thy hand to that also if thou art so minded. But hasten, I prythee, for I would get back to mine inn betimes."

So Little John came to where the three youths stood trembling, and, putting his face to the first fellow's cheek as though he were listening to him, he whispered softly in his ear, "Stand still, brother, when thou feelest thy bonds cut, but when thou seest me throw my woollen wig and beard from my head and face, cast the noose from thy neck and run for the woodlands." Then he slyly cut the cord that bound the youth's hands, who, upon his part, stood still as though he were yet bound. Then he went to the second fellow, and spoke to him in the same way and also cut his bonds. This he did to the third likewise, but all so slyly that the Sheriff, who sat upon his horse laughing, wotted [knew] not what was being done, nor his men either.

Then Little John turned to the Sheriff. "Please your worship," said he, "will you give me leave to string my bow? for I would fain help these fellows along the way, when they are swinging, with an arrow beneath their ribs."

"With all my heart," said the Sheriff, "only, as I said before, make thou haste in thy doings."

Little John put the tip of his bow to his instep, and strung the weapon so deftly that all wondered to see an old man so strong. Next he drew a good smooth arrow from his quiver and fitted it to the string; then, looking all around to see that the way was clear behind him, he suddenly cast away the wool from his head and face, shouting in a mighty voice, "Run!" Quick as a flash the three youths flung the nooses from their necks and sped across the open to the woodlands as the arrow speeds from the bow. Little John also flew toward the covert like a greyhound, while the Sheriff and his men gazed after him all bewildered with the sudden doing. But ere the yeomen had gone far the Sheriff roused himself. "After him!" he roared in a mighty voice; for he knew now who it was with whom he had been talking, and wondered that he had not known him before.

Little John heard the Sheriff's words, and seeing that he could not hope to reach the woodlands before they would be upon him, he stopped and turned suddenly, holding his bow as though he were about to shoot. "Stand back!" cried he fiercely. "The first man that cometh a foot forward, or toucheth finger to bowstring, dieth!"

At these words the Sheriff's men stood still as stocks, for they knew right well that Little John would be as good as his word, and that to disobey him meant death. In vain the

Sheriff roared at them, calling them cowards, and urging them forward in a body; they would not budge an inch, but stood and watched Little John as he moved slowly away toward the forest, keeping his gaze fixed upon them. But when the Sheriff saw his enemy thus slipping betwixt his fingers he grew mad with his rage, so that his head swam and he knew not what he did. Then of a sudden he turned his horse's head, and plunging his spurs into its sides he gave a great shout, and, rising in his stirrups, came down upon Little John like the wind. Then Little John raised his deadly bow and drew the gray goose feather to his cheek. But alas for him! For, ere he could loose the shaft, the good bow that had served him so long, split in his hands, and the arrow fell harmless at his feet.

Seeing what had happened, the Sheriff's men raised a shout, and, following their master, came rushing down upon Little John. But the Sheriff was ahead of the others, and so caught up with the yeoman before he reached the shelter of the woodlands, then leaning forward he struck a mighty blow. Little John ducked and the Sheriff's sword turned in his hand, but the flat of the blade struck the other upon the head and smote him down, stunned and senseless.

"Now, I am right glad," said the Sheriff, when the men came up and found that Little John was not dead, "that I have not slain this man in my haste! I would rather lose five hundred pounds than have him die thus instead of hanging, as such a vile thief should do. Go, get some water from yonder fountain, William, and pour it over his head."

The man did as he was bidden, and presently Little John opened his eyes and looked around him, all dazed and bewildered with the stun of the blow. Then they tied his hands behind him, and lifting him up set him upon the back of one of the horses, with his face to its tail and his feet strapped beneath its belly. So they took him back to the King's Head Inn, laughing and rejoicing as they went along. But in the meantime the widow's three sons had gotten safely away, and were hidden in the woodlands.

Once more the Sheriff of Nottingham sat within the King's Head Inn. His heart rejoiced within him, for he had at last done that which he had sought to do for years, taken Little John prisoner. Quoth he to himself, "This time to-morrow the rogue shall hang upon the gallows tree in front of the great gate of Nottingham Town, and thus shall I make my long score with him even." So saying he took a deep draft of Canary. But it seemed as if the Sheriff had swallowed a thought with his wine, for he shook his head and put the cup down hastily.

"Now," he muttered to himself, "I would not for a thousand pounds have this fellow slip through my fingers; yet, should his master escape that foul Guy of Gisbourne, there is no knowing what he may do, for he is the cunningest knave in all the world—this same Robin Hood. Belike I had better not wait until tomorrow to hang the fellow." So saying, he pushed his chair back hastily, and going forth from the inn called his men together. Quoth he, "I will wait no longer for the hanging of this rogue, but it shall be done forthwith, and that from the very tree whence he saved those three young villains by stepping so boldly betwixt them and the law. So get ye ready straightway."

Then once more they sat Little John upon the horse, with his face to the tail, and so, one leading the horse whereon he sat and the others riding around him, they went forward to that tree from the branches of which they had thought to hang the poachers. On they went, rattling and jingling along the road till they came to the tree. Here one of the men spake to the Sheriff of a sudden. "Your worship," cried he, "is not yon fellow coming along toward us Guy of Gisbourne?"

At these words the Sheriff shaded his eyes and looked eagerly. "It is!" he cried. "Now, Heaven send that he hath slain the master thief, as we will presently slay the man!"

When Little John heard this speech he looked up, and straightway his heart crumbled away within him. Not only were the man's garments all covered with blood, but he wore Robin Hood's bugle horn and carried his bow and broadsword.

"How, now!" cried the Sheriff, when Robin Hood, in Guy of Gisbourne's clothes, had come nigh to them. "What luck hath befallen thee in the forest? Why, man, thy clothes are all over blood!"

"An thou likest not my clothes," said Robin, in a harsh voice like that of Guy of Gisbourne, "thou mayst shut thine eyes. Marry, the blood upon me is that of the vilest outlaw that ever trod the woodlands, and one whom I have slain this day, albeit not without wound to myself."

Then out spake Little John, for the first time since he had fallen into the Sheriff's hands. "O thou vile, bloody wretch! I know thee, Guy of Gisbourne, for who is there that hath not heard of thee and cursed thee for thy vile deeds of blood and rapine? Is it by such a hand as thine that the gentlest heart that ever beat is stilled in death? Truly, thou art a fit tool for this coward Sheriff of Nottingham. Now I die joyfully, nor do I care how I die, for life is nought to me!" So spake Little John, the salt tears rolling down his brown cheeks.

But the Sheriff of Nottingham clapped his hands for joy. "Now, Guy of Gisbourne," cried he, "if what thou tellest me is true, it will be the best day's doings of thy life."

"What I have told thee is sooth [truth], and I lie not," said

Robin, still in Guy of Gisbourne's voice. "Look, is not this Robin Hood's sword, and is not this his good bow of yew, and is not this his bugle horn? Thinkest thou he would have given them to Guy of Gisbourne of his own free will?"

Then the Sheriff laughed aloud for joy. "This is a good day!" cried he. "The great outlaw dead and his right-hand man in my hands! Ask what thou wilt of me, Guy of Gisbourne, and it is thine!"

"Then this I ask of thee," said Robin. "As I have slain the master I would now kill the man. Give this fellow's life into my hands, Sir Sheriff."

The Sheriff scowled. "I like ill to let this fellow pass from my hands, but as I have promised, thou shalt have him."

"I thank thee right heartily for thy gift," cried Robin. "Take the rogue down from the horse, men, and lean him against yonder tree, whilst I show you how we stick a porker whence I come!"

At these words some of the Sheriff's men shook their heads; for though they cared not a whit whether Little John were hanged or not, they hated to see him butchered in cold blood. But the Sheriff called to them in a loud voice, ordering them to take the yeoman down from his horse and lean him against the tree, as the other bade.

Whilst they were doing this Robin Hood strung both his bow and that of Guy of Gisbourne, albeit none of them took notice of his doing so. Then, when Little John stood against the tree, he drew Guy of Gisbourne's sharp, double-edged dagger. "Fall back! fall back!" cried he. "Would ye crowd so on my pleasure, ye unmannerly knaves? Back, I say! Farther yet!" So they crowded back, as he ordered, many of them turning their faces away, that they might not see what was about to happen.

"Come!" cried Little John. "Here is my breast. It is meet that the same hand that slew my dear master should butcher me also! I know thee, Guy of Gisbourne!"

"Peace, Little John!" said Robin, in a low voice. "Twice thou hast said thou knowest me, and yet thou knowest me not at all. Couldst thou not tell me beneath this wild beast's hide? Yonder, just in front of thee, lie my bow and arrows, likewise my broadsword. Take them when I cut thy bonds. Now! Get them quickly!" So saying, he cut the bonds, and Little John, quick as a wink, leaped forward and caught up the bow and arrows and the broadsword. At the same time Robin Hood threw back the cowl of horse's hide from his face and bent Guy of Gisbourne's bow, with a keen, barbed arrow fitted to the string. "Stand back!" cried he, sternly. "The first man that toucheth finger to bowstring dieth! I have slain thy man, Sheriff. Take heed that it is not thy turn next." Then, seeing that Little John had armed himself, he clapped his bugle horn to his lips and blew three blasts loud and shrill.

Now when the Sheriff of Nottingham saw whose face it was beneath Guy of Gisbourne's hood, and when he heard those bugle notes ring in his ear, he felt as if his hour had come. "Robin Hood!" roared he, and without another word he wheeled his horse in the road and went off in a cloud of dust. The Sheriff's men, seeing their master thus fleeing for his life, thought that it was not their business to tarry longer; so, clapping spurs to their horses, they also dashed away after him. But though the Sheriff of Nottingham went fast, he could not outstrip a clothyard arrow. Little John twanged his bowstring with a shout, and when the Sheriff dashed in through the gates of Nottingham Town at full speed, a gray goose shaft stuck out behind him like a moulting sparrow with one feather in its tail. For a month afterward the poor Sheriff could sit upon nought but the softest cushions that could be gotten for him.

Thus the Sheriff and a score of men ran away from Robin Hood and Little John; so that when Will Stutely and a dozen or more of stout yeomen burst from out the covert, they saw nought of their master's enemies, for the Sheriff and his men were scouring away in the distance, hidden within a cloud of dust like a little thunderstorm.

Then they all went back into the forest once more, where they found the widow's three sons, who ran to Little John and kissed his hands. But it would not do for them to roam the forest at large any more; so they promised that, after they had gone and told their mother of their escape, they would come that night to the greenwood tree, and thenceforth become men of the band.

CHAPTER 15 • • •

King Richard in Sherwood Forest

NOT more than two months had passed and gone since these stirring adventures that have just been told befell Robin Hood and Little John, when all Nottinghamshire was in a mighty stir and tumult. King Richard of the Lion's Heart was making a royal progress through merry England, and everyone expected him to come to Nottingham Town in his journeying. Messengers went riding back and forth between the Sheriff and the King, until at last time was fixed upon when his majesty was to stop in Nottingham, as the guest of his worship.

And now came more bustle than ever; a great running hither and thither, a rapping of hammers and a babble of voices sounded everywhere through the place, for the folk were building great arches across the streets, beneath which the King was to pass, and were draping these arches with silken banners and streamers of many colors. Great hubbub was going on in the Guild Hall of the town, also, for here a grand banquet was to be given to the King and the nobles of his

train, and the best carpenters were busy building a throne
where the King and the Sheriff were to sit at the head of the
table, side by side.

It seemed to many of the good town folk of the place as if
the day that should bring the King into the town would never
come; but all the same it did come in its own season, and
bright shone the sun down into the stony streets, which were
all alive with a restless sea of people. On either side of the
way great crowds of town and country folk stood packed as
close together as dried herring in a box, so that the Sheriff's
men, halberds in hands, could hardly press them back to leave
space for the King's riding.

"Take care whom thou pushest against!" cried a great,
burly friar to one of these men. "Wouldst thou dig thine
elbows into me, sirrah? By'r Lady of the Fountain, an thou
dost not treat me with more deference I will crack thy
knave's pate for thee, even though thou be one of the mighty
Sheriff's men."

At this a great shout of laughter arose from a number of
tall yeomen in Lincoln green that were scattered through
the crowd thereabouts; but one that seemed of more authority
than the others nudged the holy man with his elbow. "Peace,
Tuck," said he; "didst thou not promise me, ere thou comest
here, that thou wouldst put a check upon thy tongue?"

"Ay, marry [indeed]," grumbled the other, "but I did not
think to have a hard-footed knave trample all over my
poor toes as though they were no more than so many acorns
in the forest."

But of a sudden all this bickering ceased, for a clear sound
of many bugle horns came winding down the street. Then all
the people craned their necks and gazed in the direction
whence the sound came, and the crowding and the pushing

and the swaying grew greater than ever. And now a gallant array of men came gleaming into sight, and the cheering of the people ran down the crowd as the fire runs in dry grass.

Eight and twenty heralds in velvet and cloth of gold came riding forward. Over their heads fluttered a cloud of snow-white feathers, and each herald bore in his hand a long silver trumpet, which he blew musically. From each trumpet hung a heavy banner of velvet and cloth of gold, with the royal arms of England emblazoned thereon. After these came riding fivescore noble knights, two by two, all fully armed, saving that their heads were uncovered. In their hands they bore tall lances, from the tops of which fluttered pennons of many colors and devices. By the side of each knight walked a page clad in rich clothes of silk and velvet, and each page bore in his hands his master's helmet, from which waved long, floating plumes of feathers. Never had Nottingham seen a fairer sight than those fivescore noble knights, from whose armor the sun blazed in dazzling light as they came riding on their great war-horses.

Behind the knights came the barons and the nobles of the midcountry, in robes of silk and cloth of gold, with golden chains about their necks and jewels at their girdles. Behind these again came a great array of men-at-arms, with spears and halberds in their hands, and, in the midst of these, two riders side by side. One of the horsemen was the Sheriff of Nottingham in his robes of office. The other, who was a head taller than the Sheriff, was clad in a rich but simple garb, with a broad, heavy chain about his neck. His hair and beard were like threads of gold, and his eyes were as blue as the summer sky. As he rode along he bowed to the right hand and the left, and a mighty roar of voices followed him as he passed; for this was King Richard.

Then, above all the tumult and the shouting a great voice was heard roaring, "Heaven, its saints bless thee, our gracious King Richard! And likewise Our Lady of the Fountain bless thee!" Then King Richard, looking toward the spot where the sound came, saw a tall, burly, strapping priest standing in front of all the crowd with his legs wide apart as he backed against those behind.

"By my soul, Sheriff," said the King, laughing, "ye have the tallest priests in Nottinghamshire that e'er I saw in all my life. If Heaven never answered prayers because of deafness, methinks I would nevertheless have blessings bestowed upon me, for that man yonder would make the great stone image of Saint Peter rub its ears and hearken unto him. I would that I had an army of such as he."

To this the Sheriff answered never a word, but all the blood left his cheeks, and he caught at the pommel of his saddle to keep himself from falling; for he also saw the fellow that so shouted, and knew him to be Friar Tuck; and, moreover, behind Friar Tuck he saw the faces of Robin Hood and Little John and Will Scarlet and Will Stutely and Allan a Dale and others of the band.

"How now," said the King hastily, "art thou ill, Sheriff, that thou growest so white?"

"Nay, your majesty," said the Sheriff, "it was nought but a sudden pain that will soon pass by." Thus he spake, for he was ashamed that the King should know that Robin Hood feared him so little that he thus dared to come within the very gates of Nottingham Town. Thus rode the King into Nottingham Town on that bright afternoon in the early fall season; and none rejoiced more than Robin Hood and his merry men to see him come so royally unto his own.

Eventide had come; the great feast in the Guild Hall at

Nottingham Town was done, and the wine passed freely. A thousand waxen lights gleamed along the board, at which sat lord and noble and knight and squire in goodly array. At the head of the table, upon a throne all hung with cloth of gold, sat King Richard with the Sheriff of Nottingham beside him.

Quoth the King to the Sheriff, laughing as he spoke, "I have heard much spoken concerning the doings of certain fellows hereabouts, one Robin Hood and his band, who are outlaws and abide in Sherwood Forest. Canst thou not tell me somewhat of them, Sir Sheriff? I hear that thou hast had dealings with them more than once."

At these words the Sheriff of Nottingham looked down gloomily, and the Bishop of Hereford, who was present, gnawed his nether lip. Quoth the Sheriff, "I can tell your majesty but little concerning the doings of those naughty [wicked] fellows, saving that they are the boldest law-breakers in all the land."

Then up spake young Sir Henry of the Lea, a great favorite with the King, under whom he had fought in Palestine. "May it please your majesty," said he, "when I was away in Palestine I heard ofttimes from my father, and in most cases I heard of this very fellow, Robin Hood. If your majesty would like I will tell you a certain adventure of this outlaw."

Then the King laughingly bade him tell his tale; whereupon he told how Robin Hood had aided Sir Richard of the Lea with money that he had borrowed from the Bishop of Hereford. Again and again the King and those present roared with laughter, whilst the poor Bishop waxed cherry red in the face with vexation, for the matter was a sore thing with him. When Sir Henry of the Lea was done, others of those present, seeing how the King enjoyed this merry tale, told other tales concerning Robin and his merry men.

"By the hilt of my sword," said stout King Richard, "this is as bold and merry a knave as ever I heard tell of. Marry, I must take this matter in hand and do what thou couldst not do, Sheriff, clear the forest of him and his band."

That night the King sat in the place that was set apart for his lodging whilst in Nottingham Town. With him were young Sir Henry of the Lea and two other knights, and three barons of Nottinghamshire; but the King's mind still dwelt upon Robin Hood. "Now," quoth he, "I would freely give a hundred pounds to meet this roguish fellow, Robin Hood, and to see somewhat of his doings in Sherwood Forest."

Then up spake Sir Hubert of Bingham, laughing: "If your majesty hath such a desire upon you it is not so hard to satisfy. If your majesty is willing to lose one hundred pounds, I will engage to cause you not only to meet this fellow, but to feast with him in Sherwood."

"Marry, Sir Hubert," quoth the King, "this pleaseth me well. But how wilt thou cause me to meet Robin Hood?"

"Why, thus," said Sir Hubert. "Let your majesty and us here present put on the robes of seven of the Order of Black Friars, and let your majesty hang a purse of one hundred pounds beneath your gown; then let us undertake to ride from here to Mansfield Town tomorrow, and, unless I am much mistaken, we will both meet with Robin Hood and dine with him before the day be passed."

"I like thy plan, Sir Hubert," quoth the King merrily, "and tomorrow we will try it and see whether there be virtue in it."

So it happened that when early the next morning the Sheriff came to where his liege lord was abiding, to pay his duty to him, the King told him what they had talked of the night before, and what merry adventure they were set upon undertaking that morning. But when the Sheriff heard this he smote his forehead with his fist. "Alas!" said he, "what evil counsel is this that hath been given thee! O my gracious lord and king, you know not what you do! This villain that you thus go to seek hath no reverence either for king or king's laws."

"But did I not hear aright when I was told that this Robin Hood hath shed no blood since he was outlawed, saving only that of that vile Guy of Gisbourne, for whose death all honest men should thank him?"

"Yea, your majesty," said the Sheriff, "you have heard aright. Nevertheless"—

"Then," quoth the King, breaking in on the Sheriff's speech, "what have I to fear in meeting him, having done him no harm? Truly, there is no danger in this. But mayhap thou wilt go with us, Sir Sheriff."

"Nay," quoth the Sheriff hastily, "Heaven forbid!"

But now seven habits such as black friars wear were brought, and the King and those about him having clad themselves therein, and his majesty having hung a purse with a hundred golden pounds in it beneath his robes, they all went forth and mounted the mules that had been brought to the door for them. Then the King bade the Sheriff be silent as to their doings, and so they set forth upon their way.

Onward they traveled, laughing and jesting, until they passed through the open country; between bare harvest fields whence the harvest had been gathered home; through scattered glades that began to thicken as they went farther along, till they came within the heavy shade of the forest itself. They traveled in the forest for several miles without meeting anyone such as they sought, until they had come to that part of the road that lay nearest to Newstead Abbey.

"By the holy Saint Martin," quoth the King, "I would that

I had a better head for remembering things of great need. Here have we come away and brought never so much as a drop of anything to drink with us. Now I would give half a hundred pounds for somewhat to quench my thirst withal."

No sooner had the King so spoken, than out from the covert at the roadside stepped a tall fellow with yellow beard and hair and a pair of merry blue eyes. "Truly, holy brother," said he, laying his hand upon the King's bridle rein, "it were an unchristian thing to not give fitting answer to so fair a bargain. We keep an inn hereabouts, and for fifty pounds we will not only give thee a good draft of wine, but will give thee as noble a feast as ever thou didst tickle thy gullet withal." So saying he put his fingers to his lips and blew a shrill whistle. Then straightway the bushes and branches on either side of the road swayed and crackled, and three-score broad-shouldered yeomen in Lincoln green burst out of the covert.

"How now, fellow," quoth the King, "who art thou, thou naughty rogue? Hast thou no regard for such holy men as we are?"

"Not a whit," quoth merry Robin Hood, for the fellow was he, "for in sooth all the holiness belonging to rich friars, such as ye are, one could drop into a thimble and the good wife would never feel it with the tip of her finger. As for my name, it is Robin Hood, and thou mayest have heard of it before."

"Now out upon thee!" quoth King Richard. "Thou art a bold and naughty fellow and a lawless one withal, as I have often heard tell. Now, prythee, let me, and these brethren of mine, travel forward in peace and quietness."

"It may not be," said Robin, "for it would look but ill of us to let such holy men travel onward with empty stomachs. But I doubt not that thou hast a fat purse to pay thy score at our inn since thou offerest freely so much for a poor draft of wine. Show me thy purse, reverend brother, or I may per-chance have to strip thy robes from thee to search for it myself."

"Nay, use no force," said the King sternly. "Here is my purse, but lay not thy lawless hands upon our person."

"Hut, tut," quoth merry Robin, "what proud words are these? Art thou the King of England, to talk so to me? Here, Will, take this purse and see what there is within."

Will Scarlet took the purse and counted the money. Then Robin bade him keep fifty pounds for themselves, and put fifty back into the purse. This he handed to the King. "Here, brother," quoth he, "take this half of thy money, and thank Saint Martin, on whom thou didst call before, that thou hast fallen into the hands of such gentle rogues that they will not strip thee bare, as they might do. But wilt thou not put back thy cowl? For I would fain see thy face."

"Nay," said the King, drawing back, "I may not put back my cowl, for we seven have vowed that we will not show our faces for four and twenty hours."

"Then keep them covered in peace," said Robin, "and far be it from me to make you break your vows."

So he called seven of his yeomen and bade them each one take a mule by the bridle; then, turning their faces toward the depths of the woodlands, they journeyed onward until they came to the open glade and the greenwood tree.

Little John, with threescore yeomen at his heels, had also gone forth that morning to wait along the roads and bring a rich guest to Sherwood glade, if such might be his luck, for many with fat purses must travel the roads at this time, when such great doings were going on in Nottinghamshire; but though Little John and so many others were gone, Friar Tuck and twoscore or more stout yeomen were seated or lying around beneath the great tree, and when Robin and the others came they leaped to their feet to meet him.

"By my soul," quoth merry King Richard, when he had gotten down from his mule and stood looking about him, "thou hast in very truth a fine lot of young men about thee, Robin. Methinks King Richard himself would be glad of such a bodyguard."

"These are not all of my fellows," said Robin proudly, "for threescore more of them are away on business with my good right-hand man, Little John. But, as for King Richard, I tell thee, brother, there is not a man of us all but would pour out our blood like water for him. Ye churchmen cannot rightly understand our King; but we yeomen love him right loyally for the sake of his brave doings which are so like our own."

But now Friar Tuck came bustling up. "Gi' ye good den [good evening], brothers," said he. "I am right glad to welcome some of my cloth in this naughty place. Truly, methinks these rogues of outlaws would stand but an ill chance were it not for the prayers of Holy Tuck, who laboreth so hard for their well being." Here he winked one eye slyly and stuck his tongue into his cheek.

"Who art thou, mad priest?" said the King in a serious voice, albeit he smiled beneath his cowl.

At this Friar Tuck looked all around with a slow gaze. "Look you now," quoth he, "never let me hear you say again that I am no patient man. Here is a knave of a friar calleth me a mad priest, and yet I smite him not. My name is Friar Tuck, fellow—the holy Friar Tuck."

"There, Tuck," said Robin, "thou hast said enow. Prythee, cease thy talk and bring some wine. These reverend men are athirst, and sin' they have paid so richly for their score they must e'en have the best."

Friar Tuck bridled at being so checked in his speech, nevertheless he went straightway to do Robin's bidding; so presently a great crock was brought, and wine was poured out for all the guests and for Robin Hood. Then Robin held his cup aloft. "Stay!" cried he. "Tarry in your drinking till I give you a pledge. Here is to good King Richard of great renown, and may all enemies to him be confounded."

Then all drank the King's health, even the King himself. "Methinks, good fellow," said he, "thou hast drunk to thine own confusion."

"Never a whit," quoth merry Robin, "for I tell thee that we
of Sherwood are more loyal to our lord the King than those
of thine order. We would give up our very lives for his bene-
fiting, whilst ye are content to lie snug in your abbeys and
priories, let reign who will."

At this the King laughed. Quoth he, "Perhaps King
Richard's welfare is more to me than thou wottest of, fellow.
But enough of that matter. We have paid well for our fare,
so canst thou not show us some merry entertainment? I have
oft heard that ye are wondrous archers. Wilt thou not show us
somewhat of your skill?"

"With all my heart," said Robin. "We are always glad to
show our guests all the sport that is to be seen. As Gaffer
Swanthold sayeth, ' 'Tis a hard heart that will not give a
caged starling of the best,' and caged starlings ye are with us.
Ho, lads! Set up a garland at the end of the glade, and we
shall see if we have archers here."

Then, as the yeomen ran to do their master's bidding, Tuck
turned to one of the mock friars. "Hearest thou our master?"
quoth he, with a sly wink. "Whenever he cometh across some
poor piece of wit he straightway layeth it on the shoulders of
this Gaffer Swanthold—whoever he may be—so that the poor
good-man goeth traveling about with all the odds and ends and
tags and rags of our master's brain packed on his back." Thus
spake Friar Tuck, but in a low voice so that Robin could
not hear him, for he felt somewhat nettled at Robin's cutting
his talk so short.

In the meantime the mark at which they were to shoot was
set up at sixscore paces distant. It was a garland of leaves and
flowers two spans in width, which same was hung upon a
stake in front of a broad tree trunk. "There," quoth Robin,
"yon is a fair mark, lads. Each of you shoot three arrows

thereat; and if any fellow misseth by so much as one arrow, he shall have a buffet of Will Scarlet's palm."

"Hearken to him!" quoth Friar Tuck. "Why, master, thou dost bestow buffets from thy strapping nephew as though they were love taps from some bouncing lass. I warrant thou art safe to hit the garland thyself, or thou wouldst not be so free with his cuffing."

First David of Doncaster shot, and lodged all three of his arrows within the garland. "Well done, David!" cried Robin. "Thou hast saved thine ears from a warming this day." Next Midge, the Miller, shot, and he, also, lodged his arrows in the garland. Then followed Wat, the Tinker, but alas for him! One of his shafts missed the mark by the breadth of two fingers.

"Come hither, fellow," said Will Scarlet, in his soft, gentle voice. "I owe thee somewhat that I would pay forthwith." Then Wat, the Tinker, came forward and stood in front of Will Scarlet, screwing up his face and shutting his eyes tightly, as though he already felt his ears ringing with the buffet. Will Scarlet rolled up his sleeve, and standing on tiptoe to give the greater swing to his arm, he struck with might and main. "*Whoof!*" came his palm against the Tinker's head, and down went stout Wat to the grass, heels over head, as the wooden image at the fair goes down when the skillful player throws a cudgel at it. Then, as the Tinker sat up upon the grass, rubbing his ear and winking and blinking at the bright stars that danced before his eyes, the yeomen roared with mirth till the forest rang.

As for King Richard, he laughed till the tears ran down his cheeks. Thus the band shot, each in turn, some getting off scot free, and some winning a buffet that always sent them to the grass. And now, last of all, Robin took his place, and all was hushed as he shot. The first shaft he shot split a piece from the stake on which the garland was hung; the second shaft lodged within an inch of the other. "By my halidom," said King Richard to himself, "I would give a thousand pounds for this fellow to be one of my guard!" And now, for the third time Robin shot; but, alas for him! The arrow was ill-feathered, and, wavering to one side, it smote an inch outside the garland.

At this a great roar went up, those of the yeomen who sat upon the grass rolling over and over and shouting with laughter, for never before had they seen their master so miss his mark; but Robin flung his bow upon the ground with vexation. "Now, out upon it!" cried he. "Give me a clean arrow, and I will engage to split the wand with it."

At these words the yeomen laughed louder than ever. "Nay, good uncle," said Will Scarlet, in his soft sweet voice, "thou hast had thy fair chance and hast missed thine aim out and out. I swear the arrow was as good as any that hath been loosed this day. Come hither; I owe thee somewhat, and would fain pay it."

"Go, good master," roared Friar Tuck, "and may my blessings go with thee. Thou hast bestowed these love-taps of Will Scarlet's with great freedom. It were pity an thou gottest not thine own share."

"It may not be," said merry Robin. "I am king here, and no subject may raise hand against the king. But even our great King Richard may yield to the holy Pope without shame and even take a tap from him by way of penance; therefore I will yield myself to this holy friar, who seemeth to be one in authority, and will take my punishment from him." Thus saying, he turned to the King. "I prythee, brother, wilt thou take my punishing into thy holy hands?"

"With all my heart," quoth merry King Richard, rising from where he was sitting. "I owe thee somewhat for having lifted a heavy weight of fifty pounds from my purse. So make room for him on the green, lads."

"An thou makest me tumble," quoth Robin, "I will give thee back thy fifty pounds; but I tell thee, brother, if thou makest me not feel grass all along my back, I will take away every farthing thou hast in fair payment for thy boastful speech."

"So be it," said the King. "I am willing to venture it." Thereupon he rolled up his sleeve and showed an arm that made the yeomen stare. But Robin, with his feet wide apart, stood firmly planted, waiting the other, smiling. Then the King swung back his arm, and, balancing himself a moment, he delivered a buffet at Robin that fell like a thunderbolt. Down went Robin headlong upon the grass, for the stroke would have felled a stone wall.

Then how the yeomen shouted with laughter till their sides ached, for never had they seen such a buffet given in all their lives. As for Robin, he presently sat up and looked around him, as though he had dropped from a cloud and had lit in a place he had never seen before. After a while, still gazing about him at his laughing yeomen, he put his finger-tips softly to his ear and felt all around it tenderly. "Will Scarlet," said he, "count this fellow out his fifty pounds; I want nothing more either of his money or of him. A murrain [plague] seize him and his buffeting! I would that I had taken my dues from thee, for I verily believe he hath deafened mine ear from ever hearing again."

Then, while gusts of laughter still broke from the band, Will Scarlet counted out the fifty pounds, and the King dropped it back into his purse again. "I give thee thanks, fellow," said he, "and if ever thou shouldst wish for another box of the ear to match the one thou hast, come to me and I will fit thee with it for nought."

So spake the merry King; but, even as he ended, there came suddenly the sound of many voices, and out from the covert burst Little John and threescore men, with Sir Richard of the Lea in the midst. Across the glade they came running, and as they came, Sir Richard shouted to Robin: "Make haste, dear friend, gather thy band together and come with me! King Richard left Nottingham Town this very morning, and cometh to seek thee in the woodlands. I know not how he cometh, for it was but a rumor of this that reached me; nevertheless, I know that it is the truth. Therefore hasten with all thy men, and come to Castle Lea, for there thou mayst lie hidden till thy present danger passeth. Who are these strangers that thou hast with thee?"

"Why," quoth merry Robin, rising from the grass, "these are certain gentle guests that came with us from the highroad over by Newstead Abbey. I know not their names, but I have been right well acquainted with this lusty rogue's palm this morning. Marry, the pleasure of this acquaintance hath cost me a deaf ear and fifty pounds to boot!"

Sir Richard looked sternly at the tall friar, who, drawing himself up to his full height, looked fixedly back at the knight. Then of a sudden Sir Richard's cheeks grew pale, for he knew who it was that he looked upon. Quickly he leaped from off his horse's back and flung himself upon his knees before the other. At this, the King, seeing that Sir Richard knew him, threw back his cowl, and all the yeomen saw his face and knew him also, for there was not one of them but had been in the crowd in the good town of Nottingham and had seen him riding side by side with the Sheriff. Down they

fell upon their knees, nor could they say a word. Then the King looked all around right grimly, and, last of all, his glance came back and rested again upon Sir Richard of the Lea.

"How is this, Sir Richard?" said he, sternly. "How darest thou step between me and these fellows? And how darest thou offer thy knightly Castle of the Lea for a refuge to them? Wilt thou make it a hiding-place for the most renowned outlaws in England?"

Then Sir Richard of the Lea raised his eyes to the King's face. "Far be it from me," said he, "to do aught that could bring your majesty's anger upon me. Yet, sooner would I face your majesty's wrath than suffer aught of harm that I could stay to fall upon Robin Hood and his band; for to them I owe life, honor, everything. Should I, then, desert him in his hour of need?"

Ere the Knight had done speaking, one of the mock friars that stood near the King came forward and knelt beside Sir Richard, and throwing back his cowl showed the face of young Sir Henry of the Lea. Then Sir Henry grasped his father's hand and said, "Here kneels one who hath served thee well, King Richard, and, as thou knowest, hath stepped between thee and death in Palestine; yet do I abide by my dear father, and here I say also, that I would freely give shelter to this noble outlaw, Robin Hood, even though it brought thy wrath upon me, for my father's honor and my father's welfare are as dear to me as mine own."

King Richard looked from one to the other of the kneeling knights, and at last the frown faded from his brow and a smile twitched at the corners of his lips. "Marry, Sir Richard," quoth the King, "thou art a bold-spoken knight, and thy freedom of speech weigheth not heavily against thee with me.

This young son of thine taketh after his sire both in boldness of speech and deed, for, as he sayeth, he stepped one time betwixt me and death; wherefore I would pardon thee for his sake even if thou hadst done more than thou hast. Rise all of you, for ye shall suffer no harm through me this day, for it were pity that a merry time should end in such a manner as to mar its joyousness."

Then all arose and the King beckoned Robin Hood to come to him. "How now," quoth he, "is thine ear still too deaf to hear me speak?"

"Mine ears would be deafened in death ere they would cease to hear your majesty's voice," said Robin. "As for the blow that your majesty struck me, I would say that though my sins are haply many, methinks they have been paid up in full thereby."

"Thinkest thou so?" said the King with somewhat of sternness in his voice. "Now I tell thee that but for three things, to wit, my mercifulness, my love for a stout woodsman, and the loyalty thou hast avowed for me, thine ears, mayhap, might have been more tightly closed than even a buffet from me could have shut them. Talk not lightly of thy sins, good Robin. But come, look up. Thy danger is past, for hereby I give thee and all thy band free pardon.

"But, in sooth, I cannot let you roam the forest as ye have done in the past; therefore I will take thee at thy word, when thou didst say thou wouldst give thy service to me, and thou shalt go back to London with me. We will take that bold knave Little John also, and likewise thy cousin, Will Scarlet, and thy minstrel, Allan a Dale. As for the rest of thy band, we will take their names and have them duly recorded as royal rangers; for methinks it were wise to have them changed to law-abiding caretakers of our deer in Sherwood than to leave them to run at large as outlawed slayers thereof. But now I fain would see how ye live here in the leafy woodlands."

So Robin bade his men make ready a grand feast; and straightway great fires were kindled and burned brightly, at which fires savory things roasted sweetly. While this was going forward, the King bade Robin Hood call Allan a Dale for he would hear him sing. So word was passed for Allan, and presently he came and sang for the King.

But now one came forward and said that the feast was ready; so Robin Hood brought King Richard and those with him to where it lay all spread out on fair white linen cloths which lay upon the soft green grass. Then King Richard sat him down and feasted and drank, and when he was done he swore roundly that he had never sat at such a lusty repast in all his life before.

That night he lay in Sherwood Forest upon a bed of sweet green leaves, and early the next morning he set forth from the woodlands for Nottingham Town, Robin Hood and all of his band going with him. You may guess what a stir there was in the good town when all these famous outlaws came marching into the streets. As for the Sheriff, he knew not what to say nor where to look when he saw Robin Hood in such high favor with the King, whilst all his heart was filled with gall because of the vexation that lay upon him.

The next day the King took leave of Nottingham Town. Robin Hood and Little John and Will Scarlet and Allan a Dale shook hands with all the rest of the band, kissing the cheeks of each man, and swearing that they would often come to Sherwood and see them. Then each mounted his horse and rode away in the train of the King.

Fiction for Young People

ROY ROGERS
The Enchanted Canyon
The Brasada Bandits
King of the Cowboys

GENE AUTRY
The Golden Stallion
The Ghost Riders

TARZAN
The Forbidden City
The City of Gold

**TROY NESBIT'S
MYSTERY ADVENTURES**
The Indian Mummy Mystery
The Jinx of Payrock Canyon
Sand Dune Pony
The Diamond Cave Mystery

GINNY GORDON
The Mystery of the Old Barn
The Lending Library
The Broadcast Mystery

TRUDY PHILLIPS
New Girl
Headline Year

ZANE GREY
The Spirit of the Border
The Last Trail

WYATT EARP

RED RYDER
The Thunder Trail

RIN TIN TIN'S RINTY

WALT DISNEY
Legends of Davy Crockett
20,000 Leagues Under the Sea

ANNIE OAKLEY
Danger at Diablo

POLLY FRENCH
Of Whitford High
Takes Charge
The Surprising Stranger

TRIXIE BELDEN
The Red Trailer Mystery
The Gatehouse Mystery
The Mysterious Visitor
The Mystery off Glen Road

BOBBSEY TWINS
Merry Days Indoors and Out
In the Country
At the Seashore

Adventure! Mystery! Read these exciting
stories written especially for young readers